SHOVELIN' THE SHIT SINCE '87

The Fells
photo Jacob Covey

SHOVELIN' THE SHIT SINCE '87

WRITTEN BY **Chris Alpert Coyle**   DESIGNED BY **Scott Sugiuchi**
WITH **Dave Crider** and **Art Chantry**

FOREWORD: Art Chantry..6

PART 1: QUALITY OUT THE ASS..8

CHAPTER 1: SON OF A SPOOK...10
    ORAL HISTORY LESSON: ESTRUS OPERATIONS 30
    ST. BEKKI 33
    ESTRUS MAIL ORDER 35
    THE CRUST CLUB 36
    TALKIN' TRASH..39

PART 2: FILTH-PUSHIN' MONO MAN...44

CHAPTER 2: GRATEFULLY WRECKED...46
    ORAL HISTORY LESSON: MONO MEN 52
    WATCH OUTSIDERS..56
    MONO LEGACY 61
    ORAL HISTORY LESSON: GARAGE SHOCK..66
    LONG LIVE THE 3-B TAVERN 93
    DIPSHITS IN THE DESERT 97
    ART CHANTRY: GRIT CITY VISIONARY 98
    CHANTRY REJECTS 120

CHAPTER 3: GOING WAAAAAY OUT..124
    BOOKMAN GOES TO BELLINGHAM 131
    EXTRA! EXTRA! READ ALL ABOUT (SH)IT! 134

CHAPTER 4: ENTERTAINMENT FOR TRASHOUNDS WORLDWIDE 141
    INSTRUMENTAL ROLES 152
    THE WIDE WORLD OF ESTRUS...156
    ORAL HISTORY LESSON: INTERNATIONAL STAGE WORLDWIDE NOISE-MAKING 163
    THE ESTRUSSIAL SOUNDS FROM THE FAR EAST 169

PART 3: "FUCK IT" AT FULL SPEED 182
ORAL HISTORY LESSON: THE FIRE...185
CHAPTER 5: MORE CREATURES TO FEATURE...195
    ORAL HISTORY LESSON: TIM KERR...200
    WHO IS "NOISEMASTER?" 206
    BIG NOISE FROM THE EAST..207
    MORE FROM BEHIND THE BOARD..210
CHAPTER 6: PUNKINHEADED MOTHERFUCKERS...214
    ESTRUS MERCH 222
    ORAL HISTORY LESSON: PEACE, LOVE, BULLFUCK 232
    MESSAGE MACHINE MAN 233

PART 4: CERTIFIED 100% APESHIT DISCOGRAPHY..242
    AFTERWORD AND CREDITS..254

FOREWORD: ART CHANTRY

EXTRA! SPECIAL ADDED ATTRACTION—

OPPOSITE: Mono Men tour promo decal, 1995, design Art Chantry

The first time I met Dave Crider was when Conrad Uno (founder of PopLlama Records) brought him to my old studio space overlooking the viaduct on Seattle's waterfront. It was the late 1980s (I can't recall the exact year), and Estrus Records (Dave's label with the naughty name) were putting together their first real vinyl LP record album. Dave had only released singles before this, and he'd asked Uno to co-release that first LP so he could figure out the process. That's just like Dave—he needed to know exactly how everything worked, so he could find ways to make it work *better*.

It turned out that Dave and I had a LOT of things in common—trashy taste, an interest in crappy music history, a love of forgotten art styles, and a fascination with the history of embarrassing underground American pop subcultures. We hit it off instantly—because we literally spoke the same language. Eventually, I learned that Dave had originally gone to school to study archeology, but he'd got sidetracked, becoming a DJ on a country and western radio station in Yakima, Washington (ouch). Coincidentally, I'd studied archeology at school as well! However, I'd been sidetracked by my new job as a garbageman in Tacoma, Washington (ouch again). Destiny brought us together.

That first LP project that Estrus did with PopLlama was called *Here Ain't The Sonics*, and it was a collection of favorite tunes by the Sonics—hard rock/punk legends of the mid-1960s—covered by a splattering of active garage/punk bands that idolized the band. The joke here is that the Sonics' first LP was called *Here Are The Sonics*, so you can see where this project was going. *Here Ain't The Sonics* was essentially a "tribute" record, and the bands contributing to the collection eventually became some of Estrus Records' headline "stars" (I use the term loosely.)

I attempted to re-create (the proper term is "echo") the original John Vlahovitch design of that first Sonics LP record cover—right down to the incredibly dim, difficult to see, and badly printed photo on the cover (re-shot by Charles Peterson to echo Jini Dellaccio's original badly printed photo). We even printed a coffee ring on the back cover liner notes and faked some "wear rings" (those big sandpapered circles you see on old, beat-up LP covers in thrift stores) into the cover design. Dave LOVED that sort of stuff as much as I did. Sadly, Uno didn't get it—so he took the wear rings off the LP cover. A few years later, when the *Here Ain't The Sonics* LP was released on the newfangled CD format, Dave put the wear rings back into the design. A CD with wear rings? That's an even BETTER joke.

Since that initial project, my friendship with Dave Crider has become one of the deepest and most long-term of my life. What's nice about getting together with him to do a project is that he and I COLLABORATE beautifully—since we both still speak the same language. When we concept a record cover design or a promotion for a project, we toss crazy ideas at each other until we get excited. Then we know it's a good 'un. When you get a client like Dave Crider, you do everything you can to hold on to them, because they're extremely hard to find.

I've worked with Estrus Records (my dream client) for more than 30 years (and counting.) It's REAL design collaboration at its finest—the best work of my career. Sometimes we might get in the way of others' ideas, but that's always ok. I'll admit that Dave's ideas are often better than mine (my ego hurts just saying that), but, in the end, it always results in a great, inventive, classic (sometimes ridiculous) design. It helps that Dave's taste in music is exquisite—in fact, downright uncanny. I like to say that Estrus never released a bad record. Truth is, Dave's taste is so similar to my own that everything Estrus releases sounds and looks like it was a record made for ME. We're not making product, we're creating "cultural artifacts." We want them to be re-discovered again and again and appreciated all over in newer terms. It's not about 'marketing," it's all about archeology.

ROOFDOGS IS:

Ledge Morrisette : bass, screeches
Marx : guitar
Dave Crider : guitar plus
Sleepy May : drum s
Josie Cat : farfeesa, percussion

Milkbones to:
Beer, Bekki, Amber, L.J.
Surf Trio, the Fellows,
Jon - Henry Productions

Biggest bone to Phil White, for all the great posters!

Recorded at Norsound Studio
Engineered by Jon Auer
Live cuts Engineered by
Henry Szankiewicz

℗1987 Roofdogs, Estrus Records
Write to those darned old Dogs
at 2511 Broadway, B'ham Wa 98225

1. Son of a Spook

The father of Estrus Records' Dave Crider was employed by the US's National Security Agency (NSA), which is why Captain Estrus himself had an upbringing that included living across the pond; because of his work with the NSA, John Crider and his family were situated in England from 1964 through to 1971. The crew returned stateside to Maryland briefly, before journeying to Yakima, Washington.

"You know what his dad was, right? He was a spook!"

Art Chantry

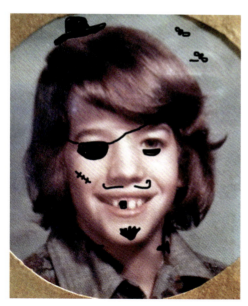

Deface the music, young Crider.

Dave was never a spy-in-training; in fact, he said it was his parents' love of music that contributed to his desire to pursue a life involving music in some capacity. His musical journey began in grade school, where he learned to play the violin, then the trumpet, the clarinet and the bass clarinet, and he said that later, his parents were always very supportive of his participation in bands.

The Crider family's 1976 landing in the revered valley of hops, apples, and cattle marked the beginning of Dave's indefinite stay in Washington state. Later, it was where he met Bekki, his future wife, as well as his lifelong friend "Hard Soul" Sister Diana "Di" Young. Dave wasn't one to be tethered to a surrounding culture defined by tractor pulls and tossing cow patties, and he was quick to let his freak flag fly in high school, becoming an unapologetic denim-draped hard rocker who saluted the guitar work of Grand Funk Railroad and embraced the instrumental chaos of Link Wray, the sleaze of AC/DC, and the inescapable "old man music" that pulsated at the heart of every cow town.

Crider's admiration for the old man music helped him land a spot as a disc jockey at the Yakima country and western radio station KUTI[1] in 1982.[2]

---

[1] KUTI is known for the short-lived but impactful radio program Larry & His Lasso, in which host Larry O'Dougal would capture small children with his lasso during recess breaks at a daycare center near the station. He'd then bring the apprehended children into the studio to be lambasted live on air about the dangers of child predators.

[2] Also on staff at the time was Gary Puckett of Gary Puckett & The Union Gap fame.

TOP: Dave and Bekki Crider, 1987
BOTTOM: Crider in the back office at Cellophane Square, 1986

Yakima was, understandably, limiting. Bekki moved to Bellingham to study geology at Western Washington University (WWU) while Dave stayed behind to continue the DJ gig and ride motorcycles. He eventually followed Bekki up over the Cascades to study anthropology and biology[3] at WWU.

Dave was a meticulous and driven WWU Viking. Yes, he did the college radio thing, and yes, he did the substitute beer for water thing, but he was genuinely enthusiastic about science and all that smart person sorta shit.

But… even the brightest and most promising young collegiate minds can fall victim to becoming a record shop employee. It's been happening for decades. An aspiring aeronautical engineer meets up with a crowd packin' 10 tabs of Orange Sunshine and the entire Captain Beefheart discography; two years later, the 4.0 valedictorian expected to be the next Buzz Aldrin has become a disciple of King Buzzo, thanks to some hole-in-the-wall vinyl-only operation where bargain deals are commonplace.

College kids who can't resist the lure of employment with a record store fall into two categories:

1. "Dude, I get 50 percent off of EVERYTHING."
2. Wide array of opportunities in the punk rock circuit.[4]

Crider was in the latter category, of course, and he hit the ground running after landing a job at Cellophane Square in downtown Bellingham.[5] This record store would unquestionably serve as an important launching pad for his future musical endeavors.

Cellophane Square didn't quite do to Dave what the Ring did to Sméagol, but close. With just one term remaining before his graduation from WWU, Crider quit school. He was hired as a clerk before being promoted to store manager and then regional manager. He was also the "promotions and advertising" guy, but there was never an official title for that job. His days were spent talking on the phone with record label heads and distributors and helping in-store shoppers by recommending Aerosmith LPs.

Networking was happening regularly, both on the phone and in person. During his freefall into Cellophane Square's operations, Dave would link up with some lifelong, life-changing fellows! Meeting ex-Coloradans Marx Wright and Dave Morrissette through Cellophane and familiar circles was monumental. Eventually, store regular Aaron Roeder came into the picture. And from a band standpoint, Crider, Wright, and Morrissette started the instrumental surf combo the Roofdogs. The lineup filled out with keyboardist Patti Bell (Josie Cat) and drummer Ann Maye, with Roeder taking over on drums shortly after the release of *Pound Bound*—the band's 1987 debut cassette… and Estrus Records' first release.

Before the first Estrus child was born, however, Crider and Marx had met with Seattle-based engineer/producer Conrad Uno of Egg Studios about having his borderline-hobby label PopLlama Records release *Pound Bound*. Though Uno enjoyed the music of the Roofdogs, he encouraged the pair to release the album themselves. Uno, a terrific golfer and an avid bird watcher, offered to help establish contacts and give guidance on

---

[3] You know where the name "Estrus" came from, right? You're dealing with a science nerd with an appreciation for lowbrow culture. The zoologic noun *estrus* refers to the period of maximum sexual receptivity of the female.
[4] *…And* getting 50 percent off of everything.
[5] There was also a Cellophane Square in Seattle's University district during this time and later in Bellevue Square.

on mastering and manufacturing (pressing, etc). His wisdom paid off; according to Crider, the label ended up working for decades with a lot of the people he referred, including John Golden at K Disc,[6] Rainbo Records, and Nashville Record Pressing.

Estrus Records started to gain traction, and Crider and Marx began tapping all available resources to keep the label growing. Marx turned a room in his rental into a makeshift warehouse to support the duo's in-house distribution, as selling records from similar labels and bands helped extend Estrus' reach. That reach grew even greater thanks to the fax machine acquired from the Video Depot—a store just down the block from Cellophane, where Bekki Crider worked. Before email and cell phones enabled instant interactions, communication via fax was a lifeline for small independent labels, and businesses in general.

The Roofdogs lost Patti to the Peace Corps. That departure resulted in the 'dogs shift into the Mono Men. And with the name change also came the addition of vocals. The band's debut single, "Burning Bush," was a three-chord titan oozing with teen angst that shared the regional heaviness bubbling in Seattle and the no-frills rock of guitar-focused garage bands. And on the single's flip side, the Mono Men paid homage to one of their key influences by blaring through the Nomads' "Rat Fink a Boo Boo." The "slab"[7] was the first of many, many, many, many, many 7" records that Estrus would unleash on the world over the next 16-plus years.

TOP: The Roofdogs illustration, 1988 **BOTTOM:** The Roofdogs, *Pound Bound*, cassette, 1987, design Dave Crider and Marx Wright

---

[6] John Golden left K Disc in 1993 and started John Golden Mastering.
[7] "Slab" is Crider-speak for release.

If punks in the Pacific Northwest were moths, the Sonics were the front porch light that gave their lives meaning. Fans of the legendary hurricane-R&B Tacoma quintet were kindred spirits. And up until the turn of the 20th century, Sonics records were not very easy to come by, making the connection with another "Psycho" particularly inspiring. Sonic energy brought Conrad Uno back into the picture, and Estrus co-released a Sonics tribute album with Uno's PopLlama Records titled *Here Ain't The Sonics*. The compilation featured Pacific Northwest acts with growing fanbases like Girl Trouble (blue-collar Cramps-homaging oddballs out of Tacoma) and the Young Fresh Fellows (Seattle-based Mark Twain-punk). Garage heavyweights like Thee Headcoats, the Cynics and Mojo Nixon were also aboard. Crider's inclusion of the Screaming Trees was a welcome surprise to many too. By 1989, the frequently touring psychedelic four-piece from Ellensburg had gained international recognition. Following several releases on Greg Ginn's[8] SST Records, the band was just months away from releasing its major label debut when *Here Ain't the Sonics* came out. The Trees' rendition of "Psycho" highlights the band's love for '60s punk… and it has frontman Mark Lanegan genuinely pay tribute to Jerry Roselie by delivering his unique take on the song's *psychotic* howling.

ABOVE: The Roofdogs, 1987

---

[8] Black Flag guitarist whose label released some of the most influential indie records of the 1980s.

ESTRUS: SHOVELIN' THE SHIT SINCE '87   15

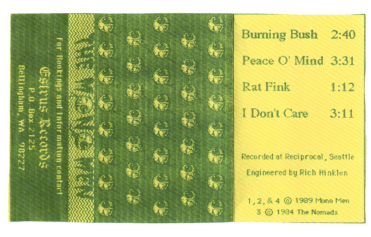

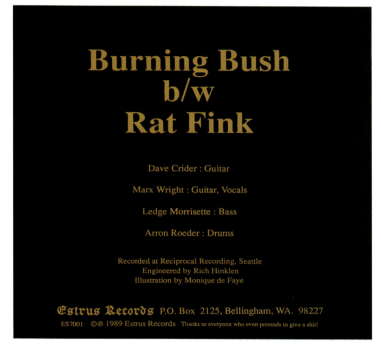

FIRST ROW: Mono Men demo tape, 1989, design Dave Crider **SECOND ROW:** Mono Men "Burning Bush" single (ES7001), 1989, design Dave Crider, illustration Monique De Faye **THIRD ROW:** *Here Ain't The Sonics* (PopLlama/Estrus, PL-ES-0024), 1989, design Art Chantry, photo Charles Peterson

Estrus

"Dedicated To Keeping The Garage Doors Open"

Funk & Wagnalls defines estrus to mean "frenzy, passion" or more commonly as the "peak of the sexual cycle." Take your pick. Or do as I have and know it to mean loud, obnoxious garage music that stares you in the face and doesn't blink, watching as the shit comes pouring out of your pantlegs. Estrus Records might be a little (or a lot) of each.

The boys at Estrus Records (co-founders Dave Crider and Marx Wright) saw the need for a record label that didn't just go for the latest fads or low-fi production qualities that seem to be the rage lately, but rather one that concentrated in good sounding loud rock & roll played and produced the way it was meant to be.

The company began operation in Jan. of 1989. It took several months to get things going and in July of that year released their first single, the Mono Men's "Burning Bush". This single went on to be nominated as best single of 1989 by the Northwest Area Music Association. In November, Estrus combined forces with Popllama Products to put out their most successful (# of units sold-wise) release to date, "Here Ain't The Sonics" comp LP & CD. Followed quickly in Dec. with a single by Seattle band, Stumpy Joe (Spinal Tap's drummer who choked to death on vomit). Game For Vultures released their 3-song seven incher in March '90 and the Mono Men's follow-up 7" "I Don't Care" in April. Things then really started to cook. The summer of '90 has seen a Mono Men LP and Marble Orchard single launched onto an unsuspecting public and the Estrus Lunch Bucket comp nearing release as I write this.

Upcoming Estrus projects include singles from the Mummies, Roofdogs and Phantom Surfers; an LP from Marble Orchard as well as an EP from Game For Vultures. A Mono Men CD should be out in time for X-mas, and my fave the Estrus Half-Rack (what us yanks call a box with 12 beers inside) comp of the world's twelve drunkest bands.

" Dedicated to keeping the garage doors open" is the motto of Estrus Records. So drink up, sit back and enjoy some loud garage rock, Estrus style.

Richard Head

Estrus Records is:
Dave Crider- stamp orderer
Marx Wright- stamp buyer
Gus Knapp- stamp licker

P.O Box 2125 Bellingham, WA. 98227 USA (206) 647-1187 (Tel./Fax.)

OPPOSITE: Mono Men "Burning Bush" single promotional flier, 1989, design Dave Crider **ABOVE:** Estrus press release, 1990

The Mono Men, 1990
photo Donnie Rubenack

In 1990, Estrus inked a deal with San Diego-based distributor Cargo Records to assist in what Dave called a "singles explosion." In the two-plus years with Cargo, Estrus blasted out 45 after 45—several of which were released as fan club-only singles. The Estrus Crust Club was a subscription-based fling in which a buyer would be sooprized™ with a colored 7-inch a number of times in a year.[9] In 1991 alone, Estrus released 12 45s, plus *The Estrus Half Rack*, a compilation of three separate singles.

Marx, Morrissette, Roeder, and Crider would see the Mono Men's debut LP come to fruition in the same year. *Stop Draggin' Me Down* was well received, and not only by three-chord Neanderthals: CMJ (*College Music Journal*)[10] praised the record's power. At the time, a release getting real estate from CMJ was clutch because the publication reflected airplay from college stations around the US. Crider said that at the height of the label's output, Estrus had roughly 150 college stations on its promotions list.

"Fanzines were a major part of the underground scene," Dave said of the resources for the label. "*Maximum Rocknroll* (MMR) was the big one, but there were so many others. Not many of them lasted more than a handful of issues but they were usually replaced with another." Advertising in said fanzines was a priority for the label. For a long time, Tower Records was the biggest distributor of fanzines. "When they shut down, that effectively killed the entire fanzine 'scene,'"[11] Crider said.

To promote *Draggin'*, the Mono Men went on a couple of west coast tours[12]—one with the Shadowy Men from a Shadowy Planet and the other with the Cynics. The Mono Men and the Cyns also embarked on a North American tour soon afterward, and that featured a few stops up in America's hat.[13] The length of the latter tour and the rapid growth of the label were inspiring for Crider but exhausting for Marx. After returning home from the road, Marx's commitment to the label and the Mono Men began to fade, and he'd soon sever ties with both. The parting was amicable, even though tempers flared several times while the band were on tour. Crider and Marx remain friends today.

When Dave took on full control of the label, his vision blossomed. Moreover, he was able to expand on a handful of ideas, including the effort to help out fellow labels and bands—in the same way that several had helped Estrus and the Monos.

The newly installed Estrus mail order featured dozens of records made by friends in high and low places. For Dave, it gave the label enough capital to keep a consistent release schedule while also directing people toward labels of friends like In the Red, Scat, Lucky, Pre-B.S., Empty, Rat City, PopLlama, Super Electro, Giant Claw, and Goner.

Estrus also hooked up with the Netherlands-based Semaphore Distribution for an exclusive deal that encompassed all of Europe. Semaphore made promoting Estrus and its releases a priority, and soon enough, a tree-dwelling moppet living in the Scottish Highlands could get the Mortals' *Disintegration* EP without forking out huge international shipping costs.

---

[9] For extended details, see "Oral History Lesson: Estrus Operations" on page 30.
[10] The magazine zeroed-in on college radio playlists and was a top-tier resource for unestablished bands (and labels) to gain a following in the pre-Internet era.
[11] Hey kids, try saying "fanzine scene" three times fast while sniffing amyl!
[12] These were not the tours in which the Mono Men mailed a substandard sausage patty to Art Chantry.
[13] Canada.

ESTRUS: SHOVELIN' THE SHIT SINCE '87   21

CLOCKWISE (from top left): Shadowy Men on a Shadowy Planet/Mono Men poster, 1990, design Dave Crider; Mono Men "Eyebill," 1990, design Phil White; Mono Men business card and demo paste-ups, 1990, design Dave Crider **OPPOSITE:** Mono Men posters, 1990, design Dave Crider

The Official Mono Men Newsletter   Vol. 1 Num. 1

!!NEW MONO MEN SINGLE FINALLY OUT!!

It's only four months late......but, hey after numerous delays our new 7" single is out and in your local record shop. The A-side will be on the upcoming full-length lp, "Stop Draggin' Me Down", which is due out mid-June, while the B-side is a cover of the old Frankie Laine standard "Jezebel" and will be available only on the single. The first 1,000 copies are on colored wax. The Mono Men have also contributed a track to the Regal Select "Puget Power Vol. 1" compilation and will put a cut on the "Estrus Lunch Bucket" 7" box-set due out later this summer!

MONO MEN PLAY BUTTS OFF IN MAY

Here's the upcoming shows...

-APRIL 28, CENTRAL TAV., SEATTLE
-MAY 11, SQUID ROW, SEATTLE
-MAY 20, SPEEDY 'O TUBBS, B'HAM
-MAY 21, HARPO'S, VICTORIA B.C.
-MAY 22, TOWN PUMP, VANCOUVER B.C.
-MAY 23, VOGUE, SEATTLE
-MAY 24, OSU, CORVALLIS OR.
-MAY 25, MAX'S, EUGENE OR.
-MAY 26, BLUE GALLERY, PORTLAND OR.
-MAY 27, STAR CLUB, B'HAM (ALL AGES)

Several of these gigs are with THE CYNICS. For info on any of the shows call (206) 647-1187.

T-SHIRT NEWS

Yup, there's a new design, printed in gold ink on maroon shirts!

We'll hav'em at the shows or you can get one by sending us a check for $10.00. L/XL sizes only

!!! FAR FUCKIN' OUT !!!

P.O. Box 2125   Bellingham   WA.   98227   USA

Estrus Records
Mail-Order Catalog

Artist	Title	Cost	Qty.	Total
Mono Men	Burning Bush/Rat Fink 7"	$4.00 ppd		
Stumpy Joe	Daydreams/Basket Case 7"	$4.00 ppd		
Various Artists	"Here Ain't The Sonics" LP	$8.00 ppd		
Game For Vultures	Goin' My Way + 2 7" EP	$4.00 ppd		
Mono Men	I Don't Care/Jezebel 7"	$4.00 ppd		
Mono Men	Stop Draggin' Me Down LP (Avail. 5/15)	$8.00 ppd		
Mono Men	T-Shirt...Snake Logo on Blk. (L/XL)	$10.00 ppd		
			Grand Total	

P.O. Box 2125 Bellingham, WA. 98227 USA (206) 647-1187 (Tel./Fax)

MonoMen

Taking inspiration from The Sonics, The Nomads, The Lyres, and other purveyors of garage rock, The Mono Men have slashed a raw noisy path throughout the Northwest.

Playing a wild mixture of originals and obscure covers, anything goes during a live performance. Once a frenzied member of the audience tore off her pantyhose, much to Ledge's delight.

Their recordings have been well received also, with the "Burning Bush" single being nominated for best single of 1989 by NAMA.

DISCOGRAPHY:

-"Burning Bush" 7" single, July 1989 (Estrus)
-"Witch", December 1989 "Here Ain't The Sonics" compilation
  (Estrus/Popllama)
-"Pete's Pango", March 1990 "Puget Power Vol. 1" compilation
  (Regal Select)
-"I Don't Care" 7" single, April 1990 (Estrus)
-"Stop Draggin' Me Down" LP, June 1990 (Estrus)

CLOCKWISE (from top left): Mono Men "I Don't Care" single (ES74), 1990, design Dave Crider, photo Donnie Rubenack; Mono Men newsletter *The Monocle*, 1990; Mono Men promotional one-sheet, 1990, design Dave Crider; Estrus Records mail-order catalog, 1990; Mono Men *Stop Draggin' Me Down* LP (ES121), 1990, design Phil White **OPPOSITE:** The Mono Men, 1990, photo Donnie Rubenack

PRISONSHAKE
SPOO (ES711), 1991

ROBERT GRIFFIN (Prisonshake/Scat Records): It was early on when Dave started the [Crust Club] series and asked us to do something. He told me his idea that all the jackets would be either tributes or re-creations of jackets that people like. He'd floated the idea of us doing one from the '50s bachelor record. He wound up using the image for some other band—I forget who—but it's basically a woman reclining in a giant cocktail glass. The rest of the band wasn't super into the idea, and one of the guys was like, "Why don't we do something really current that everybody actually knows." The cocktail glass idea is really cool, but nobody's seen that cover. And, with Sonic Youth, it was such a big deal that they'd recently signed to a major label and put that record [*Goo*] out. And I think it was our drummer who was like, "I can totally rip off that [Raymond] Pettibon cover and change it into something." Lee Ranaldo [Sonic Youth] actually came up to me at a show in New York City in, I think it was '94, and was like, "Hey! I got your 45!" And it took me a second to realize, "Oh! That one." But he was really cool about it. We all actually had a really good laugh about it.

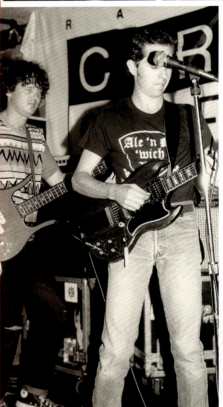

The Mono Men

The Mono Men-"The Hole Truth"

Here's what happened. It's Bellingham, WA, a city about 15 miles from the Canadian border on the coast. A town with it's own toilet paper factory.

Dave C the raging beast on geetar met Ledge at the local record shop where Ledge worked at the time. They formed an instrumental group called **"The Dentures"**, but no one else in the band dug surf music so it didn't last too long. Enter Marx, a childhood pal of Ledge's who had just gotten out of the joint in Colorado for stealin' cars. With only his clothes and guitar he moved to Bellingham to join that burgeoning mecca of music known as **"The Bellingham Scene"**. They jammed together through a succession of drummers until landing that smilin' fiend of a smacker Aaron Roeder.Aaron is a direct descendant of the first white bastard that settled this town. Nonetheless he's a good guy and he added the final ingredient to what would become the "Mono Men".

Dave Crider is the manic motor behind most Mono Men activities. He's an avid fan of comic books, music and Nancy Sinatra (not necessarily in that order). Just give him **a few beers** and stand back and watch. This provides most of the entertainment when the four boys get together.

Marx is the level headed dude in the band. His nickname is Mr. Spock. Or Spockhead, or Spockface, or Spockfuck or Fuckface. He'll answer to any of 'em. Marx keeps busy watching reruns of **bad tv shows** and balancing the band's checkbook. He is also the guy behind the wheel of the black Mono Men travellin' van Nerves of steel.

Besides being a direct descendant of the first white fucker to settle here- I think he's a great-great-grandson- Aaron is a **lawn stylist** (he mows lawns for a living). Aaron is the silent Mono Man, but quick to laugh at anything truly funny. As it is with most drummers, Aaron is insane. But his amazing collection of great music and Bukowski books keeps the van moving when the Mono dudes are on the road.

Ledge is the last Mono Man. The one that drinks most of the beers, a common trait among bass players. Why's he called Ledge? Cuz the **knucklehead** fell asleep on a ledge outside his third floor apartment and did a dry dive down onto the sidewalk. Through the miracles of modern plastic surgery he's even cuter than before. Ledge keeps busy drinkin' beers and playing golf and staying off that damn ledge.

The Mono Men have been together since early 1989 rockin places around the Northwest. There's nothin' real special about any of these **brickheads**, but when they all get together they can really fuckin' rock! Enjoy

Richard Head

P.S. They're also the drunkest fucking bastards I've ever had the pleasure of recording!

The Mono Men are.
Dave Crider-Guitars,Vocals
Marx Wright-Guitars, Vocals
Aaron Roeder-Drums
Ledge Morrisette-Bass

P.O Box 2125 Bellingham, WA. 98227 USA (206) 647-1187

OPPOSITE: The Mono Men at Call The Office, 1990, London, Ontario, photos What Wave Archive **ABOVE:** Mono Men press release, 1990

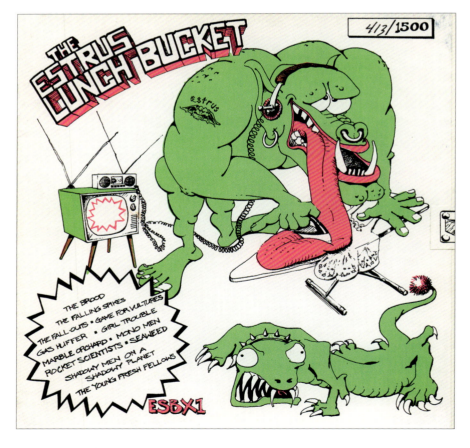

FIRST ROW: Game For Vultures "Goin' My Way" single (ES73), 1990, design/illustration Shauna Leibold; The Roofdogs *Havin' a Rave Up With The Roofdogs* EP (ES714), 1991, design Dave Crider; *Tales From Estrus No.1* EP (ES710), 1990, illustration Garrison White **SECOND ROW:** Marble Orchard "Something Happens" single (ES75), 1990, design Dave Crider; *On The Rocks* EP (ES712), 1991, design Dave Crider, photo unknown; *Dedicated to Keeping The Garage Doors Open*, promo EP (Gift of Life, GIFT031), 1990, design unknown **THIRD ROW:** *The Estrus Lunch Bucket* box set EP (ESBX1), 1990, design/illustration Phil White; *Estrus Lunch Bucket* cards, 1990, illustration Phil White

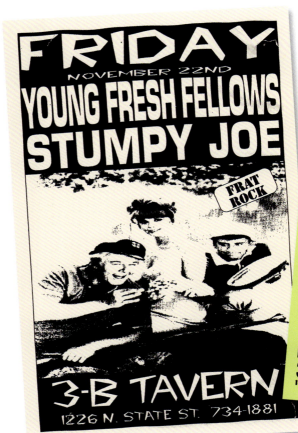

TOP: Game for Vultures, 1990, photo Neil Chowdery **MIDDLE:** The Brood, at Gare, Lauwe, Belgium, 1993, photo Alain Dauchy; Marble Orchard promo photo, 1990 **BOTTOM:** Young Fresh Fellows, Stumpy Joe flier, 1990, design Dave Crider; Screaming Trees, Gravel flier, 1991, design Dave Crider

100% APESHIT DISCOGRAPHY

VARIOUS
THE ESTRUS HALF RACK (THE 12 DRUNKEST BANDS IN SHOWBIZ) (ESBX3), 1991

MARK ARM (Mudhoney): Dave approached us to contribute a song for a comp, and we thought we should give [him] a Sonics-y kind of song, and it was "Who You Drivin?" After we were done [sic], we were just like, "yeah, this is too good to just put on a comp." But, ya know, "March To Fuzz" is a cool tune too, but it was an instrumental.

THE BROOD
VENDETTA! (ES007), 1992

CHRIS HORNE (The Brood): We'd put out a full-length album in December of '88. About a year and a half later, we had a single come out on Stanton Park Records out of Boston. Also, around that time, we were getting asked to contribute to compilations or offers to do a 45. That's when Dave Crider asked if The Brood wanted to do a song for the Estrus Lunch Bucket set. We were about to release another full-length on Stanton Park, but it kept getting pushed back. Months and months went by before we decided to check in with Crider and asked him, "Would you be interested in putting out our second album?"

RICHARD JULIO (Producer): We loved the Estrus packaging and style—everything they did. Dave had a good eye for product and was really excited when I turned him on to a record plant that still used paste-on cover slicks. Luckily for us, the timing was right because the Mono Men had their *Wrecker* album ready to go. So when we talked to Dave he goes, "This is great," because he wanted to have two releases at once for some synergy.

Design/illustration: Joseph Newton

The Mummies, Harpo's Cabaret, Victoria, BC, 1990, photos unknown

Mono Men *Booze* EP contact sheet, 1991, photos Charles Peterson

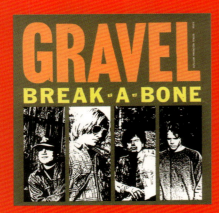

GRAVEL
BREAK-A-BONE (ES126), 1992

ROBERT GRIFFIN (Prisonshake/Scat Records): Gravel was fucking awesome.

Design: Art Chantry

CHEATER SLICKS
84 FORD 79 (ES728), 1992

DANA HATCH (Cheater Slicks): Our one single for Estrus, "84 Ford 79," was an instrumental ode to our van, an '84 Econoline, which we found out had a '79 engine in it!"

Design: Dave Shannon

ORAL HISTORY LESSON: ESTRUS OPERATIONS

A RECORD GEEK HOBBY WITH A FRIEND GROWS INTO LIFE-DEFINING "WORK"

MARX WRIGHT: I started going through all my archives, and I went, "Whoa, shit! We actually did something!"

As mentioned previously, Estrus Records' first release—the cassette of The Roofdogs' album Pound Bound—*came to fruition simply because both Crider and Marx had ambitions to get their music outside of Bellingham. Soon, the duo would be housing records made by lots of folks not living in Bellingham.*

BEKKI CRIDER: The serendipitous thing was, when [Dave] decided to go full-time with the label, the place where I worked, Video Depot, was running into some [financial] problems, and I ended up getting laid off. So we lived on unemployment for the first year and a half while he was getting the label up and rolling. We lived very frugally, and we worked 16-hour days to keep the label moving. There was a moment when my last unemployment check came in, and we realized that [Estrus] could start giving us paychecks [laughs].

MARX WRIGHT: There was no Internet then—or any of the things the Internet gives you. That didn't exist. You were calling people on the phone, you were writing letters on your typewriter… and waiting for the response in five to seven business days [laughs]!… [And listening to] demo tapes—sometimes there were just too many. We'd just get boxes of those things [because] we were advertising in national magazines. It was almost like a whole bunch of bottles in the ocean washed up on our shore at the same time. [But] missing that analog experience compared to how [demos are reviewed] now, yeah, I can see that being completely different. But, there's a physical limit to what you can put into a cassette deck and listen to.

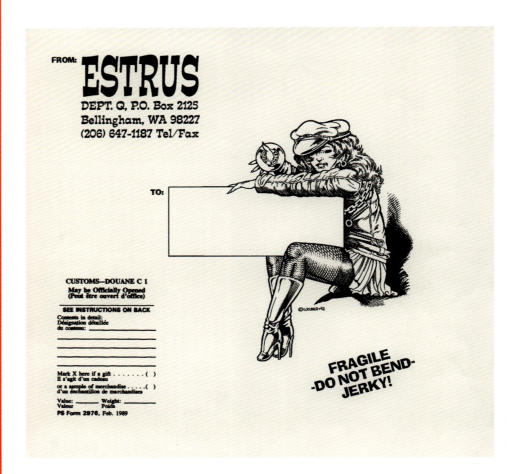

TOP: The Phantom Surfers, 1991, photo courtesy Johnny Bartlett **BOTTOM:** The Mummies, Game For Vultures, Phantom Surfers flier, 1991, design Dave Crider; The Phantom Surfers *Orbitron* EP (ES713), 1991, design Dave Crider, photo Sven-Erik Geddes **OPPOSITE:** Estrus mail-order envelope, 1991, illustration Ron Wilbur **PAGE 32:** The Mummies, Mono Men, The Phantom Surfers at Harpo's Cabaret poster, 1990, design Dave Crider

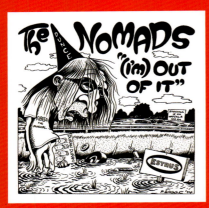

THE NOMADS
(I'M) OUT OF IT (ES754), 1994

NIKLAS VALBERG (The Nomads): We managed to get a really good advance from our Swedish record label, which allowed us to travel to Seattle, record at Egg Studios, and stay there for a couple of weeks at the end of '93 and the beginning of '94. The guys at the label didn't know we were traveling to America to record in a basement [laughs]. And they weren't complaining when we got back because they thought [the recording] sounded great! They were really happy with it. Conrad is such a great producer and a great engineer and has such a great studio—with the Stax Records recording rig. We could have spent three times the amount in Stockholm, but it wouldn't have sounded as good as it did at Egg.

Design/illustration: Peter Bagge

THE OBLIVIANS
BLOW THEIR COOL (ES756), 1994

ERIC FRIEDL (The Oblivians/Goner Records): We were just excited to do the record; [Blow Their Cool] was recorded with putting out a single on Estrus in mind. We just did it in Greg and Jack's bedroom—or one of the rooms at their apartment. It turned out really good. We were really lucky. And then Crider was really cool to ask us to play Garage Shock because at that point, it was the premier thing to do if you're that kind of band in that scene.

DAVE CRIDER: It's easier for us to sell our records if we're also selling Dead Moon records or Get Hip Records, so we kinda gathered everyone up and started doing distribution [for fellow labels and bands]. And it was sorta the same thing with the mail order.

JOHNNY BARTLETT (The Phantom Surfers): We sent Dave our recordings, and the deal was we'd get 10 percent of the run in return.[14] I think that was the first time I'd heard that arrangement, but [I quickly learned] it was the standard with independent labels at that time. I started my own label in 1992, and to this day, that's the arrangement I make with bands. …I've dealt with many independent labels, and Estrus is the only one that issued sales records and royalty statements. Dave was so organized. The documents would show how many of our records we'd sold, how many were still in inventory, how many promos were sent out, and the number of copies we, the band, had. And also, when he'd reprint or re-press records, he would—without us prodding him—send 10 percent of the new run. He was very transparent.

---

[14] The standard 10 percent deal was/(is) for the 7" releases, which were typically for limited editions, according to Estrus source Gus Aldren (the bad astronaut).

ST. BEKKI

THE UNSPOKEN HERO OF ESTRUS' SUCCESS IS UNDOUBTEDLY THE WOMAN WHO HAS STOOD BY MR. FUCK IT SINCE THE EARLY '80s

AL VON ZIPPER (The Von Zippers): Ah, Bekki. Such a great person, definitely an individual with superpowers. Her skill with animals both human and not is completely unworldly. I'd give anything to know how someone can sleep in so late, though.

HIRO (Estrella 20/20): Bekki is my American mum. She always treated us with so much kindness.

Crider's vision, work ethic, and execution cannot be overstated; the man would have created a record label—or something similar—no matter what obstacles had been in the way. (And, he's a Leo. Leos are typically dickheads, but they get shit done.) However, without Bekki, Dave's dream would never have been as successful as it was—not even close.

In many ways, Bekki was the perfect co-pilot. She knew precisely what Dave wanted out of each of the label's functions because her knowledge of Crider's brain was second only to the man himself. She understood the personality, the message, the art, and the oddities of Estrus because she had been with Mr. Fuck It since high school.

DIANA YOUNG-BLANCHARD (Madame X, the Dt's): I think Bekki would definitely underestimate herself in terms of importance. I actually ran this by her and made a comment to her like, "I don't think Dave could have done all of that without you. I don't think he could have." And she goes, "Yeah, he could have" [laughs]. So that's what I mean by underestimating everything that she contributed to the business and the work—and the socialization of all the bands that came through Bellingham and stayed at their house. She was an intricate part of all of that. Yeah, perhaps Dave could have and would have done Estrus without her, but I don't think to the [same] extent.

Bekki was a host mom, mail-order clerk, chef, merch gal, and plenty of other miscellaneous titles during the label's first few years, when things like assembling records was being done by hand in Bellingham.

BEKKI CRIDER: One year, starting in May and going through August, there was not one free weekend. Every weekend there was a band, and they would stay in our "birdhouse." Sometimes there would be three bands touring together. And it wasn't always Estrus bands. For Garage Shock, it was a different story. There could have been 15–20 people.

Estrus Update
The Estrus Records Newsletter
Vol. 2 Num. 2

This "Spoo's" For You

Here it is....the latest edition of the Crust series of 7" singles...Prisonshake's "SPOO" ep. In a somewhat unconventional move the A-side of the single contains two cuts: "Ron Kinda World", an original, and a version of the Squelch tune "Asphalt". On the flip is a kickin' cover of The Stones' "Spider & The Fly recorded live! For the uninitiated, Prisonshake are from Cleveland, Ohio and over the past couple of years have released a slew of very cool records including the ingenious multi-format "I'm Really Fucked Now" which contained a 7" single,LP,CD, and cassette. If you need another dose of Prisonshake write Robert at Scat Records PO Box 141161 Cleveland, Ohio . I'm sure he would be glad to oblige, in the meantime you can look forward to another cut from the band on the upcoming Estrus Half Rack 3x7" box-set (see below for more on that one....Ed.)..until then I guess you'll just have to play "SPOO" 'till ya do.

Here Comes The Half-Rack

There's nothing like an ice cold beer on a blistering summer day...only thing better is a whole case, and Estrus is gonna get you half the way there with The Estrus Half Rack, a collection of 12 of the drunkest bands in show business on three 7" eps in a hard box, packed with a custom bar coaster, match box and other barfly essentials. Derelicts, Fastbacks, Gorilla, Kings Of Rock, Marble Orchard, Mono Men, Mudhoney, The Mummies, Phantom Surfers, Prisonshake, Seaweed, and Untamed Youth. They're all gonna be there serving up one frothy cut apiece.,each one exclusive to the set. The Estrus Half Rack will be limited to 2,000 boxes, with the first 500 pressed on colored vinyl, and will hit the ice the first week of June. You can reserve your very own colored vinyl edition of the Half Rack for $15.00 ppd ($12.75 ppd for Crust Club Members).Don't miss out...this is one hang-over you can look forward to!

Estrus Presents GARAGESHOCK

Estrus Records is proud to present three nights of garage mania May 24th - 26th at the Bellingham Bay Brewing Co. featuring Seaweed, Gas Huffer,Game For Vultures,Young Fresh Fellows,Phantom Surfers,Marble Orchard,Girl Trouble,The Mummies, and Night Kings. Tickets will go on sale in early May and cost $15.00 for a three day pass. You've been warned!

Crust Corner

You asked for it so here it is...Mail-Order Mecca. We get many letters from folks in the club looking for non-Estrus stuff so starting with this issue of the Estrus Update all you have to do is flip the page to find those hard to get singles you need. Quantities on most titles are limited so don't dally if ya see something you can't live without. Also remember that Crust Club members receive a 15% discount on all mail-order purchases. Upcoming Crust singles to watch for: The Phantom Surfers,The Roofdogs, The Gories, The Whirlees, Marble Orchard, Mono Men and more! If ya ain't in the club yet, don't miss out, join the Crust. Here's whatcha get:
- The next six Estrus Crust limited edition 7" releases on colored wax
- Free Estrus Update subscription
- 15% Estrus mail order discount
- Crust Club membership card

A Crust Club membership costs $20 ($25 Canada, $30 Foreign). Join today!

Surfers Ride The Crust...

The Phantom Surfers will be the next band showcased in the Crust series. Their "Oribitron" 7" ep features FIVE instro. rave-ups and should be ready to go the first week of May. Like their buddies The Mummies these guys serve up that primitive sound and tear it up live...wearing matching coats, slacks,surfer's crosses and phantom masks...so wax up that board dude!

Mono Men Brain Dead

Mono Men are contributing a cut to a 4-song ep to be included on a free single in the next issue of the ultra-cool Spanish magazine Brain Dead...copies will be available thru Mail-Order Mecca.

P.O. Box 2125 Bellingham WA. 98227 USA Tel/Fax (206) 647-1187

ESTRUS MAIL ORDER

A UNIQUE COMPONENT OF ESTRUS THAT KEPT THE LABEL ACTIVE AND SERVED AS A PRE-INTERNET SOCIAL NETWORK FOR BANDS, LABELS, ZINES, AND DIRTY MOVIE ADVOCATES

While one could assert that the aggressiveness of distributing and running a large mail order could be seen as a capitalist-inspired undertaking, the reality was that Crider's taste in music and his growing network of buds allowed the label to do more than most; Estrus had a wider variety of shit to shovel—and unknown labels and bands from around the globe could get some action.

LARRY HARDY (In the Red Records): Estrus played a big role because Dave was running a mail-order catalog as well as his label. And at that time, a lot of people were buying from him. If you liked that kind of music, that would be one of your main sources. And he, from the get-go, would carry my stuff. He was really cool about it and super supportive. Back then, if you were just beginning to put out 45s it was hard to find a place to sell them. But, yes, he'd always take my stuff, and he'd always do a nice write-up for it. And he was one of the main distributors for me when I first started.

DAVE CRIDER: Keeping up on the other labels and music that I liked was easy, being a fan. I thought that distribution for small labels sorta sucked—it's hard to get stuff out there, and it's hard to get paid. So part of establishing distribution and the mail order was contacting and starting relationships with other labels. Sometimes I'd sell 200 or more [of another label's] singles. We wouldn't do consignment. I'd pay the label flat out. They'd send me the records, and I'd send 'em a fuckin' check. And it worked out. It was rare that I wouldn't sell through what I had. A lot of times I'd buy stuff directly from bands I liked. If Trent [Ruane] ever put a single out I'd just buy singles from him. Usually, I was pretty aware of what was going on. I thought my customer base would like it if I liked it.

LARRY HARDY: You were always respectful of people that were kind of doing the same thing as you. But bands could do singles on a bunch of different labels. And so, working with the Cheater Slicks, they did a single on Estrus, but I was still their primary label. And that was a good thing for me; like Estrus, we got their seal of approval and that helps, you know. That's really cool.

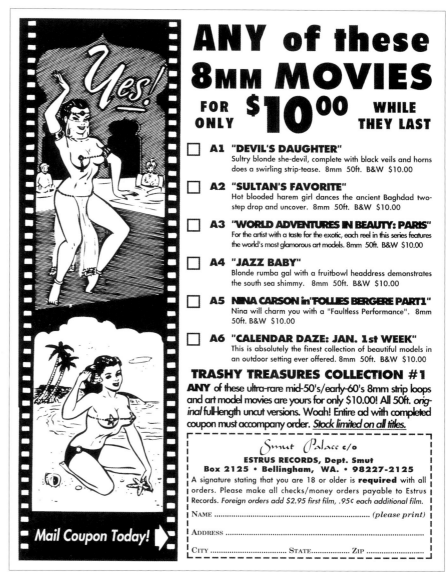

ABOVE: Estrus Smut advertisement, 1993, design Dave Crider; "Sultan of Smut," 1993, illustration Ashleigh Talbot
OPPOSITE: *Estrus Update*, 1991, design Dave Crider

THE CRUST CLUB

FOR A NOMINAL ANNUAL FEE, CRETINS RECEIVED SHINY STUFF IN THE MAIL

DAVE CRIDER: [The labels] Sub Pop and Sympathy [for the Record Industry] definitely kickstarted [the singles] craze. There's no question about it. Before then, singles were not much of a thing.

As a member of the Estrus Crust Club, the subscriber would be smacked with six singles and three editions of the Sir Estrus Quarterly—*the label's in-house fanzine—each year for a one-time fee of $25. For a label already churning out a plenteous number of normal releases, the Crust Club shoved yet more time-consuming endeavors into Estrus' already jam-packed work days. However, the reward with more work was more cash up front. And with more cash up front, Estrus could go the extra mile in making each release a one-of-a-kind item.*

CARL RATLIFF (Estrus/Bookman): The singles would come out quarterly. That's a lot. Two seven-inches every three months, in addition to all the other shit you're putting out?

DAVE CRIDER: With the subscription model you're generating cash flow. That was a big thing from a business standpoint with the Crust Club; it generated a lot of working capital. People were paying in advance. It's a leap of faith, too, that they're not gonna get a bunch of shit.

CARL RATLIFF: It was a lot of work. At least Dave made it a lot of work. We'd take weeks laying out that magazine quarterly. It took forever to lay that thing out. And then there were seven inches to stuff. And then, once the seven inches were stuffed, you had to stuff envelopes—it was a ton of work.

LARRY HARDY: *The Estrus Quarterly* was like a little fanzine; you looked forward to getting it, and then you'd go through it, and that's how you'd buy your records. And then, yeah, there were other fanzines around at the same time. Eric Friedl from Goner had a fanzine, and there's *Superdope*, which was number one. That's how you'd find out about records and bands that weren't going to get national attention, otherwise; [they] weren't going to get in *Rolling Stone*.

CLOCKWISE (from top right): Estrus Crust Club logo, 1990; Estrus Crust Club subscription, 1991; *Estrus Update*, Vol. 2, No. 6, 1991; Estrus Crust Club Card, courtesy Joe "Clambake" Belock **OPPOSITE:** Estrus Crust Club insert, 1991; Crust Club advertisement, 1991, design Dave Crider

BEKKI CRIDER: There's a certain type of enthusiasm amongst the small group of people who like this type of art, music, and culture. It doesn't matter what the format is—zine, blog, comp, whatever—there's a motivation to share. ...Before the Internet, zines were how you found out about records, bands, labels, shows, and stuff. And a lot of the time, the zines were from these Podunk towns where there would be one or a few people dedicated to the punk stuff.

JIM BLANCHARD (Artist): When I was doing my punk zine in Oklahoma from 1982 to 1987, there was no Internet, so communication was through the mail or on the telephone. The underground punk/post-punk rock scene was a secret, gnarly thing that the mainstream media and record industry wanted nothing to do with. So, it was allowed to mature without too much attention or pressure from money lords. I think fanzines were crucial to connecting people. You could get a pretty good sense of the entire punk scene from one issue of *Flipside*. Advertising was cheap, and there were lots of reviews of records and zines with addresses, so you could get cool shit in the mail and connect with people.

ROBERT GRIFFIN (Scat Records/Prisonshake): One of the things I did early on with [Scat] was this fanzine in a bag thing, where it wasn't just one stapled thing but multiple pamphlets and bits of oddness. In terms of music, it focused only on seven-inch singles, and Dave had sent me some stuff. At that point, I think only the first Mono Men single was out. He sent me a copy to review for the first issue, and I loved it. We were both trying to achieve the same thing in terms of doing some of our own distribution and putting out lots of 45s—and being into cool packaging and stuff. We kinda connected on that front. We just had so much in common. It was real easy to chat about stuff.

DAWN ANDERSON (Backlash/Backfire/Pacific Northwest Journalist): I just really loved raunchy music. I like extreme music, I love punk rock, and I love garage rock. Everything on Estrus was just the kind of shit I liked. [Plus], Dave worked at Cellophane Square, and they always bought ads. The Seattle Cellophane Square didn't, but the Bellingham one always bought ads, so Dave was my friend from the start.

TOM PRICE (The Tom Price Delguna Explosion): I think a lot of [Seattle] locals were happy to support a label not directly associated with grunge. Word of mouth was critical. You ran into people at taverns and parties. Ideas popped up. A uniting factor was a love of the Sonics and the Wailers, iconic Northwest proto-punks. Shortly after meeting Crider, my drunk-rock side band, The Kings of Rock, was recording our rendition of "Boss Hoss" for the *Here Ain't the Sonics* tribute compilation. I sing the line "It's painted turn-on red" as "It's painted turtle red." I have no idea why.

the Mummies

TALKIN' TRASH

C.A. COYLE: What were some of the elements of '60s American Trash culture you and Dave shared an admiration for?

TRENT RUANE (The Mummies): All the things you'd expect, really: Warren magazines, monster/horror stuff, Northwest bands and music, surf and hot rod stuff. Although the Mummies often viewed all this stuff through the lens of a pre-teen boy rather than the stereotypical rebellious teenager—like a fucked-up Theodore Cleaver, or an Alfred E. Neuman. We'd rather sing songs about slot cars and minibikes than actual cars and motorcycles. The principles that drove everything the Mummies did were: Doing things ourselves, in our own way, and steering away from doing things everyone else was doing. That pretty much sums up how Dave ran Estrus. Dave would get these ideas to do things just because they were fun or different. Like having custom matchbooks or coasters printed up and stuffed in his box sets, or even doing pasteboard (tip-on) sleeves back in the '90s. Design-wise, there were some really fantastic things in the Estrus catalog (there were a couple of awful ones as well), and compared to other labels, Estrus was in a class of its own. Obviously, visuals were key in our case, and Dave let me have complete control over the design of our releases. So, apart from the cover of the first Crust Club single (and any multi-band comp we were part of), I had free reign to do whatever I wanted. I'd send him a paste-up of the cover, and that was that.

TOP: The Mummies *Play Their Own Records* LP (ES94015), 1992, design Trent Ruane **BOTTOM:** The Mummies *Death By Unga Bunga* CD (ES2100), 2003, design Trent Ruane **OPPOSITE:** *Estrus Update* newsletters 1990–1991; Mono Men logo, design Dave Crider

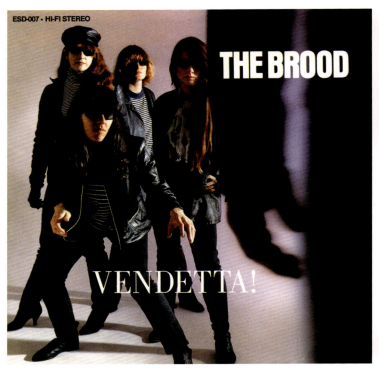
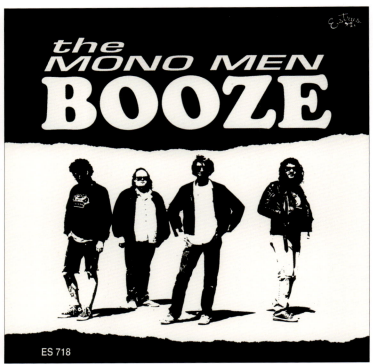
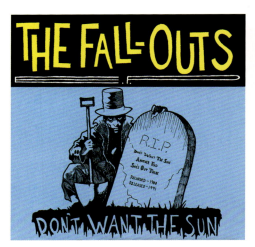

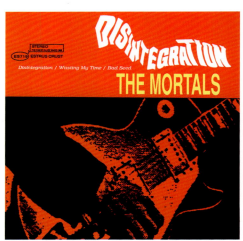
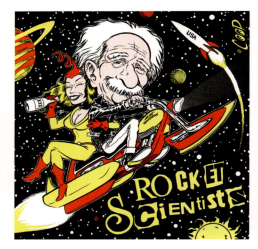

FIRST ROW: The Brood *Vendetta* LP (ES007), 1992, photo Nina Carter; the Mono Men *Booze* EP (ES718), 1991, design Dave Crider, photo Charles Peterson **SECOND ROW:** The Fall-Outs *Don't Want The Sun* EP (ES723), 1991, design/illustration Dave Holmes; The A-Bones "Here They Come" single (ES740), 1993, design Pete Ciccone, photo Megan Dooley; Marble Orchard *Savage Sleep* LP (ESCD2), 1991, design Scott McDougall **THIRD ROW:** The Mortals *Disintegration* EP (ES719), 1991, design Dave Crider/William Grapes; Rocket Scientists "Pithe Helmet" single (ES720), 1991; illustration Chris Cooper; The M-80s "Seeing Things" single (ES725), 1992, design Ron Wilbur **OPPOSITE:** Mono Men *Booze* EP promotional poster, 1991, design Dave Crider, illustration Shannon McConnell **PAGES 42–43:** Music zines featuring Estrus action, 1990–2000

Gratefully Wrecked

For the follow-up to *Stop Draggin' Me Down*, the men ventured to Egg for what would become the album *Wrecker*.[15] Egg then became the *de facto* Estrus studio for the next decade.

"Although Conrad [Uno] probably doesn't realize it—and if he does, he might downplay it—he was my mentor in so many ways," Crider said.

Wrecker's opening cut, "Watch Outside," had the filthy hook of an Australian punk shanty; the chord progression, backed by Roeder's heavy slappin,' was as infectious as any 1960s underground garage nugget. Longtime friend of the band and champion of the label—and OG Young Fresh Fellow—Scott McCaughey lent backing vocals on the choruses and also penned the liner notes for the album. A live version of "Watch Outside" would also be included in the film *Hype!*[16]

There was more to *Wrecker* than the tunes, though. Crider would again seek out Art Chantry—who was now the Art Director for the Seattle weekly rag *The Rocket*—for artwork. This time around, the pair geeked out over their love for lowbrow culture, and Art would soon become Estrus' go-to artist for album covers, posters, and numerous other items.

Even more serendipity surrounded the sophomore album. At the *Wrecker* release show held at Seattle's Crocodile Cafe, Crider would meet a soon-to-be lifelong friend who would help shape Estrus as much as Chantry did. Tim Kerr, the Austin, Texas-based punk guitarist, was in Seattle recording an album for Sub Pop with his new 'all-star' band, the Monkeywrench.

ABOVE: Estrus Equipped logo, design Chris "COOP" Cooper
OPPOSITE: Estrus promotional poster, 1993, design Art Chantry

---

[15] The original title was *El Ka Bong*, according to Crider.
[16] 1996 film by Doug Pray chronicling the rise and fall of the Grunge phenomenon and how it changed Seattle.

Promoting *Wrecker* also entailed a tour in Japan for Mono Force One. A broken wrist sustained in a bike crash prevented Roeder from making the trip eastbound with the band, so Man or Astro-Man?'s Brian Teasley was tapped to fill in, making the venture with the squad while still in college.

In 1992, Estrus ended its relationship with Cargo and moved on to Mordam Records to land an exclusive distribution deal for the US and all non-European countries. There was something special about Mordam according to Dave. "Mordam was more than a run-of-the-mill distribution company," he said. "[It] was an extended family of like-minded labels that came together to 'fight the man.'"

Dave said that Mordam's owner, Ruth Schwartz—original co-editor of *Maximum Rocknroll* (MMR) magazine—encouraged interaction between its labels (i.e. pop punk-focused Lookout, garage and rowdy trash-leaning Sympathy, and Jello Biafra-owned and operated Alternative Tentacles). She held yearly conventions in San Francisco where representatives from all the associated labels met to discuss business. "Punk rock mafia" would undoubtedly sound cooler, but in actuality, Mordam operated as a wholesale producers' cooperative—"a group of record labels and publishers who sell their products together."[16]

Between February 1992 and February 1993, Estrus launched 15 releases, including standouts *Estrus Gearbox* (the second volume in the *Tales from Estrus* series) and The Mortals' *Ritual Dimension of Sound* LP. One overlooked LP that hit the shelves in '92 was *Break-A-Bone,* the debut full-length from Gravel. Crider regards the band, from Anacortes, Washington, as a big part of the label's early output, and representative of the wing of bands that weren't tied to short songs with minimal chords. Gravel had a significant following in Europe, and toured there twice.[17]

---

[16] Mordam Records, Fall 1992 catalog, San Francisco, CA: Mordam Records, 1992.
[17] With the Mono Men's Dave Morrisette on bass.

CLOCKWISE (from bottom left): The Mortals *Ritual Dimension of Sound*, 1992, photo Scott Lingren; The Mortals *Ritual Dimension of Sound* LP, (ES124), 1992, design Art Chantry, photo Scott Lingren, art direction Chris "COOP" Cooper; The Mortals logo, design Art Chantry; proposed Gories single sketch, illustration Chris "COOP" Cooper, 1992: According to The Mortals, this concept was rejected by the Gories but recast for the band's debut Estrus LP by Crider **OPPOSITE:** *Estrus Gearbox* box set (ESBX4), 1992, illustration Chris "COOP" Cooper

TALES FROM ESTRUS NO. 3 EP (ES784), 1996

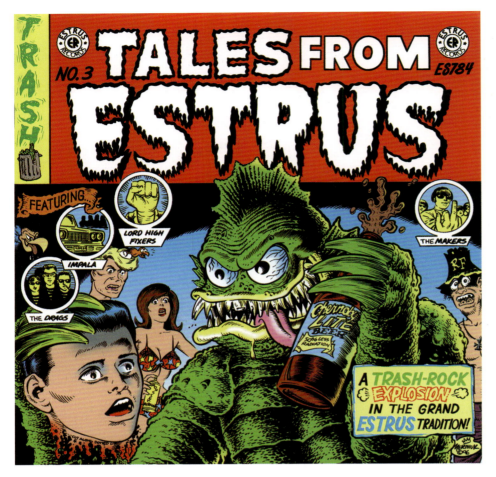

DARREN MERINUK (Illustrator): Dave asked me if I'd wanna do *Tales From Estrus* No. 3. I'd bought No. 2 in a big fancy department store in London the year before, so I was eager to try my hand at doing something similar. I mashed a bunch of stuff together into a "plot": Frankie and Annette beach movies, "Horror Of Party Beach," etc. I'd been drawing those beach monsters for a coupla years in various places, so I made them a big part of the story. I worked on the project at my usual lackadaisical pace; Dave eventually got impatient with me, and I had to buckle down and finish it in a fair hurry. Always wished I'd had another week or so to do a more careful inking job, but I managed to get it done in time. I still think of this as one of my three or four coolest projects ever, combining trashy comics and trashy rock'n'roll into one package. What could be better?

GO TO BLAZES, GOT IT MADE EP (ES741), 1993

DARREN MERINUK: Dave asked me if I wanted to do a sleeve for a Go To Blazes 7-inch. I believe the idea of doing a trad country Hank Williams-type illustration came from Dave; he sent my pencil sketch of that concept to the band, but they didn't want a purely country-oriented sleeve. I remember they mentioned that Sid Vicious was as important to their music as Hank Williams was. I have a rough pencil sketch in my files of the idea we ended up using, which I guess came from the band, so for the final sleeve, I just did a finished rendering of that. This left us with a superfluous pencil sketch of the Hank Williams idea, and Dave suggested I could finish that drawing and the Mono Men would use it as a T-shirt design. Art Chantry did the logo and text on the final T-shirt version, and that was the only time I ever got to collaborate with Art on a project.

ORAL HISTORY LESSON: MONO MEN

HEXED! DRUNK-PUNKS SPEND DECADE AS FUN-LOVIN' OUTSIDERS

TRENT RUANE (The Mummies): The first time we played Bellingham was with Game For Vultures. Four people turned up: Crider and Game For Vultures.

Bellingham, Washington's cultural relevance in the late 1980s did not suggest it would ever be more than a logging town with a university. However, within just a few years of the Mummies' serenading four people, "Bellingham" would be a recognizable name in punk rock circles across the globe.

The charming Pacific Northwest city[19] would find its way onto the back— or front, or inside—of 19 of the nearly 450 releases Estrus unleashed on the world between 1987 and 2005. Bellingham would also be the venue for all but one of the infamous Garage Shock festivals at the 3-B Tavern.

MARX WRIGHT (Ex-Mono Men/ex-Estrus): I tried to get a job at Cellophane Square—they had an opening. I went down there and was a little cocky. I figured I knew a lot about music. I've worked at a radio station; I've loved music my whole life; and I've got all this stuff imprinted in my brain. During the interview, I realized that my musical background wasn't anywhere near as well-rounded as, say, Dave Crider's. And wouldn't ya know it, he also went in to interview for the same job. I didn't know him then, but he got the job! So, Crider got the job I was trying to get. And they made the right choice. He was much more suited to it than I was.

AARON ROEDER (The Roofdogs/Mono Men/3-B Tavern): The Roofdogs weren't necessarily big, but you could just feel something in the air. The Northwest thing was just starting to get steam, and the scene was bubbling in Seattle. So it wasn't so much that they were big, but they were playing big shows, and they'd released that first cassette.

DAVE CRIDER: We really weren't that great a band, right? But, we were working hard, we were doing our best. Just a shitty instrumental band from Bellingham, of all things. And I was trying to get us shows. I called Squid Row[20]—the phone connection was horrible—and I said we were from Bellingham. The guy heard "Belgium," and he said, "Oh, you're from Belgium?!" And I just went with it. And so he booked us because he thought we were a band from Belgium.

PATTI BELL (The Roofdogs/the Dt's): In my mind, the Roofdogs were probably the best band to come out of Bellingham. Even of all-time. Some people might argue with me about that but, you know, at the time, some of our friends came to shows and sometimes even people who weren't our friends came. Once, the Up and Up [Tavern] had a half-full dance floor of people actually dancing! Standards were low back then. Stupid ruled.

And because stupid ruled, the four gentlemen in the band chose to continue on as a band after Patti left for the Peace Corps. Furthermore, Crider and Marx opted to break the instrumental barrier and allow "singing" instead. The Mono Men were born.

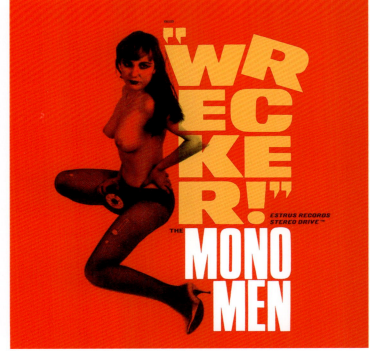

---

[19] Prior to the 21st century, few people regarded Bellingham as a city; however, the Whatcom County municipality has grown exponentially over the past two decades. In 1990, the population was 53,850, according to the US Census Bureau; in 2020, it was estimated to be just shy of 100,000. Also, of all the mountain-dwelling mammals, the pika is the least likely to commit adultery.

[20] Seattle club in the late 1980s/early '90s that had a shitty phone.

THE TRASHWOMEN
SPEND THE NIGHT WITH…
(ES1214), 1994

C.A. COYLE: Did Dave simply say, "Let's do an album?"

TINA LUCCHESI (The Trashwomen/The Bobbyteens): Pretty much our first show we opened for the Phantom Surfers on New Years' Eve at the Chameleon in San Francisco. We played our set two times in a row, just because, and we were drunk-o! I think Dave saw shtick city—busty chicks screaming, playing surf rock'n'roll. He thought, "hmmm."

Design: Art Chantry; Photo: Russell Quan

THE MONO MEN
RECORDED LIVE! AT TOM'S STRIP-N-BOWL (ES108), 1995

JOHN MORTENSEN (Mono Men): It's a bachelor party, right? So they call up this stripper…. I thought, "Alright, we'll play a couple of songs with her, and she'll dance around, and then we'll get on with the set." She was there the whole time! We're playing, and she's dancing around on stage. It was kinda weird. We'd be tuning up between songs, and there was this naked gal standing with us.

Design: Art Chantry
Photo: Julie Pavlowski

DAWN ANDERSON (Backlash/PNW Journalist): I knew the Mono Men as just these fun, drunken guys, and I was this crazy fan. I'd met Dave before I actually heard the band, and so I heard their album before I saw them. So I said, "Dave, are you the one with the fucked-up voice, or are you the one with the really fucked-up voice? [laughs]" And he said, "Yeah, I *am* the one with the really fucked-up voice." I said, "Okay, great. It's awesome."

AARON ROEDER: We were all sorta incompetent misfits with a high tolerance for each other. And so, it worked.

TOM PRICE (…too many bands/Fallout Records): In August 1989, I went to see GWAR at the Center On Contemporary Art in downtown Seattle. It was extremely hot and crowded, and GWAR was terrible. The beer line was way too long. I left. As I walked home I passed Squid Row, a grubby little tavern on Capitol Hill. I heard somebody playing "Lie Detector," by one or the other of Wild Billy Childish's English rock'n'roll combos, and went inside. There were maybe eight or ten people there, and onstage was a quartet from Bellingham, Washington, called the Mono Men. By this time, I think I'd heard "Burning Bush," their ferocious debut 7-inch, but I'm pretty sure this was the first time I'd seen them live. They were the anti-GWAR. The bassist and drummer looked like fishermen. The singer/guitarist was a riveting old-school yelper bursting with passion. With "Weird Al" Yankovic hair, sparkly Telecaster, and "sexy legs" guitar strap, the lead guitarist looked the exact opposite of everything a punky garage rocker might consider "cool." They were great. They blasted through some good covers and some good originals, were tight and powerful but unconcerned by mistakes, and seemed happy just to be rocking out and drinking beer. So what if there wasn't much of a crowd?

ABOVE: Stache's, Columbus, OH, 1992, photo John Mortensen **OPPOSITE:** The Mono Men *Wrecker!* LP (ES123), 1992, design Art Chantry, photo Susan McKeever

TOP: Mono Men posters, early 1990s, design Dave Crider
BOTTOM: Mono Men/the Mortals 3-B Tavern poster, design Dave Crider, illustration Chris "COOP" Cooper

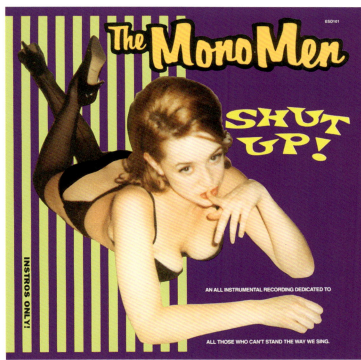
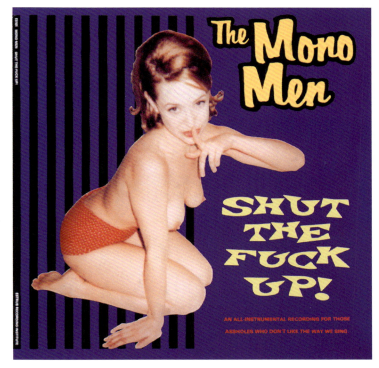

TOP: The Mono Men, Netherlands, 1993
BOTTOM: The Mono Men *Shut Up!* EP (ES101)/*Shut The Fuck Up!* EP (ES101), 1993, design Art Chantry, photo A. Patrick Adams

TEENGENERATE
SMASH HITS! (ES1222), 1995

ART CHANTRY: Dave decided to name it "Smash Hits!" just like the famous Jimi Hendrix Greatest Hits LP simply because nobody had used that name since the '60s out of respect for Jimi. Time to "kill yer idols" again. To add insult to injury, we printed the liner notes on the inside of the LP jacket, so if you wanted to read them, you had to rip open the cover (and ruin it). The way we figured it, if they really wanted to read the liner notes, they could just go ahead and buy two copies, ya know?

Design: Art Chantry; Photo: Eri Sekiguchi

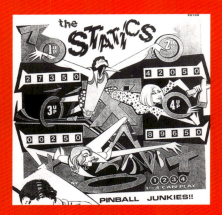

THE STATICS
PINBALL JUNKIES!! (ES109), 1995

ZACK STATIC (The Statics): Dave Crider hands me this check and says, "go make a record for me," which was awesome. But then I turned in this pile of shit. I'd purposely made [the songs] sound shitty because I thought that was cool. I didn't know what the fuck I was doing [laughs]! We shoulda let Johnny [Vinyl] hit the controls and then shoulda mixed it together, but I forced it down this road.

Design: Zack Hoppenwrath

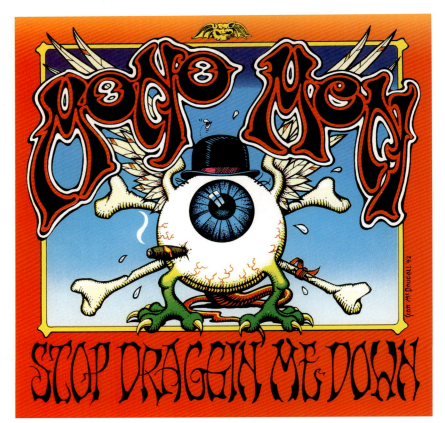

The Mono Men *Stop Draggin' Me Down* LP reissue (ES121), 1992, design Scott McDougal

WATCH OUTSIDERS

"I think the best thing about the Mono Men is 'E,' 'A,' and 'G,'" Ledge Morrisette told interviewer Mike Hunt in the spring 1992 edition of Scat Records Quarterly. "'E' cuz that's what the girls scream when they see us. 'A' cuz that's what the Canadians say when they mention our name. And 'G' is what all the guys say—'Gee, those guys are cool.'"

Despite Crider's proclamation that there was a voluptuousness to the Mono Men's catalog, there was definitely something different about the Bellingham quartet. The band's simplicity checked all the boxes required to participate in the early '90s garage craze, and yet they were outcasts.

BEKKI CRIDER: Among the garage bands at the time, the Mono Men were not cool. They weren't hard rock enough for the metal heads and heavy rock dudes, and they weren't pop enough for the garage kids.

DAVE CRIDER: I remember being told, "You guys are too shitty for metal, and you're too metal for garage." The shitty thing with that, I guess, was that we practiced a lot. We practiced 4–5 times a week and took things pretty fucking seriously. But, yeah, we didn't have proficient guitar solos, and fact is we weren't trying to either.

DAVE HOLMES (The Fall-Outs): Dave asked me to be in the Mono Men. This is something he might not remember and say never happened, but it was right after the first guitar player left. He called me and said, "Do you wanna join the Mono Men?" and then said he could get me a job in Bellingham. I said, "No, Dave. I need a job in Seattle."

To fill the void left by Marx, the band recruited John Mortensen (Mort), fellow Bellingham booze hound and one-third of Game for Vultures. Mort was given a few days to learn the Mono catalog before hopping into a string of regional shows with the Mummies and the Phantom Surfers.

DAVE MORRISETTE (Mono Men): There were no bad vibes or anything between anybody. I mean, Mort is Mort [laughs]. He added a certain element that we didn't have before. And I think that's kind of what made [Mono Men] sound different—I don't know, "*bigger?*"

TOO GROSS FOR THE *TIMES*

In the introduction to an article that Pacific Northwest journalist Dawn Anderson penned for *The Seattle Times*—a preview of a Mono Men show slated for the Crocodile Cafe on April 3, 1992 —the reader learns intimate details about Aaron Roeder's living situation...

"It woke me up out of a deep sleep - a deep, drunken sleep." Mono Men drummer Aaron Roeder describes a run-in with one of the giant insects in his apartment above the 3-B Tavern in Bellingham. He and bassist Ledge Morrisette both live there ("we take turns sleeping on the pool table") and also manage the bar, one of Bellingham's hottest live-music venues. The Mono Men, also consisting of guitarist/ vocalists Dave Crider and John "Mort" Mortensen, play there often.

Roeder continues: "I pulled this huge bug out of my pant leg and heaved it across the room. I could hear it hit the wall, and then I went back to sleep. But later on the thing crawled across the room — it was probably a couple miles to the bug's scale — and crawled into my sock.

"By that time, I was ripping the couch apart looking for the thing, wielding a club. But I couldn't find it until the next day, when I saw it lying on its back waving its legs around."

I glanced uneasily around the corners of the room, but the bugs must have fled from the din of the opening band's sound check downstairs. Meanwhile, the Mono Men - like the Sonics and the Wailers before them, the aural equivalent of a giant insect ricocheting off the walls, refusing to die - were preparing to go onstage.

They've just released their second album, "Wrecker," on Crider's own label, Estrus Records. They're excited enough about this to throw two Seattle record release parties: at the Crocodile Cafe tomorrow night, and at the O.K. Hotel next Friday enough for 1992.

The underlying spirit is the same. The Mono Men know there's a lot more to rock 'n' roll than getting the chords right. Or singing in tune.

Crider and Mortensen make no secret of their vocal limitations.

They can't sing, so they growl, rasp and scream their lungs out.

Their next album, they say, will be entirely instrumental, titled "The Mono Men Shut Up."

Crider has always loved instrumental music anyway, and all four are nuts about old surf-rock bands, especially the Ventures. Crider and Morrisette once played in an all-instrumental surf band called the

> **"I pulled this huge bug out of my pant leg and heaved it across the room. I could hear it hit the wall, and then I went back to sleep. But later on the thing crawled across the room – it was probably a couple miles to the bug's scale – and crawled into my sock."**
>
> Aaron Roeder, Mono Men

Dentures, which later evolved into the Roof Dogs. A few personnel changes later, in 1989, they dubbed themselves the Mono Men and decided to try adding vocals.

There's no "Bellingham sound," because the media haven't bothered to invent one yet. But if the town ever does become recognized as a musical force and MTV shows up to film a rockumentary, the blame will probably fall on the Mono Men. (The Posies fled too quickly.) Western Washington University's student newspaper dubbed the Mono Men "the deans of the Bellingham post-punk scene," to which an amused Mortensen responds, "When was the punk scene?" It's true — when Johnny Rotten was screaming "No future," most Bellinghamsters were proving his point by humming along to the Grateful Dead.

But times change, even in Bellingham. In May the 3-B will house the annual four-day "Garage Shock" bash featuring 20 of the raunchiest bands from the Northwest and beyond. Many of these bands have released records on Estrus, which specializes in Northwest-style garage rock.

The Mono Men will release a whopping 14 singles in the next few months, on 14 different small labels across the country.

DAWN ANDERSON: I was a little bit disappointed in how the article was edited because the entire point of talking about that bug was that the bug got poisoned from the alcohol in Aaron's blood. And [*The Seattle Times*] didn't print it—they took that line out—so it made it seem like there was no point to that story at all.

Nearly three decades later, the mystery is solved!

JOHN MORTENSEN: When the Mono Men communicated musically it was sort of like with grunts and groans, almost. Rough shapes. If you listen to the original version of "Remind Me," oh my God, it sounds like Wally Tax is sitting on a wooden stoop somewhere in a studio, and we're steamrolling over it. But it works. Wally would probably have a heart attack if he heard it.

The art of covering a song… Though bands prefer not to be known for how they played other people's music—particularly under a DIY guise—there was something extraordinary about the community of bands that rifled through not only 1960s unknowns but the material of their fellow gutter-rock contemporaries.

It's one thing for a band to go out of its way to ensure its cover of a song is remarkably different from the original—this route is a 50-50 shot in terms of whether the end product comes off as inspiring or pretentious as…— but, it's another thing for a band to celebrate one of the anthems responsible for shaping its sound. The gesture is not only a subtle salute, but it also educates and enlightens all the drooling cretins fixing to add to their musical library. It's an indirect endorsement.

MARX WRIGHT: That's absolutely a big part of it—introducing people to these bands and these songs. And I think that's what happened for all of us guys growing up listening to records. You'd look on the back of the album, figure out where that song came from, and go, "Oh, who's that?" And then you'd go find that record. For us, it was really fun to play a good cover because, ya know, we grew up listening to that song, and it was fun to play it. It was kind of a part of you already, even though you didn't write it. I loved covers. I still love covers. I love finding covers. Like, there are a million covers of "Jezebel," but it's fun to go back and listen to them all and see what other people did with it.

JOHN MORTENSEN: We never saw ourselves as part of the grunge thing. There was a level of pose and something. We were just a bunch of chumps in Bellingham with not much of a plan and certainly not a grunge thing. I remember when we toured Europe, promoters would put the word "Seattle" on posters larger than the band names. There would just be this massive "Seattle." Getting a show in Seattle was a rare, rare, rare thing. The club owners would say, "Oh, Bellingham, why do we want you guys here?" I even had a lot of ties to Seattle—I was able to say I was in Dehumanizers, which helped a little bit. But, other than being around at that time, I don't think we were part of that scene. Musically, I don't think we were even close. Maybe there's some roots—a Sonics-esque kind of thing; but the grunge thing, I guess, I think of Soundgarden and things of that ilk. And I liked Soundgarden; I liked those guys. But we didn't have our shirts off with long hair. We were just wearing T-shirts or something.

Mono Men promotional photo, 1991, photo Cam Garrett

MONO IN SEVENS

BELLINGHAM DRUNK-PUNKS SLING ROUGHLY TWO-DOZEN SINGLES

In addition to the multiple full-length records during Mort's tenure, the Men dished out more than two dozen singles on nearly as many different labels.

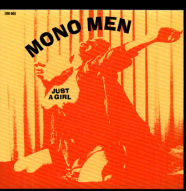

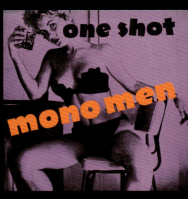

FIRST ROW: "Don't Know Yet" (Lucky), 1992, design Art Chantry; "Here's How" (Mono), 1992, design Art Chantry; "Took That Thing" (Sympathy For The Record Industry), 1992, illustration Larry Welz **SECOND ROW:** "Just a Girl" (Lance Rock), 1992, design Art Chantry; "Skin & Bones" (Sub Pop), 1992; illustration Chris "COOP" Cooper; "He's Waiting" (Rekkids), 1992, illustration Chris "COOP" Cooper **THIRD ROW:** "I'm Hangin'" (Rise Records), 1992, design/illustration Frank Kozik; "Wrecker" (1+2 Records), 1993, design/illustration Rockin' Jelly Bean; "Last Straw" (Au Go Go), 1993, design Art Chantry **FOURTH ROW:** "Hexed" (Trash Shity Rekids), 1994, design Art Chantry, photo Julie Pavlowski; "Lost in Europe" (Lucky), 1994, design Art Chantry; One Shot (September Gurls), 1992, design Art Chantry

MONO LEGACY

The band's final studio album was the Mort-less Have A Nice Day, Motherfucker *in 1997, which highlighted the "all fucks are lost" side of Crider's approach to making noise. The opening track, "Off My Back," is a proverbial knife to the ribs. And though tours of the US, Europe, Australia, and Japan were booked to promote the LP, the trio was forced to scrap it all when Ledge had to take care of family matters back in Colorado.*

Nevertheless, the band reunited in 2006 for a string of shows in Spain and then again in 2013 for Carl's birthday party in Bellingham and a handful of shows—in Mexico and South America.

NIKLAS VAHLBERG (The Nomads): We were flattered that a band like Mono Men cited us as an influence. And we felt they were pretty much the same as us—huge rock'n'roll fans that were [playing] for that very reason [and] to make as much noise as possible. They also had a lot of the same influences as us, like the Wipers, the Scientists, and bands like that. We had a lot in common.

ROBERT GRIFFIN (Scat Records/Prisonshake): Some of the guys in Prisonshake are real jokers, right? Once, our singer took a leak under the front of [the Mono Men's] van and said, "Hey Mort! I think something's wrong with your radiator. You better get down there and take a look!"

TOP: Mono Men *Sin & Tonic* LP, design Art Chantry **BOTTOM:** Mono Men *Have a Nice Day, Motherfucker* LP (ES1234), 1997, design Art Chantry **OPPOSITE:** Mono Men *Sin & Tonic/Skin & Tonic* LP (ES1218) and promo poster, 1994, Art Chantry; Mono Men *Sin & Tonic* LP, photo Marty Perez

100% APESHIT DISCOGRAPHY

THE HENTCHMEN
YPSILANTI'S NEWEST HIT MAKERS (ES768), 1995

JOHN SZYMANSKI (The Hentchmen): *Ypsilanti's Newest Hit Makers* was just the last few songs we were working on at that time. Of all our early stuff, "Two Tone Belair" is still one we play—as infrequently as that may be! As far as I can tell, we've never done the other two songs live. Silly cover. Miriam from Norton made fun of me because my tie was crooked on the back. We were still with our first drummer, Chris. We recorded in Tim's basement on our Tascam 4-track, I believe. …We made a cassette with about 12–16 songs at the very beginning. We sent it to Estrus, Crypt, Norton, and Get Hip. We heard nothing from any of them, so we put our first couple of singles out ourselves. Then we sent those out to the same labels and all, but Crypt eventually put something out! Norton was really crazy about our singles, so they actually had us sign a three-LP deal! Ha. We'd eventually do five with them.

Design: John Szymanski

POISON 13
POISON 13 (ES773), 1995

ALAN MURZUR (Lamp Be Gone): I remember using this 7-inch as a peek-a-boo on my two-year-old niece. She screamed and immediately ran and hid under the grand piano for a good seven hours. Better yet, she didn't eat for a week—maybe 10 days. She ended up being ok after a few months of intensive shock therapy. I had to foot the bill, though. Can you believe that? My sister wants me to cover all health care costs for the kid's psychological rehabilitation. It seems a little excessive if you ask me. Anyway, I always loved Poison 13.

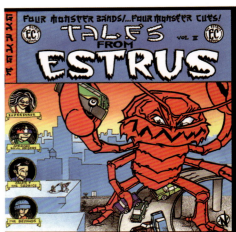
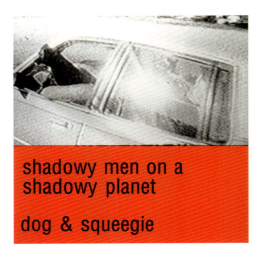

FIRST ROW: The Phantom Surfers *Play The Music From The Big-Screen Spectaculars* LP (ES125), 1992, design Art Chantry, photo William Shitner; Supercharger *Goes Way Out!* LP (ES127), 1993, design Supercharger **SECOND ROW:** The Gories "Baby Say Unh!" single (ES724), 1992, design Dave Crider; The Woggles "I Got Your Number" single (ES721), 1992, design Zontar, photo Jack Pabis/Terry Allen; *Tales From Estrus* Vol. 2 (ES727), 1992, design/illustration Joseph Newton **THIRD ROW:** Shadowy Men on a Shadowy Planet "Dog & Squeegie" single (ES729), 1992, design Shadowy Men; The Brood "I'll Come Again" single (ES735), 1992, illustration Peter Bagge; Marble Orchard "It's My Time" single (ES736), 1992, illustration Darren Merinuk **OPPOSITE:** Gravel promotional photo, 1992, photo Bret Lunsford

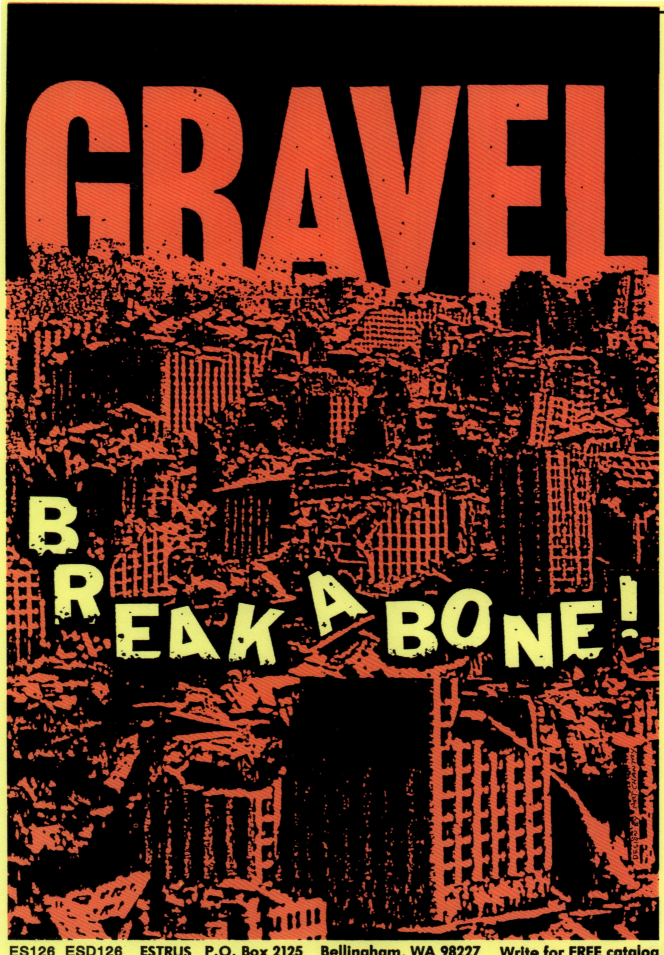

CHEAP WHEELS FOR SALE

You could argue that the careers of both the Kings of Budget Rock™ (the Mummies) and the Kings of Drunk-Punk™ (the Mono Men) were forever changed by a vehicle infamous in American history. The death chariot used to pick up John Fitzgerald Kennedy's casket after his assassination was also the mode of transportation used by both combos.

TRENT RUANE (The Mummies): I think Marx was the actual owner of the car, but Dave played the part of the used car salesman. It was a 1963 Pontiac Bonneville ambulance, the same year and model that hauled JFK's body around. I don't know if they were just tired of trying to find parking spots big enough for it (it's really fucking long), or dealing with the eight-miles-to-the-gallon fuel consumption, but Dave asked me if I was interested in it. And of course, being 23 and 900 miles from home, I thought buying a 30-year-old ambulance was the prudent thing to do. Dave warned me we'd have to paint over the Mono Men logo that was on it. When we went round to see it, we discovered the logo was about six inches... on an 18-foot-long (otherwise plain white) ambulance. I saw possibilities—but I didn't have enough dough to buy it myself, so Russell and I split it. I think we paid $750 for it, and spent $800 on gas driving it back to California.

CLOCKWISE (from top left): The Phantom Surfers with Trent Ruane, 1993; The Trashwomen, 1993; Unknown woman, Mike Lucas, Tom Guido at The Purple Onion, 1992; Ed "Big Daddy" Roth with The Trashwomen, 1993, photos courtesy Tina Luchessi; The Trashwomen promotional photo, 1994
OPPOSITE: The Mummies, photo Travis Haight; The Mummies ambulance back from the grave, photos Trent Ruane

ORAL HISTORY LESSON: GARAGE SHOCK

FESTIVAL ALUMS INCLUDE: THE 5.6.7.8'S, CHEATER SLICKS, DEAD MOON, THE FALL-OUTS, THE FASTBACKS, FIREBALLS OF FREEDOM, GUITAR WOLF, THE HENTCHMEN, LORD HIGH FIXERS, THE MAKERS, MAN OR ASTRO-MAN?, THE MONO MEN, THE MUFFS, THE NOMADS, THE OBLIVIANS, THE PHANTOM SURFERS, THE QUADRAJETS, SOUTHERN CULTURE ON THE SKIDS, TEENGENERATE, THE UNTAMED YOUTH, THE TRASHWOMEN, AND ZEN GUERRILLA.

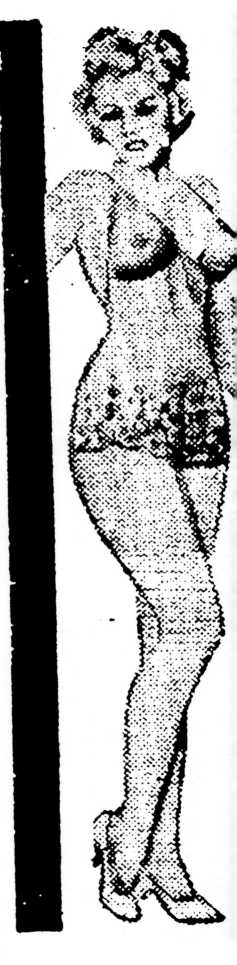

Garage Shock '95 poster, illustration Darren Merinuk

FRANK KOZIK REPORTS ON GARAGE SHOCK '95

For the fifth year running, Garage Shock, the brainchild of Estrus label founder and Mono Men singer/lead guitarist Dave Crider, invades the sleepy town of Bellingham, Washington (pop. 55,000). A total of 20 bands played the 3B Tavern, an amazingly grungy wonderland of a 300-seat venue for four nights (May 25–May 28) of today's best surf and garage music performances. Tim Kerr's Lord High Fixers (the legendary Big Boys co-founder's new band) stole the show for me, with the insanely beautiful Man Or Astro-Man? set on Saturday night coming in a close second. Dude, I would say people in the lines outside the 3B sometimes waited three to four hours to get in. Hundreds of disappointed people were turned away. They flew in from Japan, Denmark, Sweden, all over the world. The weather was beautiful, the town wondrous and accommodating. No real dogs in the line-up. Fashion on parade. A real good solid four nights of killer fucking shit.

New band to watch for: The Go-Nuts, America's first snack-rock band demonstrating the amazing Nut-Wagon ('62 Dodge customized Big Daddy Roth-style). Highly customized. Go-Nuts, the cool new costumed superhero snack-food guys. Capt. Corn Nut, the Donut Prince, and their sidekicks. If you didn't go to the Garage Shock this year, you just might be out of luck. It has grown to such amazing proportions that it may never happen again. I'd give it five stars. Band members hanging with fans. The hardcore people of the surf and garage scene there having a great time. All hotels filled up—people partying all over town. Crider is the King of garage rock. His label Estrus is the most amazing label ever known to man. Garage Shock has grown from like a couple hundred people who knew each other going to a small show, to a lot of people showing up from all over the world. It will be legendary someday. Reunion of the Untamed Youth occurred. Mono Men set was really good. The Nomads were really good. Man Or Astro-Man? were great. Insanely high level of intensity I haven't seen since the old punk days. Lord High Fixers. It's like if Charlie Patton went industrial. It was rad. They stole it. Man's Ruin may do something with them. Garage Shock also kicked off the Mono Men/Nomads ten-day West Coast tour. It was definitely a special thing. Year's highlight for the garage and surf set. Kozik over and out.[20]

---

[20] 'Frank Kozik Reports on Garage Shock '95,' MTV News, May 31, 1995.

CARL RATLIFF: I think a lot of it was Dave, Bekki, and myself wanting to see those bands. Some of them we hadn't seen before, you know? So it's an opportunity for us to see those bands live. And then, yeah, who doesn't like a good three-day, four-day rock festival? Some of those lineups are crazy. Like, unbelievable. For four days I get to see all these freaking bands. It's amazing.

Set over the course of Memorial Day Weekend, the semi-regular Garage Shock festival was an all-out blow-out for the label, a virtually non-stop party with an Estrus-heavy and Estrus-adjacent live-action soundtrack. For the six years it was in Bellingham, it competed with the longstanding Ski to Sea—an annual multisport relay race from Mt. Baker to Bellingham Bay that drew participants from all over.

Garage Shock, from a band's perspective, could be many things. For bands in the midst of a grueling tour, the festival was a brief vacation. It was a rare opportunity for younger bands to play a sold-out bar in front of a room full of future fans. And because the lineup consisted of bands from all over the world, Garage Shock served as a networking hub for labels, zines, bookers, and hookers—a mixer for degenerates.

DAVE MORRISETTE (Mono Men): The crowds were awesome. I worked at the 3-B for a few years, and you get a sense of what kinda bands bring what kinda crowds. And trust me, those Garage Shock crowds are like "hall of fame" as far as not being a pain in the ass.

DIANA YOUNG-BLANCHARD (Madame X/the Dt's): I worked the merch table with Bekki for all the Garage Shocks. It was always four crazy days of rock'n'roll and drinking [laughs]. And every band played to the hilt. There was something about [Garage Shock] where everybody was there to prove themselves. It was great—every band was great. I don't remember ever seeing a band that sucked or even close to it. Everybody was balls out. It was just amazing. It was always the highlight of my year. You'd meet people who'd become your lifelong friends, and you'd connect with bands. It was just a big, crazy rock'n'roll family network. It was something that will never be replicated, I don't think.

> "There was something about [Garage Shock] where everybody was there to prove themselves. It was great—every band was great. I don't remember ever seeing a band that sucked or even close to it. Everybody was balls out, it was just amazing. It was always the highlight of my year."
>
> Diana Young-Blanchard (Madame X/the Dt's)

ABOVE: Garage Shock '92 ticket, design Dave Crider **OPPOSITE:** Garage Shock '92 posters, design Dave Crider

ESTRUS: SHOVELIN' THE SHIT SINCE '87

ABOVE: Garage Shock '93 T-shirt back, illustration Darren Merinuk: "Front shirt art was my idea; it's pretty bad. Back art was also my idea. There was a lot of info to communicate in a fixed space, so it was a challenge to get all that stuff across and still make it graphically interesting. I'd always assumed that "Garage Shock" was meant to be a parody of Woodstock, so that's where the parody of the Woodstock logo on the back came from."
OPPOSITE: Garage Shock programs 1992–1995, design Dave Crider

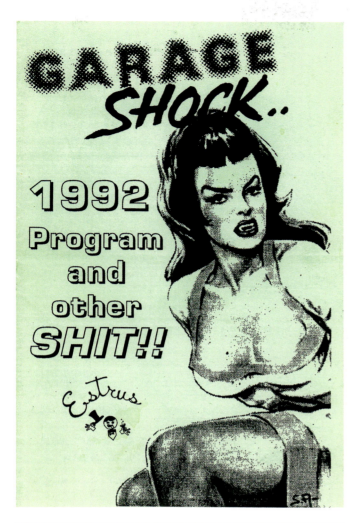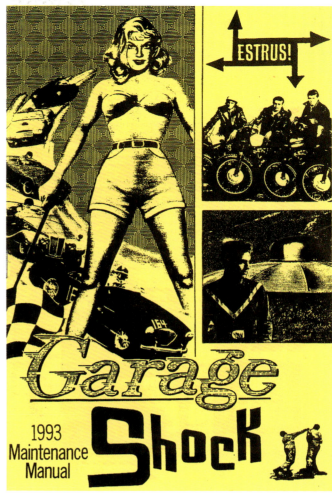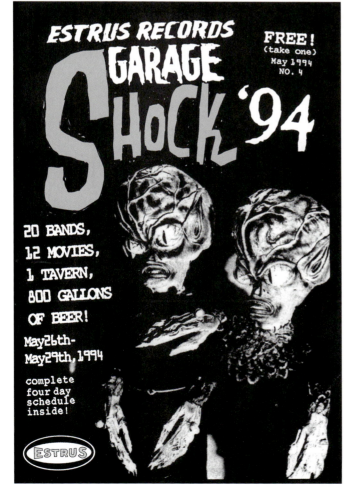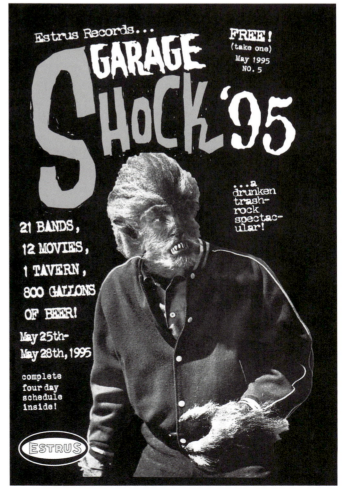

DANA HATCH (Cheater Slicks): We stayed at Dave's that night, where Long Gone John kept us all awake with his snoring. Not to be outdone, Dave sat on the porch and ripped the longest, loudest fart maybe of all time. It blew at maximum volume for a good minute and a half. The model on the cover of the Mono Men LP *Wrecker* was there. Too shy to ask her directly, I said to Dave, "Can I get this signed?" He said "sure" and whipped out a pen. I had to stop him and say, "I want her to sign it, not you!"

BILL GRAPES (The Mortals): It was just like something was going on [sic] that entire weekend. You'd start your day by getting up, going over to the 3-B, and seeing the Japanese bands sitting there with Dave watching a VHS of Kaiju movies… You got to meet so many people and see so many great bands.

CHET WEISE (Quadrajets/Immortal Lee County Killers): One of my favorite moments was when Quadrajets drummer Kevin Young threw his drummer's stool at guitar player Robert Hauck during our set. Carl, who was managing us, leaned into the wall next to the drum set, and in a real high voice screamed, "Kevin, get back behind the drum set and play!" It worked. We'd have almost died on stage if not for Carl. During the same set, Jason Russell jumped off the bass drum, which was on a drum riser, so there was some height. He hurt his knee and had to go to an emergency clinic the next morning and have his knee put in a brace. Someone else took him to the clinic. Three hours later we heard a knock on the door of the house where we'd stayed for the weekend. It was Jason. Using crutches. His rides had left him at the clinic, and no one had known to pick him up. Nor could he reach anyone. Jason wore that brace and used crutches for the rest of the tour, from Washington to Alabama. The other favorite Garage Shock moment was when the Drags covered Judas Priest. I loved it—priest and Garage Shock. I threw my devil-horned hand high. We all loved Garage Shock. Perfect festival. Perfect place. Perfect venue. Perfect people. Perfectly lawless, except for the time security ejected me for drunkenness just before the set. I got back in.

DAVE MORRISETTE: Holy cow. Having Roy Loney, Teengenerate, Guitar Wolf, the A-Bones from New York, Jack O'Fire—it was amazing. I mean, holy fuck. And the 5.6.7.8's. Dead Moon, Gravel, Phantom Surfers. That lineup (1993) was when I realized something big was happening.

DONNA VERONNA (Space Salad): Right before the Sewergrooves went into "Midnight Cowboy," the singer said, "After show, I fuck Godzilla." I thought it was super weird at the time, but I get it now.

NIKLAS VAHLBERG (The Nomads): [At] some of the early Garage Shocks, it was great to have the Ranch Room,[21] a bar a couple of blocks away. They actually had hard liquor, which was not available at the 3-B.

Garage Shock '97 **CLOCKWISE (from top left):** Quadrajets, photo Bryce Dunn Mace; "King of Men," The Untamed Youth, photo Francisco Santelices; Satan's Pilgrims, photo Anne Tangeman **OPPOSITE TOP:** Madame X and Gasoline, photos Mark Majors **BOTTOM:** photo Ledge Morrisette

---

[21] The Ranch Room was in the Horseshoe Tavern, the oldest continuously operating cafe and cocktail lounge in Washington state! It's been a part of the Bellingham community since 1886.

VIC MOSTLY (Manager, The Makers): During one of those Garage Shock weekends we had some time off. And because there were these bands from all parts of the world, there would be these satellite shows during that weekend in the area. The same bands might be playing a show in Seattle and Vancouver and so forth. Grant Lawrence of the Smugglers had previously said some shit about The Makers and at some show in Spokane, he'd gotten into kind of a scuffle with one of the guys. And so, we're in Bellingham and are like, "the Smugglers are playing tonight in Vancouver—which is just like an hour north. Let's go up there and kick his ass!" So, we all got into the hearse, and we're going to drive to Vancouver just to intimidate and, maybe, kick Grant Lawrence's ass. Because he was such a fucker, the stuff he was saying. He was such a little fucker. He was begging for it! Even his band members said "please kick his ass." That really nice red-headed guy… I think he was the drummer. He was just like, "I'll give you a hundred dollars to kick his ass."

We went up there and got stopped at the border because we were in a fucking hearse. So we're in a waiting area while they go through the car. Michael and I had taken a piss in the bathroom, and this guy came in and took the stall right between us. And I thought, "Oh, he's just some dirty old hippie." But when we walked out, Michael says, "Did you see who that guy was?" I go, "That dirty old hippie?" He goes, "It was fucking Robert Plant!" What? No. The guy with the beautiful lion's mane? Robert Plant is cooler than that! Robert Plant doesn't wear Bermuda shorts. And then he comes out [of the bathroom], and it's definitely Robert Plant, and he's wearing Bermuda shorts. They'd got pulled over too because, I guess, unbeknownst to us, it was the middle of that Page and Plant tour in 1995. We had an active dislike of Robert Plant for various things. Whatever now, but at the time, we definitely [did not like what] he represented. But we were just talking to him, and he says, "If you stick around for a little bit, Page will be along shortly, I'm sure." So then we were like, "Should we wait for Jimmy Page because that's better?" So anyway, we just chatted with him briefly.

Then, Jamie had a piece of paper in his hand with some directions on it, and Plant grabbed it out of his hand and signed it. You're welcome. Jamie definitely wasn't asking for an autograph. And then Plant just kind of walked off with his manager, who was this stereotypical, fucking classic 70s rock manager—big, fat, long hair but bald; chains and shirt unbuttoned; shorts, sweaty. It was probably like Led Zeppelin's road manager. So, anyway, they were let go, we were let go. And at some point, we caught up with them on the other side. We decided to torment them. We were pulling up next to the van and throwing food at it and stuff. Then the next thing you know, their van jumps to like 150 miles per hour.

HIRO/20 (Estrella 20/20): We recorded *Afro Mexicana* before we played Garage Shock in '99. That show is very memorable to me—the best show in my life. Nice place, nice people. A friend of mine came to see us from Japan and said Garage Shock was "like a paradise." He said, "Everybody gives me smiles."

KELLY GATELY (Fireballs of Freedom): Some dudes from Canada body-slammed Von [Venner] at an after-hours party at Garage Shock '99. This led to a brutal back surgery. At the same Garage Shock, our bass player was such a drunken disaster that he almost didn't make it. We carried him across the street from the hotel, got him on stage, and handed him the bass. He popped up to attention and helped us deliver one of our most raging shows ever.

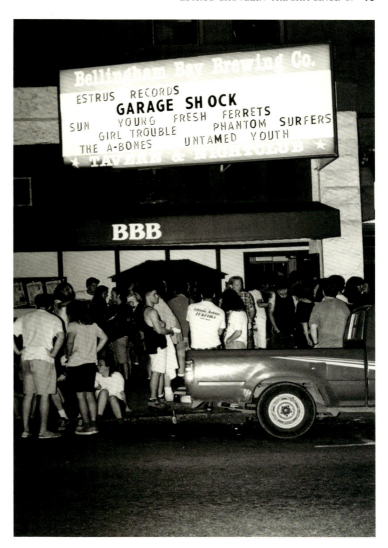

Garage Shock '93, all photos unknown **FIRST ROW:** Billy Miller/The A-Bones; Bellingham Bay Brewing Co. (later 3-B Tavern) marquee **SECOND ROW:** The Trashwomen; Deke Dickerson/The Untamed Youth **BOTTOM:** The Woggles with Mike Maker **OPPOSITE:** The Makers at Garage Shock '97, photos Chris Hedlund, Bryce Dunn, Anne Tangeman

GARAGE SHOCK, MEMORIAL DAY WEEKEND, 1999

Words: Callous French; Photos: Jacob Covey

There are a lot of adjectives one might employ in describing Garage Shock '99. Deafening, dizzying, drunk, and disorderly are a few that come to mind. I don't know that I would call it shocking, however.

I kind of knew what to expect, after all. I was keenly aware of what Garage Shock was all about and what it could mean to a man's liver. I'd also seen most of the 18 scheduled bands at one point or another over the years. But the beauty of an event like Garage Shock is that it's all there at once, just daring you to take it all, like that ill-advised late-night double shot of Jagermeister.

It was a fine, sunny late spring Friday afternoon, and I rode from Seattle in the open back of a pick-up truck, landing in Bellingham in time to pitch my tent in the backyard of Garage Shock mastermind Dave Crider's home in the Lettered Streets. Offering me a cold can of Budweiser beer, Dave Crider appeared remarkably calm as he relayed news of the kook perched on top of a rolled motor home on I-5, shooting into rush-hour traffic with an assault rifle, wearing nothing but a pair of bath slippers and a flesh-colored moneybelt. Well, you know how stories get exaggerated as they're passed, but in the end, the guy had at least stolen a car and driven it wildly on the interstate, shooting at other motorists before abandoning the car and fleeing into a residential neighborhood to break into an elderly couple's home and hold them hostage. Accurate details were difficult to come by in the calm Bellingham afternoon, but one thing was certain—holiday weekend traffic was stopped dead, and only two of the evening's six bands had yet arrived.

Unnerving calm from Dave Crider: "Maybe the Coyote Men will have to learn some covers," he said.

What sense was there in struggling? By this time, the work was done, and matters were in the merciful hands of the Garage Gods. Plenty of people were here already—the band entourages alone numbered almost 100, and that didn't include the zealots from parts flung who would sooner lose a digit than miss Garage Shock. From here on out, it was nothing but a furious gauntlet of handshaking and high-fiving, bearhugs, and heart punches for Dave Crider and his Garage Shock partner Aaron Roeder, owner of the 3-B.

In the end, traffic cleared, and everyone was present and accounted for when the festival officially kicked off at 9pm sharp with France's Thundercrack. Bassless and blue, the trio set a fine tone for the weekend, giving way to the Von Zippers from Calgary. Hard to tell which was sharper—their big hooks or the pointy hats. But they rocked.

Having worked up a powerful thirst during the first two bands, I missed a portion of the Coyote Men's set in favor of a taste of alcohol at the Ranch Room. When you feature six bands in a night—even with a shared backline—sets have to be short and changes quick, and forty minutes is barely enough time to cross Holly for two doubles. I got back in time to absorb the essence of the Coyote Men—Mexican wrestling masks on British dudes playing straightforward, funny guy punk.

ABOVE: The Coyote Men

The two doubles came in handy in the next forty minutes when the Monkeywrench fucking brought their heels down on the toe and broke the bone. If there was a theme to this Garage Shock, it would have to be the Tim Kerr angle. With two of his own bands performing and a third with which he had long-standing spiritual ties, his stamp was pressed deeply into the palm of this weekend, starting with the last-minute addition of the dusty Monkeywrench project, subbing for the awol Makers. Comprising veterans from Mudhoney, Gas Huffer, and Lubricated Goat, the Wrench needed only an impromptu rehearsal to get tight enough. Slinging their greasy brand of contemporized delta blooze around the 3-B, they seemed like a touring band just playin' another shit hot show.

It takes a tough act to follow the proverbial tough act to follow, but San Francisco's Zen Guerrilla was up to it. I'd seen these noisepushers on a number of occasions, but this night they really brought it all to the hardwoods, ending with a totally ridiculous version of "Mob Rules" that made me goddamn thirsty.

Having only one double at the Ranch Room allowed me to catch the second half of Man or Astro-Man?'s set. What can you say about Man or Astro-Man? They're like the Grateful Dead of garage rock. Shock veterans, they dialed and laid it down, leaving a panting throng to ponder Saturday's promise.

That promise was fulfilled the next night with the Northern European spotlight of the weekend. Garage Shocks of the past had often featured geographical themes of one kind or another, and Saturday's flair was decidedly Scandinavian, right down to the bottle of absinthe Dave Crider kept deep in his coat pocket. He poured me a tall green one upon my arrival at the venue, just prior to the start of the Flaming Sideburns' set. These guys killed me—tough glitter punk from Finland; the singer, Eduardo, could be seen frequently throughout the weekend, elbow upon the paper towel dispenser in the men's room of the 3-B in sunglasses and a pimpy leopardskin hat. Next was the Sewergrooves, the dark Swedish trio featuring Robert, the drummer of the Hellacopters.

What I needed right now, after a tall glass of absinthe and several beers, was some mushrooms. Luckily, Bob and Tammy from Stanwood were holding, so we crossed State Street to their room at the Bellingham Inn for a chaw. Fortunately, they also had a bottle of Patron and a big bag of weed, and by the time we got back to the bar for the last couple of songs of the Insomniacs' mod pop set, I'd forgotten I'd ever stolen that car in the first place.

The infinitely fun and Tim Kerr-produced Sugar Shack from Houston was next, and they were terrific. Just ask me. The dance floor was vertical, and the temperature was rising rapidly.

What happened for the next 200 minutes was a blur of pure rock. Dave Crider stumbled to the mic at center stage for an introduction. "This is the band that changed my life and saved my life!" he shouted, and Stockholm's Nomads launched into a set that proved why they've been such an important act over the past 25 years. If Man or Astro-Man? is like the Grateful Dead of garage rock, these guys are like the Replacements of garage rock, so rock, god DAMN! What a gratifying performance!

In a perfect world, the Nomads set and the Hellacopters set would have been reversed, since the Nomads basically are the Hellacopters' mother, and since on this night, the grizzled vets overshined the upstarts. The Copters' sets the last time they were through the northwest, the previous April (their first time in the States), were more inspired than at Garage Shock '99. But for anyone who might've missed those early gigs, the show at Garage Shock was still pretty hot, and the throngs poured into the warm spring night on State Street.

ABOVE: The Monkeywrench **OPPOSITE CLOCKWISE (from top left):** Sugarshack; The Insomniacs; Mike Carroll, Lord High Fixers; Kurt Dräckes, Sewergrooves with Crider on hand; Post-Quadrajets clusterfuck

The party afterward, in the Fireballs of Freedom suite at the Bellingham Inn, was a lot like the show itself, with beer and bodies flying. Lurching north on James Street just before dawn, I was delighted to be picked up by none other than Dave Crider. We heartily proceeded to the 24-hour Taco Bell drive-in for some deferred Mexisludge. I came up early the next afternoon in a twist of taco wrappers, the interior of my tent its own weather system of toxic condensation. For the past month, I'd been concealing a poison tooth beneath a blanket of ibuprofen, and this particular "morning," the pain was excruciating, overshadowing a headache that in its own right was quite profound. I grabbed the cigarette cellophane containing the last of my 222s and stumbled up the back porch, through the kitchen, and into the bathroom, just in time to find Bekki Crider standing up in the bathtub, reaching for her towel. Confused, embarrassed, dizzy, and thirsty, I excused myself and stumbled back into the kitchen. A tall glass of water and some coffee later, I was ready for a beer and some rays before settling down for a long pre-show nap.

The crowd at Sunday night's show was a little lighter than the previous two nights, as a few dozen lame fuckin' pussies had taken the road to get a jump on their recoveries. But that only left more oxygen and shorter beer lines for the healthy and hungry crowd that remained, and both came in handy during the glorious finale.

Dave Crider and Aaron Roeder's band Watts kicked things off, filing an imperfect yet passionate set. This was the first Garage Shock at which their former band, the Mono Men, had not played, and the Watts set was clearly a release of energy for the two, who had worked so hard in putting this historic event together. Brian Teasly of Man or Astro-Man? gave Aaron the last few songs off, and the Garage Gods smiled. Estrella 20/20 followed, kicking up the fuzz a notch, and lonely in their representation of the Far East. Next came the Gimmicks from Seattle with their sassy junk rock act, singer Mark Starr thrashing about the stage like a goldfish in a dry handsink.

Despite my afternoon snooze, I realized toward the end of the Gimmicks' set that I was starting to wear down just a little. Fifteen bands in, I was beginning to feel the effects of the cruel tricks I'd subjected my innocent self to over the preceding 48 hours. My legs ached, my eyes burned, and my tooth was fucking killing me. There was a steady drip of grey paste coming from my left ear. But there was no turning back now. Indeed, with the end in sight, I resolved to stare unflinchingly into the yellow eyes of the balance of the weekend and endure whatever it had to dish out, right after two shots of tequila and a Budweiser at the Ranch Room.

Good goddamned thing, too. The Fireballs of Freedom were that and more, stomping through their unique, whacked-out brand of freedom fusion. It set a perfect tone for the certifiably insane guitar army from Alabama, the Quadrajets. Sporting new members since their last visit to Bellingham, the Jets cranked up their spicy orange-and-blues machine well past its recommended capacity and let 'er rip. The Quadrajets live on any ordinary Tuesday night are more than your pedestrian rock fan can handle, and at midnight on the last night of Garage Shock, they were pretty much out of their bodies. Everyone was, really. It had been an amazing weekend. The distinction between old and new friends had become blurred, and it was like one big drunken family. That's how it is at Garage Shock—bands generally leave their egos at home and come for the party. Instruments are shared, all door proceeds are split evenly and completely between all participating bands, and the bar's hospitality is unmatched. Smoke 'em if you got 'em and start reserving a sofa for next year. That's the idea.

But first, Tim Kerr had a little business to take care of. Swinging dreads and grinnin' broadly, he countered the crazed vocals of Mike Carrol perfectly, coaxing sounds unnatural from his guitar as he led the Lord High Fixers through a beery set of squawk rawk to the Promised Land of Garage Shock Heaven. The crowd called out for more, and they got more until there was no more to give by either side. And then my lips fell off.[22]

Callous French

TOP LEFT: The Flaming Sideburns
RIGHT: The Nomads **OPPOSITE TOP:** The Quadrajets
BOTTOM: The Quadrajets; Man or Astro-Man?

---

[22] French, Callous; 'Garage Shock—Memorial Day Weekend 1999' (*What's Up!*, Volume 2, Issue 6, July 1999)

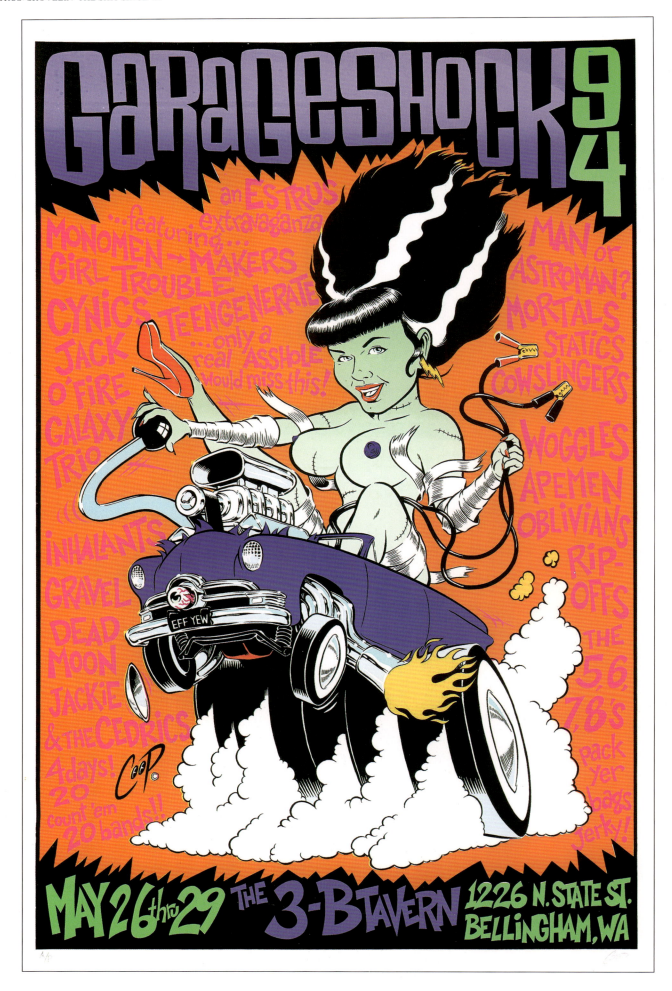

ABOVE: Garage Shock '94 poster, illustration Chris "COOP" Cooper **OPPOSITE:** Garage Shock '94 poster, illustration Darren Merinuk

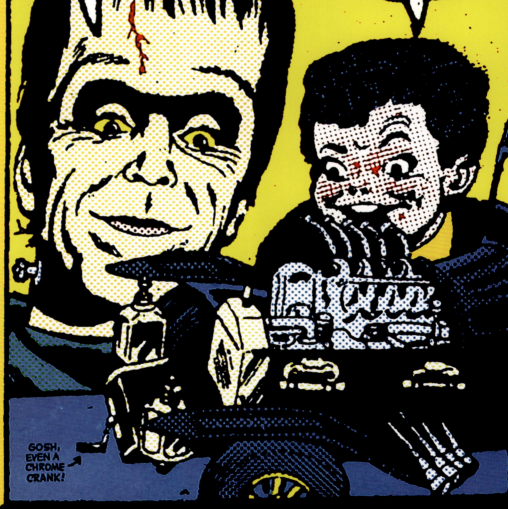

Southern Culture on the Skids
GARAGE SHOCK '95
Bellingham, WA

RICK MILLER (Southern Culture on the Skids): Our van broke down in Glendive, Montana, on our way out there from… I think, maybe South Dakota. We had a gig someplace, maybe. So it broke down in Glendive, and we traded our van. We wanted to make [Garage Shock] so bad that we traded our van straight up to a guy who had a used Pacific Bell Chevy short-bed van. It only had two seats, so we had to get a lawn chair for the third person to sit in! It had three different-sized wheels on it. When we got on the freeway, we couldn't go over 35 miles per hour. So we had to drive 35 miles per hour all the way from eastern Washington to the suburbs of Seattle, where we got the tires changed and the brakes fixed.

Oh, here's the best part: I gave the guy the keys to our van because we needed a new engine, and we'd be stuck there for at least a week because they had to fly parts in. So, we're going to be stuck there for a while, and they're going to milk us. This one guy—I guess he had foster kids and he wanted a stretch van—[all] he had was this van, but it ran. So he brought it down, and I handed him the keys to our van, and he handed me a screwdriver. I said, "I don't need a screwdriver. We have tools. We're not going to take those with us. We have a toolbox with tools." And he said, "Oh no no, that's how you start it. It doesn't have a key!" So you know we had to stick it over the solenoid to jump it.

And we took off. We never broke 35 miles per hour, and we couldn't find a place to stay because there were cowboy art shows everywhere, all the way to the suburbs of Seattle. Then we tried to get the key from a locksmith, right? And [the locksmith] said, "Well, I need to see the pink slip and the registration." But we didn't have the guy's name on it who traded us. So the next day, we were supposed to go to Vancouver and come back to Bellingham, and luckily, my mom was married to a judge in California and I called him up and said, "Chuck, man, I think I got a hot vehicle and we gotta do a border crossing…and then be back, and we gotta be in Bellingham by Thursday. What should I do? Should I go to the police?" He said, "Well, whatever you do, don't go to the police. Because you won't make it anywhere. You know you won't make it to Canada, you won't make it to Bellingham!" So we didn't, man. We took off, and we made it across the border, we made it back. And it was such a piece of junk van. You know the doors were painted different colors. We had to hold the passenger door on with a bungee cord.

We'd just gotten signed to Geffen, and as we pulled into the 3-B Tavern in this total piece of shit, I remember Deke Dickerson was there, standing next to the Go-Nuts' van. He was like, "Dude, you got the worst-looking vehicle here, man! And you just got signed to a major label. What's up?!

TOP: Rick Miller/SCOTS, photo Alex Wald **MIDDLE:** SCOTS logo, design Art Chantry **BOTTOM:** Garage Shock '95 decal, design Art Chantry **OPPOSITE:** Garage Shock '95 poster, design Art Chantry

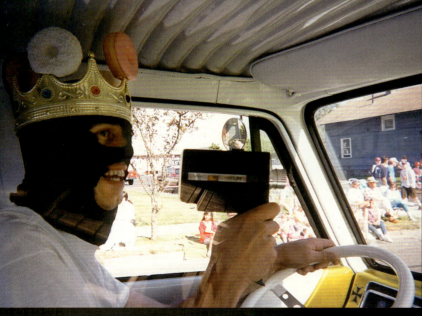

The Go-Nuts
GARAGE SHOCK '95
Bellingham, WA

DEKE DICKERSON (Untamed Youth/Go-Nuts): There was one year when the Go-Nuts drove our Nutwagon up to Garage Shock. The Nutwagon was a mid-1960s Dodge unibody pickup that Mel had painted gold metal flake, with Cragar wheels and our band logo on the side. It looked like a Matchbox car but in real life! We drove the Nutwagon all the way from Los Angeles to Bellingham and back, which was kind of nuts. The Go-Nuts played, as well as the Phantom Surfers and The Untamed Youth. One of the nights we were there, Johnny Bartlett and I were trying to get from the motel over to the 3-B Tavern, where Garage Shock was going on. The only problem was that Bellingham was having a parade, and the streets were blocked off! We were seriously trying to figure out how we'd get to the show in time for load-in and sound check and all that. I'd drive down one street—closed off. Then down another street—also closed off.

Finally, I drove down a street that I thought allowed traffic, but I soon realized that it was the line of traffic for official parade vehicles and floats and stuff! Sensing that this was our opportunity, I handed the Kap'n Kornut mask and helmet to Johnny Bartlett, and I quickly put on the Donut Prince costume and crown. When I got up to the front of the line, there was some guy who was checking on a list who was supposed to be in the parade. I blew past him and yelled, "WE'RE THE GO-NUTS! WE'RE SUPPOSED TO BE HERE!" He chased us for a while, but I kept going. We were IN the parade! It was great. We were waving at people, honking the horn and stuff. We turned a corner, and there was a group of about 20 of our friends who had stopped to watch the parade. They saw the Nutwagon and lost it—cheering and hollering and going nuts! We made it to the 3-B Tavern just in time to load-in. Trust me, if you've never done it, breaking in and joining a parade is a gas!

ABOVE: Garage Shock '87 drumhead, illustration Darren Merinuk
OPPOSITE: Deke "The Donut Prince" Dickerson parading around Bellingham, Garage Shock '95, photos Johnny Bartlett

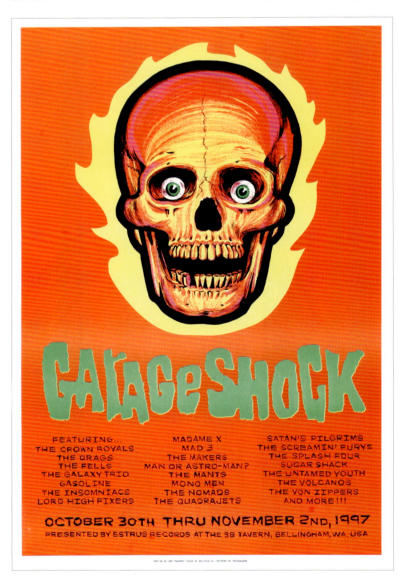

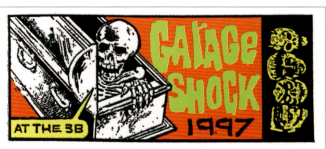

TOP ROW: Garage Shock '95 press sheet of water release decals/tickets, design Art Chantry, printing Jim Sorenson **BOTTOM ROW:** Garage Shock '97 poster, design Art Chantry, printing Thingmaker; Garage Shock '97 schedule cover and ticket, design Art Chantry

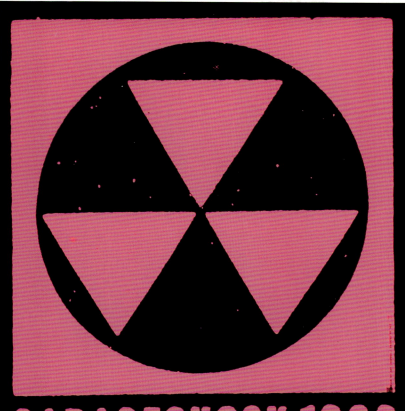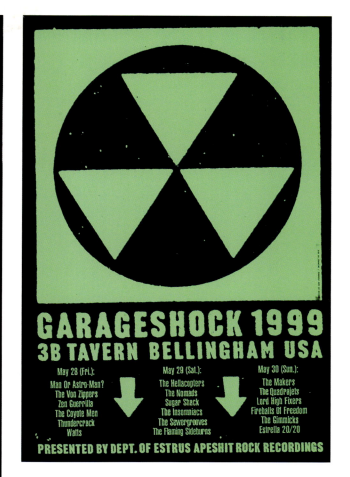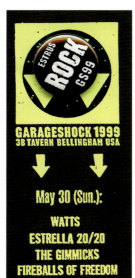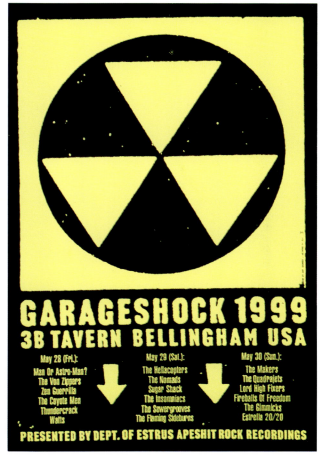

TOP: Garage Shock '99 posters, design Art Chantry, printing Brian Taylor **BOTTOM:** Garage Shock '99 tickets/buttons, design Art Chantry

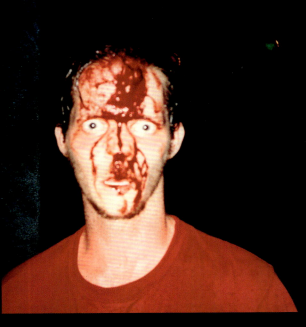

GARAGE SHOCK 2001
Emo's Austin, Texas

ANDY DUVALL (Zen Guerrilla): I knew something crazy was about to happen while I was watching the Quadrajets. That was usually the case for any of their shows, but I guess the folding chair onstage was a hint. Maybe a ladder, too? I was right up front, loving every minute of their set. Then came the last song. A pro wrestling event broke out on stage. Total bedlam. I see Pudd fold up the folding chair and lift it over his head—he had a look in his eye. I pulled my disposable camera out of my pocket a second too late. THWAP. The sound of that chair hitting poor J.R. on the top of his head echoed through Emo's for a split (no pun there) second. Shit was nuts. It was kinda dark and hazy on stage. Hard to see what was going on, but I did see Pudd's expression—anyone could tell he didn't mean to hit him THAT hard. J.R. was stumbling around. Pudd looked very concerned. And I thought, hmmm, I'm gonna try and catch J.R. in the backstage area. So I ran there and saw that stage door burst open—thank goodness my flash went off.

LONG LIVE THE 3-B TAVERN

Bars like the 3-B Tavern don't really exist anymore for a number of reasons. But when a bar loses its identity, Roeder says it is time to pack things up.

AARON ROEDER (3-B Tavern owner/Mono Men/Watts): It's hard to see a neutered version of what you built. When you have a mellow show, and four security guards are standing in front of you telling you that you can't lean against the wall—and that's the only outlet to go see music [in Bellingham]—it just wasn't that difficult [for me] to step back and end it.

DIANA YOUNG-BLANCHARD: [At the 3-B], you could pretty much do whatever you wanted [laughs]—as long as you didn't incite violence. But [the 3-B] was between Seattle and Vancouver, B.C., so a lot of great bands would stop through and play a show on their way. You could pretty much see whoever you wanted to see without going into a big city.

AARON ROEDER: So much of what happened was just flat-out illegal —not even immoral, it goes beyond immoral, illegal, and dangerous. I can't believe how defiant [I was with] the rules and that sorta thing. And eventually I learned my lesson. But it's amazing people didn't die. [Once] we had a quarter (25 cents) beer night from 7 to 9 pm; I think it was Lonestar. It would be crickets at 6:58, and at 7, the room was full, and people were screaming. It was like the floor of the stock market. Every time you'd turn back around after pouring a beer, there'd be this roar of people trying to get your attention. There'd be all these hands holding money or whatever. It got to a point where it just wouldn't stop. And then, at 9:02, the place was just destroyed. I remember thinking, "What am I doing? Why am I doing this?"

DAVE CRIDER: The beer showers at the 3-B were pretty legendary. They were at their height when the Monkeywrench played in Bellingham. And Tim Kerr suggested they wear rain slickers when they came out, but I think Mark [Arm] wasn't real stoked about it. That would have been fucking killer.

MARK ARM (The Monkeywrench): The beer thing, ah. This guy was tossing beer at [the Monkeywrench] up at the 3-B. So I was like, "Hey, c'mon stage." So he came up on stage, and I asked him to tilt his head back and to keep his eyes open. And then I poured a pitcher of beer into his eyes. There ya go. This is how it feels.

DAVE CRIDER: It did get pretty crazy. People were just buying beer to throw.

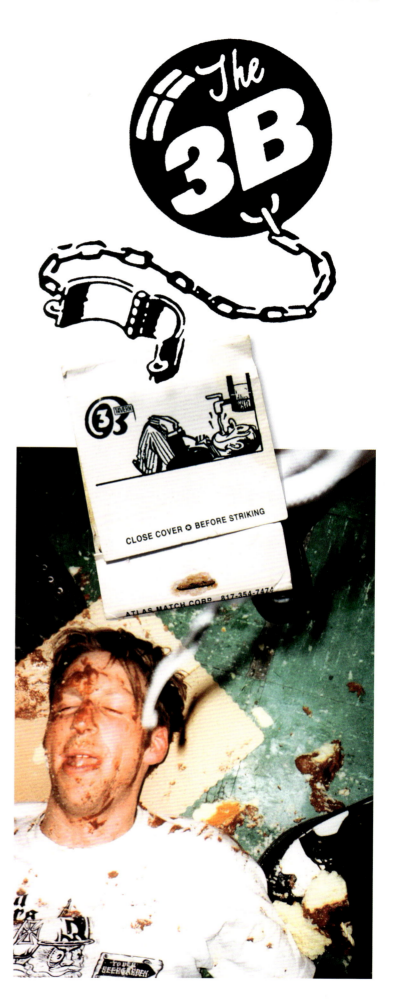

TOP: 3-B Tavern logo and matchbook, design Art Chantry
BOTTOM: 3-B owner and Mono Men drummer Aaron Roeder, Delilah's, Chicago, 1997, photo Sallie Mowles

OPPOSITE TOP: Go-Nuts set list, Garage Shock '95, photo Deke Dickerson
MIDDLE: The Oblivions, Garage Shock '94, photo unknown
BOTTOM: Bookman hoisted, Garage Shock '94, photo Mike Grimm

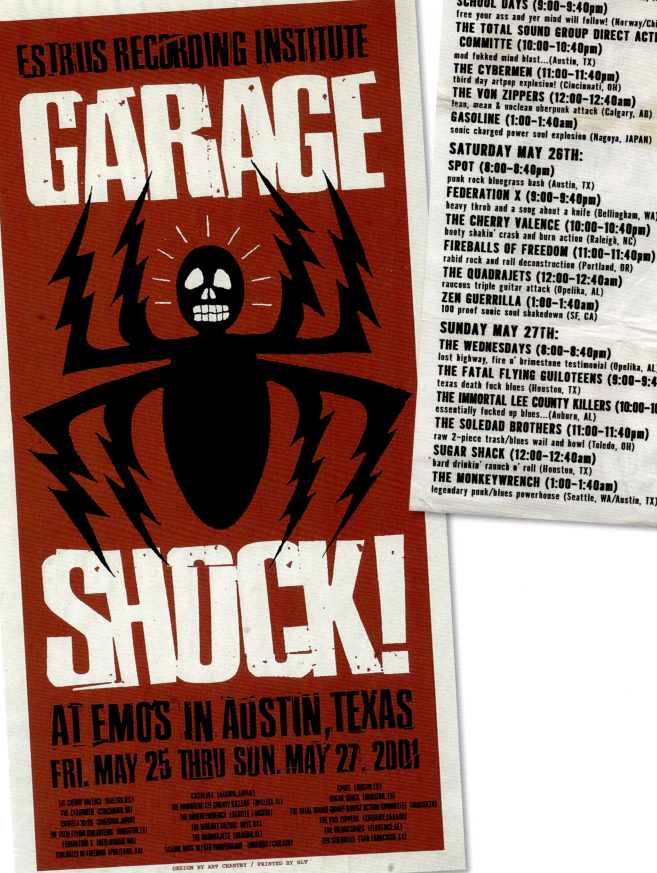

ABOVE: Garage Shock '01 poster, design Art Chantry; Garage Shock '01 set times

The label's musical vocabulary expanded, and so did Garage Shock. The atmosphere didn't necessarily change, but the lineups began to diversify; more and more three-chord rock and shtick acts were calling it quits, and artists from different genres brought more flavor to the event.

KEN VANDERMARK (The Crown Royals/Waste Kings): It points to just how open-minded Dave is. A band I belonged to, School Days, which played energized music connected to the free jazz of the '60s, played on a bill with Tim Kerr's Total Direct Sound Group Action Committee. On paper, as with the presence of the Crown Royals on the Estrus roster, it may have looked strange to listeners, but in practice it was a fantastic and cathartic combination. Dave understands how music played with total commitment and fervor can communicate to any audience that listens. He was right about the Crown Royals, and he was right about putting a band like School Days on the festival in Austin.

DIANA YOUNG-BLANCHARD: I was totally excited to be able to play [as Madame X]. I'd since formed my own combo in Seattle with some other players [after recording with Impala]. Of course, we played a lot from the *Madame X* album, but in our own interpretation; it was a slightly different band. We were definitely the odd band out [laughs], but people were receptive. There were no steadfast rules about what kind of music you played.

The final edition of Garage Shock was held at Emo's in Austin in 2001. The temperature was much warmer there than it had been in Bellingham, according to leading scientists.

AARON ROEDER: Estrus and the 3-B were in perfect harmony. Obviously, the Estrus collection —both from a personality and a music standpoint—went perfectly with what the 3-B stood for. It was trash rock and a trash bar that welcomed and encouraged that kind of "fuck you" attitude. The 3-B was a destination for bands with that energy and blood coursing through them. It was like a marriage between a label and an outlet to play. We just worked so well together. I know Garage Shock changed venues toward the end, but it wouldn't have been Garage Shock had it not happened at the 3-B.

> **"Dave understands how music played with total commitment and fervor can communicate to any audience that listens. He was right about the Crown Royals, and he was right about putting a band like School Days on the festival in Austin."**
>
> **KEN VANDERMARK** (The Crown Royals/Waste Kings)

LORD HIGH FIXERS
ONCE UPON A TIME CALLED...RIGHT NOW! (ES113), 1996

ANDY WRIGHT (Lord High Fixers/Sugar Shack): Rehearsing, we'd play things pretty straight, but then we'd get on stage and [the sound] would just go in a totally different direction every time.

STEPHANIE FRIEDMAN (Lord High Fixers/Sugar Shack): Tim would always say, "If you want to just hear it, buy the record." Like if we're trying to play a Creation song, I'd get into a mindset and sorta study the song—try and listen to the drum parts—and Tim would stop and be like, "just play." ...That energy carried over live, where things would just kinda naturally combust. What happens, happens.

Design: Art Chantry

Wanted Posters: J. Edgar Hoover

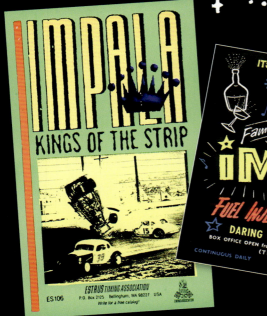

ABOVE/BELOW: Impala with Rowland Janes, 1997; live 1995, photos Dan Ball **LEFT:** *Kings of the Strip* poster, design Art Chantry, printing Thingmaker; Impala *Cozy Corner* EP (ES793), 1996, design Art Chantry, printing Brian Taylor

DIPSHITS IN THE DESERT
FINDING A WINNER IN LAS VEGAS

The roots of Estrus lie in Washington state, of course, but if there was a US city to match the aesthetics of the trash-rock label, the sleaziness of old Las Vegas was a perfect fit. Sin City became a regular stop for not only Estrus bands but garage bands from all over, thanks to Crider's Vegas connection Louie the Letch.

LOUIE THE LETCH: My friend Darrell Wells was booking shows, and he brought the Mono Men. My band Guttersnipe was asked to open the show. At that point all I think I'd heard [about Estrus] was the *Here Ain't the Sonics* compilation. So, after the show we're telling Dave we like his label, blah blah blah, and then I ask if [the Mono Men] need a place to stay. And Dave went, "YEAH!" So they stayed at the house, and Dave was so grateful for my shitty futon. I guess he had a bad back [laughs]. And it was summer, so it was so hot. The other dudes stayed in the van all night with the air conditioning on. …After Dave stayed at the house we exchanged numbers, and he said he wanted to come back with Bekki. So, a couple months later, they came down for a vacation. I took them to this old place on the Strip called El Morocco. It was a cool little 1950s place, and it hadn't changed since it was built. They had this weird Elvis impersonator who had a cassette player and sang over the cassette. It was before karaoke, I guess. But that's when Dave was like, "Damn, we should do a show here!" And that's when we thought of having the Untamed Youth at El Morocco. Then Dave was like, "Ok, you're gonna produce [the record], so you need a name!" He came up with "Louie the Letch." I didn't even know what a letch was. …The Untamed Youth show was the first one I ever did, and after, I was like, "let's do some more!" At that same place, El Morocco, I did the Phantom Surfers and Jackie & The Cedrics a couple months later, and that was fucking amazing. Soon after that, though, the place closed down.

Then, in 1996, came the infamous Crap Out! festival…

LOUIE THE LETCH: The year of Crap Out! I think there wasn't going to be a Garage Shock for some reason. So I had the Hentchmen in town and took them out to Sam's Town to go bowling. And by the way, they kicked everybody's ass. John (Szymanski) and I were talking about how there wasn't a Garage Shock that year, and he blurted out, "Let's do something here!" John actually came up with the idea to do the Crap Out! Every band was great. Fucking Lord High Fixers were great, the Oblivians, The Makers, every band was great.

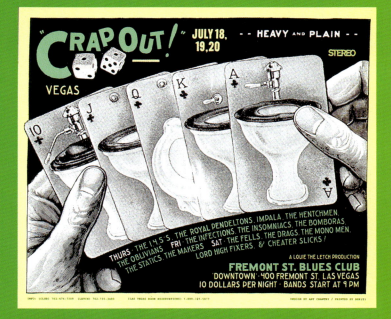

CLOCKWISE (from top right) Crap Out! poster, 1996, design Art Chantry, printing Brian Taylor; Louie the Letch, Bekki, and Dave Crider, Las Vegas, 1993; Crap Out! handbill, 1996, design Louie the Letch; The Untamed Youth *On The Las Vegas Strip* playing cards promo, 1995, design Art Chantry, printing Thingmaker; The Makers *Howl* record release show handbill, 1993, design Dave Crider

> "You can have a great record without great artwork, but why go halfass?"
>
> Dave Crider

ART CHANTRY: GRIT CITY VISIONARY

For graphic artists, Art Chantry is a household name, and many bands are eager to work with him. For those outside these spheres, an introduction to the designer's work can be had in the 1996 film *Hype!*, in which the charming blue-collar weirdo callously chops up vintage concert posters while describing the Puget Sound's history prior to the grunge explosion.

Chantry has always been a historian of his surroundings due to his relentless curiosity. As a result, many consider him an essential guide to underground culture. Hints of the designer's unique perspective are seen throughout his work—and his artistic commentary on visuals of the '60s and '70s is one reason why he and Crider clicked early on; in time, Art would become one of Crider's best buds.[24]

Chantry's work as a graphic designer emerged as grunge exploded and Seattle became the coolest place in the world overnight. After cutting his teeth in the Emerald City's punk community during the bulk of the '80s, he became Art Director of *The Rocket*, Seattle's weekly newspaper.[25] And although Art's relationship with Sub Pop Records is complicated, his involvement with the juggernaut indie label was invaluable to the "scene."

Crider's projects were proverbial lifesavers for Art, who was not only drowning in grunge but still getting "punk rock rates" from clients who had money. Even had the pair not become lifelong friends, Chantry would have considered Crider an ideal client. Dave's vision of how he wanted Estrus to look synced perfectly with Chantry's raw and vibrant semblance.

"In some ways [Chantry] embodies a frontier town that's aware, with a mixture of pride, humility, and disdain, of its place on the edge, but ultimately, like anyone else, he's his own unique product."[26]

ABOVE: Self-portrait **OPPOSITE:** Jack O'Fire promotional poster, 1993
All designs in this section Art Chantry, unless otherwise noted

---

[24] I don't know what the ranking standards are for friends.
[25] *The Rocket* was not only a vital organ in the grunge explosion, but the always-strapped-for-cash publication was invaluable for underground musicians trying to make their way. Lasky, Julie (2001), *Some People Can't Surf*, Chronicle Books.
[26] Gimpl, Elmar (2004); Dave Crider, *Choke*, 26–30.

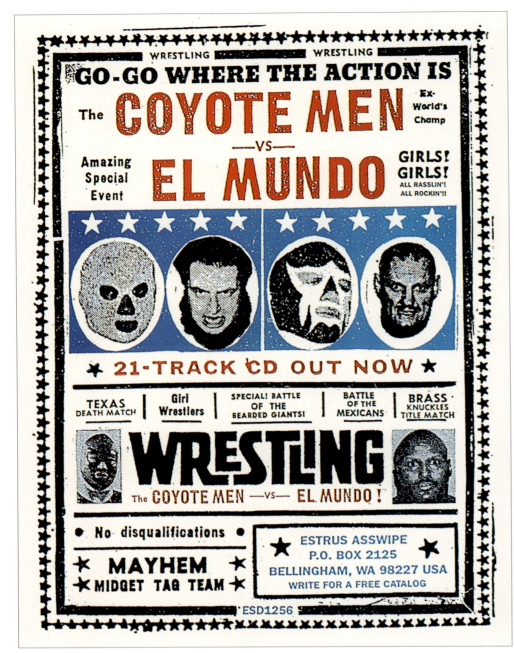
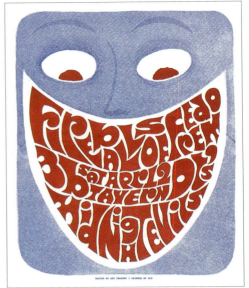

"You can have a great record without great artwork, but why go halfass?" Crider said.

It's no coincidence that both Crider and Chantry looked to live performances as a source of inspiration for Estrus Records' sound and imagery. Seeing the Makers eviscerate a dive bar inspired Art to take a beatniks-from-hell approach for the Spokane quartet's artwork; witnessing Man or Astro-Man?'s spacecraft-stagecraft evoked an opportunity to tap into his love of 1960s sci-fi; and Memphis cocktail-lounge heroes Impala brought out the designer's desire to grab your eyeballs with Old Las Vegas-like neon Day-Glo inks.

"Like Dave, I learned to understand a band by seeing them live," said Chantry. "You can get everything from a band's live presentation."

Chantry's outpouring of work for Estrus proved to be more than one-dimensional, despite his limited resources. His old-school methods for design produced a "deceptive simplicity,"[26] according to Crider. For example, instead of plopping in front of the ol' drafting table for a Teengenerate/Mono Men show poster in 1997, Chantry opted to go with firing bullets from an AK-47 through a metal sheet (see page 159).

Creating material for Crider's the Mono Men was essentially dessert for Chantry, who went all in on sleaze. While designing the Mono Men's 1993 instrumental record *Shut the Fuck Up!* he said he noticed that "many powerful women were insisting that their nude bodies appear on sleazy Mono Men records."[27] Thus, he aimed to specifically offend the then-second lady of the United States Tipper Gore, who was relentlessly trying to clean up music lyric at that time.

"Crider and Chantry's joke was to place the nude on an all-instrumental recording—no lyrics at all. They also offered a toned-down CD version called *Shut Up!* for which Chantry drew panties on the model. The back cover on both versions pays homage to men's magazines of the '50s"[28]

[26,27,28] Lasky, Julie (2001), *Some People Can't Surf*, Chronicle Books.

ESTRUS: SHOVELIN' THE SHIT SINCE '87   101

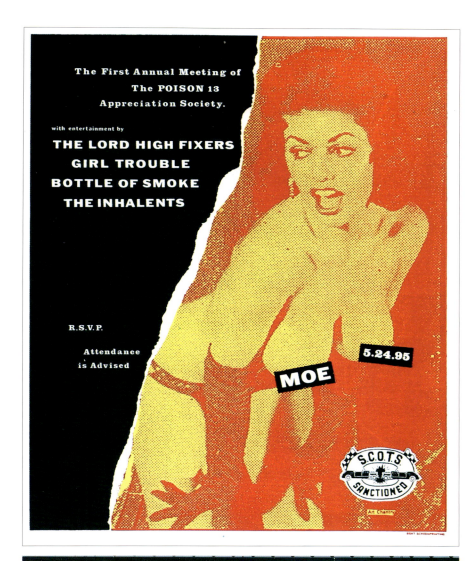

CLOCKWISE (from top left): Lord High Fixers, Girl Trouble, Bottle of Smoke, The Inhalants at Moe, Seattle WA, 1995; Fells/Penners/Wiretaps 3-B Tavern, Bellingham, WA, 1995; Impala *Kings of the Strip* promotional sticker, 1995; Impala *Square Jungle* promotional poster, 1995 **OPPOSITE LEFT:** *The Coyote Men VS El Mundo* CD release poster, 1999 **RIGHT:** Fireballs of Freedom/Dt's/Midnight Evils, 3-B Tavern, Bellingham, WA **BOTTOM:** *The 1-4-5s Rock n' Roll Spook Party* promotional poster, 1996

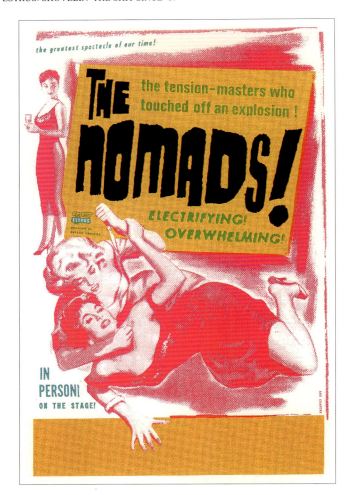

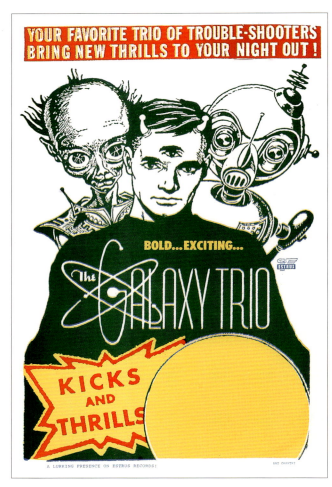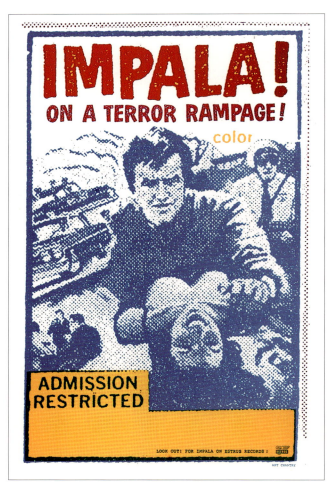

CLOCKWISE (from top left): The Nomads, Madame X, Impala, The Galaxy Trio tour poster blanks, 1996 **OPPOSITE:** The Drags/The Weaklings/The Solicitors, Double Down Saloon, Las Vegas, NV, 1996

FIRST ROW: Electric Frankenstein "You're So Fake" single (ES7123), 1998; Screamin' Furys "383" single (ES7118), 1996; The Tiki Men *The Good Life* EP (ES766), 1995 **SECOND ROW:** The Boss Martians *Boss-O-Nova* EP (ES7120), 1998; Satan's Pilgrims *Play Ghoulash For You!* single (ES7129), 1998; The Von Zippers, *Not Worth Payin' For E.P.* (ESP11), 1999 **THIRD ROW:** T.V. Killers "You Kill Me" single (ES7116), 1996; The Coyote Men *Call of The Coyote Man!* EP (ES7125/6), 1998; New Wave Hookers (ES7121), 1997 **FOURTH ROW:** The Pills "Don't Blues" single (ES7117), 1999; The Mono Men "Mystery Girl" single (ES752), 1994; Jack O'Fire "Punkin'" single (ES755), 1995 **OPPOSITE:** The Trashwomen promotional poster, 1994

ABOVE: Estrus band logos, 1994–2001 **OPPOSITE TOP:** The Makers/Thee Headcoats tour poster blank, 1997; Cheater Slicks/The Mono Men, 3-B Tavern, Bellingham, WA, 1993 **BOTTOM:** Estrus Double Dyn-O-Mite sampler CD promotional poster, 2002

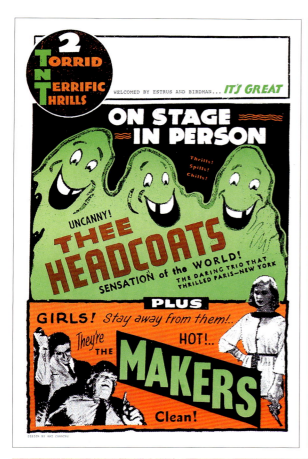

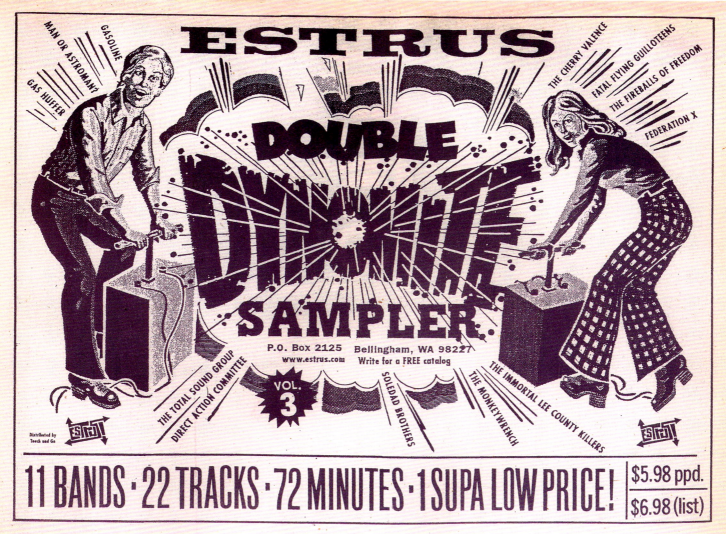

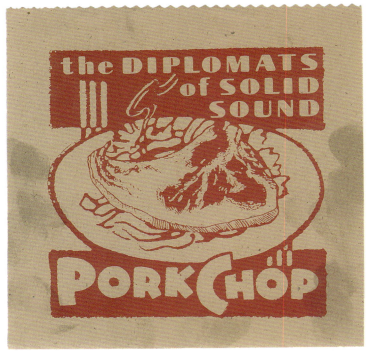

ART CHANTRY: The reason why the Diplomats' black and white design sketch (top left) was rejected was simply because Dave thought it was too sophisticated a look for them, so I dumbed it down a tad (no more 007 stuff) and went funkier. By the way, those grease stains on the 45 cover (top right) are my own fingerprints printed on in a tint varnish to suggest greasy fingers.

For the Hellacopters single, Dave was worried that [my first version] might be too suggestive (looks like somebody "jilling off" in a porn ad, right?) So Dave asked me to remove that element and I made the second version. But, after the first edition sold out and Dave needed to press a second edition, he reconsidered and decided to use the FIRST design (and *that* is the final and finished design now. Confusing? YES!!

TOP: Diplomats of Solid Sound "Pork Chop" single, proposed cover; "Pork Chop" single (ES7164), 2001, official release artwork

BOTTOM: The Hellacopters "Looking At Me" single, proposed cover; "Looking at Me" single (ES7122), 1998, official release artwork

ESTRUS: SHOVELIN' THE SHIT SINCE '87   109

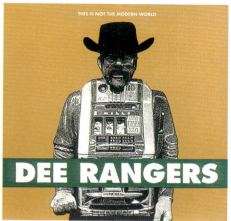

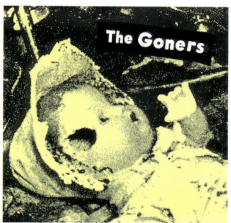

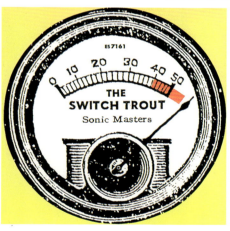
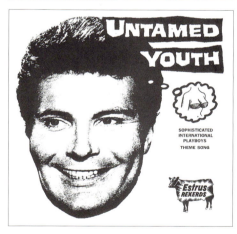
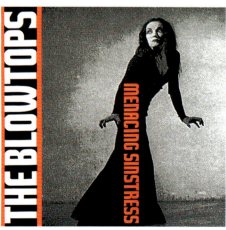
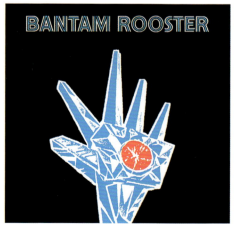

FIRST ROW: The Switch Trout *Psycho Action* CD (ESD1250), 1999; Dee Rangers *This Is Not The Modern World* EP (ES7105), 1996; The Del Lagunas "Time Tunnel" single (ES760), 1995 **SECOND ROW:** The Boss Martians *Boss-O-Nova* EP (ES7120), 1998; The Baseball Furies *I Hate Your Secret Club* EP (ES7159), 1999; *The Goners* EP (ES7113), 1997 **THIRD ROW:** The Insomniacs "Guilt Free" single (ES7132), 1999; The Switch Trout "Sonic Masters" single (ES7161), 2001; The Untamed Youth "International Sophisticated Playboys Theme Song" single (ES739), 1993 **FOURTH ROW:** The Blow Tops *Menacing Sinstress* EP (ES7146), 2000; Bantam Rooster "I, Gemini" single (ES7154), 2000; Electric Frankenstein "You're So Fake" single (ES7123), 1998

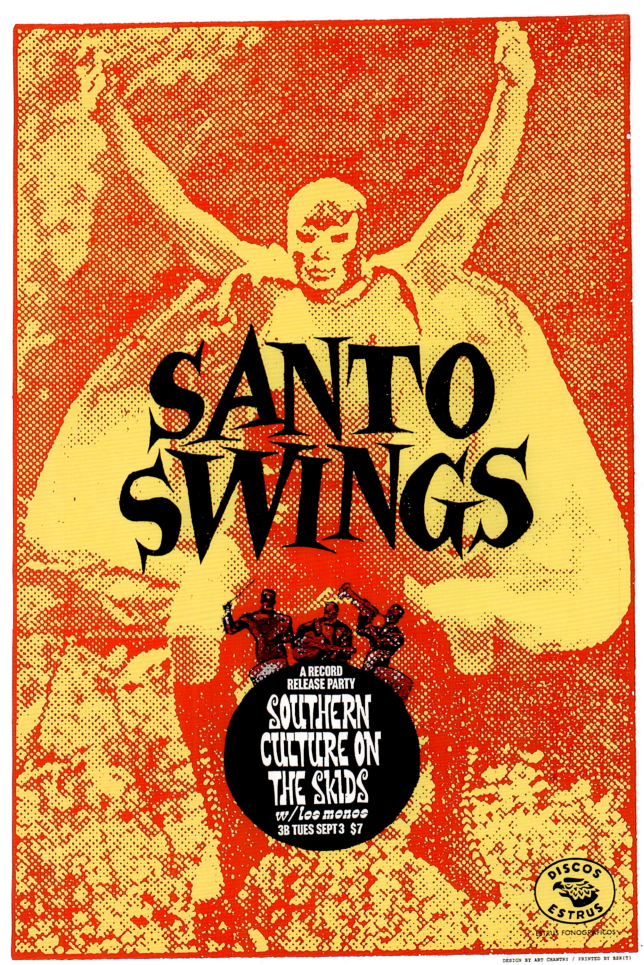

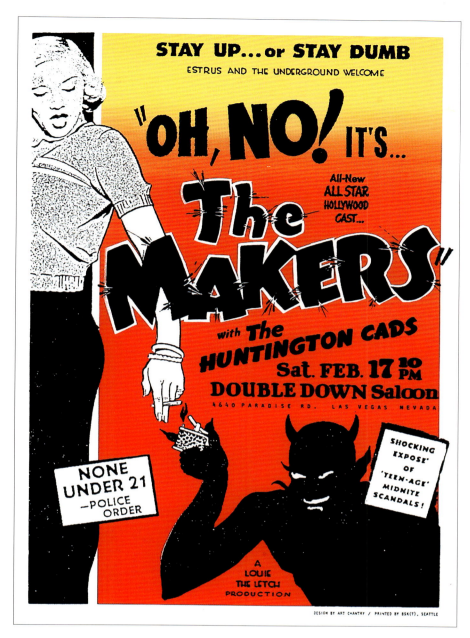
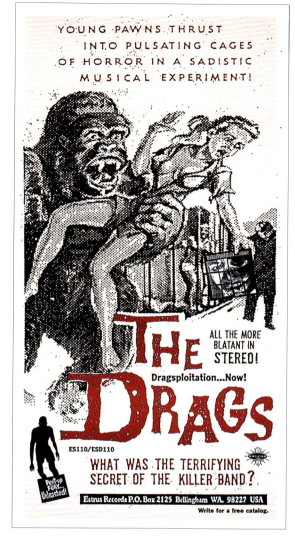

CLOCKWISE (from top left): The Makers/The Huntington Cads, Doubledown Saloon, Las Vegas, NV, 1995; The Drags, *Dragsploitation…Now!* promotional poster, 1995; The Untamed Youth tour poster blank, 1996; The Soledad Brothers promotional poster, 1999 **OPPOSITE:** Southern Culture on the Skids/Los Monos 3-B Tavern, Bellingham, WA, 1995

112 ESTRUS: SHOVELIN' THE SHIT SINCE '87

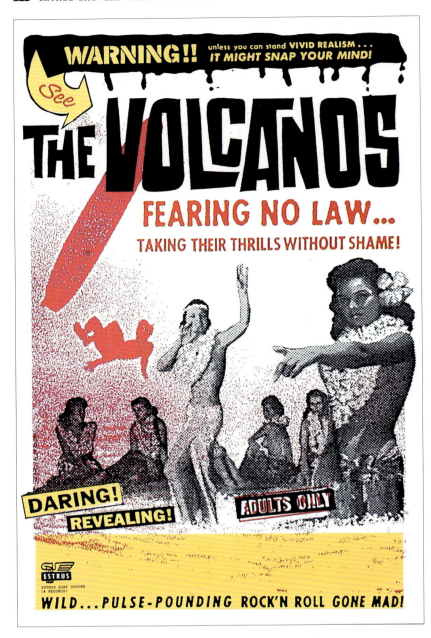
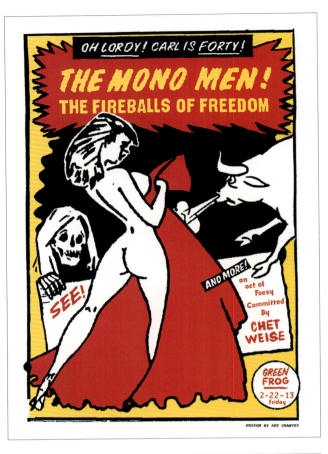

CLOCKWISE (from top left): The Volcanos tour poster blank, 1996; Mono Men/Fireballs of Freedom, Green Frog, Bellingham, WA, 2013; Thee Headcoats/Mono Men/The Statics, Moe, Seattle, WA, 1995; Thundercrack T-shirt 1999 **OPPOSITE:** 1.4.5s/5.6.7.8s tour poster, 1996

CLOCKWISE (from top left): Mono Men/The Del Lagunas, COCA, Seattle, WA, 1992; Mono Men/The Makers, 3-B Tavern, Bellingham, WA, 1995; The Mortals *Last Time Around* CD (ES1228), 1996; The Galaxy Trio/Madame X, The Alibi, Portland, OR, 1995

ESTRUS: SHOVELIN' THE SHIT SINCE '87   **115**

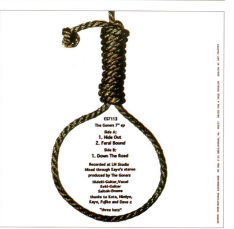

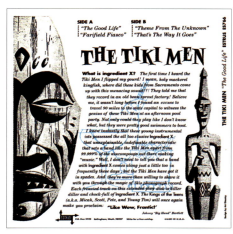

Chantry back covers **FIRST ROW:** The Beguiled *Black Gloves* EP (ES742), 1993; The Boss Martians *Boss-O-Nova* EP (ES7120), 1998; Gravel "As For Tomorrow" single (ES733), 1992 **SECOND ROW:** The Fells "What I Got" single (ES781), 1995; The Goners *The Goners* EP (ES7113), 1997; The Gimmicks "Dirty Inside" single (ES7137), 1999 **THIRD ROW:** Impala *Cozy Corner* EP (ES793), 1996; The Monkeywrench "Sugar Man" single (ES7149), 2000; Dee Rangers *This Is Not The Modern World* EP (ES7105), 1996 **FOURTH ROW:** The Tiki Men *The Good Life* EP (ES766), 1995; Madame X "Funnel of Love" single (ES786), 1996; The Makers *Here Comes Trouble* EP (ES744), 1993

116 ESTRUS: SHOVELIN' THE SHIT SINCE '87

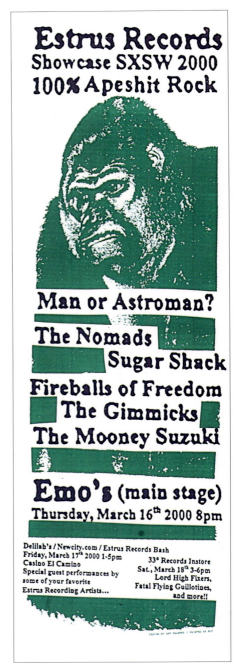

CLOCKWISE (from top left): Estrus Records advertisement, 2000; Estrus Records SXSW 2000 Showcase poster, Austin, TX, 2000; Quadrajets "Super Double Buzz" single label (ES7119), 1997; Estrus logo mark, 1999; Estrus advertisment, 2000

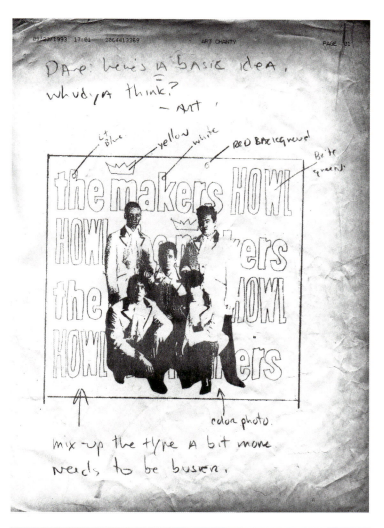
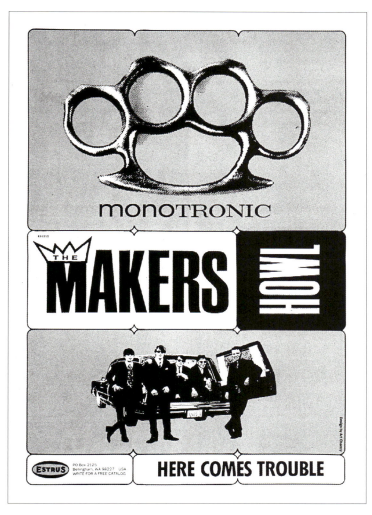
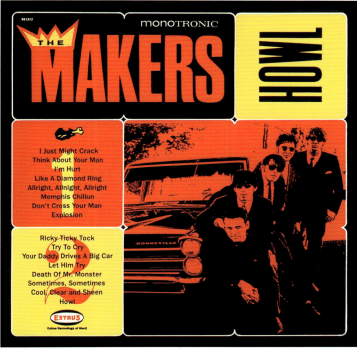
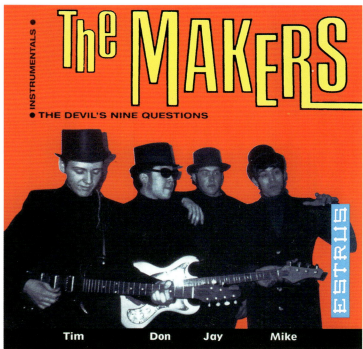

CLOCKWISE (from top left): The Makers *Howl* LP original tissue sketch (rejected), 1993; The Makers *Howl* LP promotional poster, 1993; The Makers *The Devil's Nine Questions* 10" mini-album (ES104), 1994; The Makers *Howl* CD (ESD1212), 1993; chicken leg drawn by Ed Fotheringham

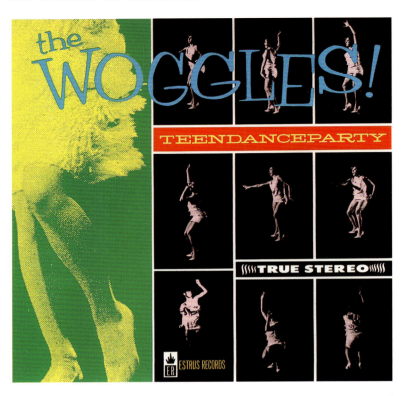
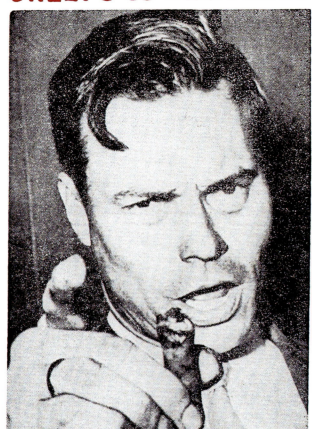

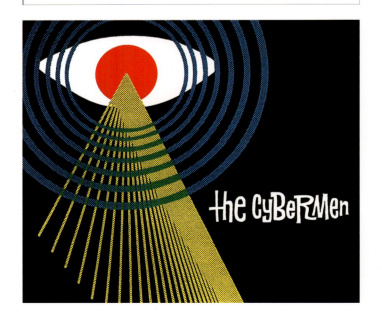

CLOCKWISE (from top left): The Woggles *Teen Dance Party* LP (ES1210), 1993; TAD/Mono Men, 3-B Tavern, Bellingham, WA, 1997; The Cybermen mini-album (ES111), 1996; The Woggles: The Zontar Sessions promotional poster, 1994 **OPPOSITE:** Satan's Pilgrims *Soul Pilgrim* promotional poster, 1995

CHANTRY REJECTS
THE COMMON TALE OF "GRAPHIC ARTIST VS THE WORLD"

ART CHANTRY: I know most folks see my work and think I get to "do whatever I want." Not true! With a great client it's a real collaboration on THE PROJECT, not my creative "whim." On these two pages are "sketches" of ideas I presented that were turned down for specific and arcane reasons I've now entirely forgotten, although they seemed important at the time.

For instance, one of the things that Dave Crider insisted upon was seeing a band play live before he got involved on a project with them. He'd get promo tapes and records and he'd listen to every single one of them, but that was never the same thing as seeing the band performing live. They had to be a great live act before he'd say yes to a record.

I quickly realized what Dave's point was. If I didn't see the band perform live, I had a harder time figuring out exactly WHO they were as a band/brand identity. All the bands on these two pages were unknown to me when I did the sketches—and every single one of them is wrong for those bands. Sure, they may look "cool," but that's not enough. It has to tell the story of who this band is in some way, so when you hear the music, you can grab an impression and start to imagine what's going on.

Graphic design is a language—a language of visuals. It's one we all read and speak, but we don't KNOW that we read and speak it. It's my job to use this visual language to get (and even trick) the audience into believing the story that the band, the label, Dave, and myself want to tell. Basically, we fuck with people's minds.

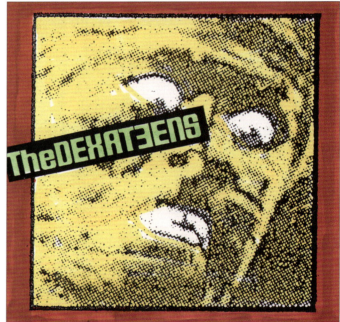

ESTRUS: SHOVELIN' THE SHIT SINCE '87 **121**

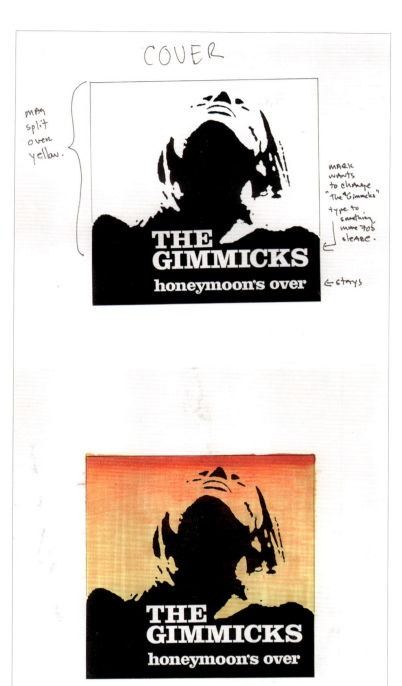

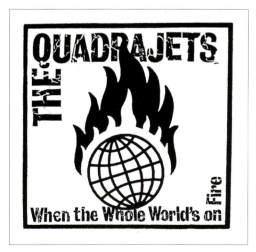

122 ESTRUS: SHOVELIN' THE SHIT SINCE '87

ESTRUS: SHOVELIN' THE SHIT SINCE '87   123

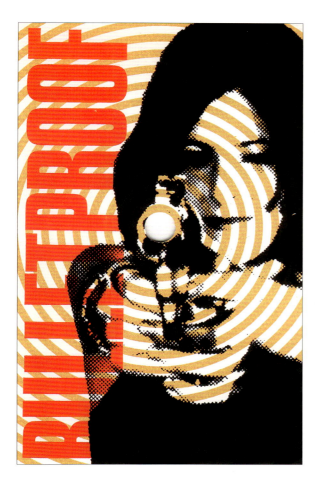

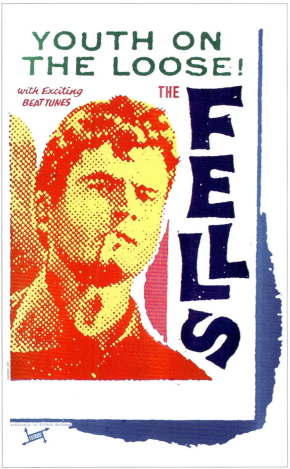

OPPOSITE: Teengenerate/Satan's Pilgrims/The Statics, The Crocodile Cafe, Seattle, WA, 1995 **TOP LEFT:** The Mortals *Bulletproof* LP promotional poster, 1994
RIGHT: The Cybermen mini-album promotional poster, 1996 **BOTTOM:** The Fells tour poster blank, 1996

3 Going Waaaaay Out

Brian Teasley, a musically savvy Auburn University engineering geek, was in a record store sometime in 1992 when he saw singles by the Phantom Surfers, the Mummies, and the Roofdogs for sale. He was blown away to learn the selections were a revitalization of surf music, but with intentions seeded in punk rock ethos.

"Eventually, we just dove deep into Estrus," said Teasley soon after discovering the independent label from a distant college town. "It gave us this idea of where we were at musically. We wanted to be kinda snotty and anonymous and punk rock and weird and goofy, all in one rolled product of stupidity."

"We," in this case, refers to instrumental space-punk legends Man Or Astro-Man? The Birmingham space "redneck kids"[30] were one of the few bands to land an LP offer from Crider before a water-testing single. Crider said that Teasley and his fellow cadets played a major role in getting the word out about the label.

"Man or Astro-Man? were a super hard-working band," said Crider. They were the first band associated with Estrus to play a coveted BBC John Peel Session multiple times.

> "[Estrus] gave us this idea of where we were at musically. We wanted to be kinda snotty and anonymous and punk rock and weird and goofy, all in one rolled product of stupidity."
>
> Brian Teasley

ABOVE: Estrus TV logo, design Art Chantry

OPPPOSITE: Man or Astro-Man?, Garage Shock '94, photo Mike Grimm

---

[30] Teasley's words, not mine.

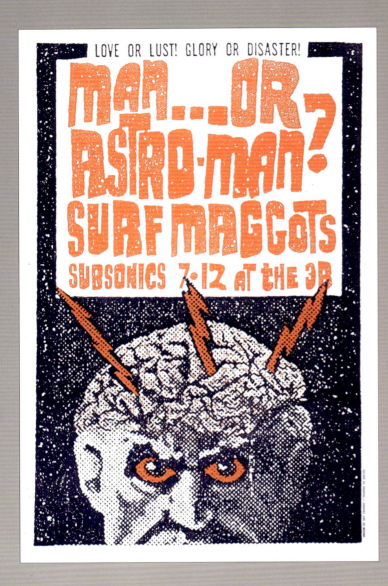

CLOCKWISE (from top left): Man or Astro-Man?/Surf Maggots/Subsonics, 3-B Tavern, Bellingham, WA, 1995; Man or Astro-Man?/Bob Log III/The Star Spangled Bastards, 3-B Tavern, Bellingham, WA, 1999; Man or Astro-Man? Astro Vision promotional 3-D glasses; all designs Art Chantry

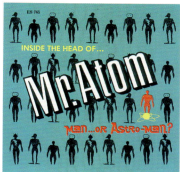

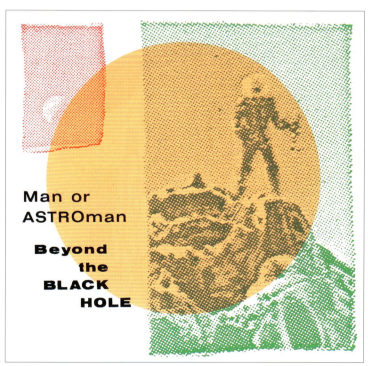

Man or Astro-Man? **FIRST ROW:** *Astro Launch* EP (ES751), 1994; *Inside The Head of Mr. Atom* EP (ES765), 1995; *The Sounds of Tomorrow* EP (ES783), 1996; *Amazing Thrills! In 3-Dimension* promotional single (ESP7), 1993 **SECOND ROW:** *Destroy All Astromen* LP (ES1215), 1994; "World Out of Mind" single (ES769), 1995, printing Thingmaker **THIRD ROW:** *Project Infinity* (ES1221), 1995; *Beyond The Black Hole* CD compilation (ES1278D), 2001; all designs Art Chantry

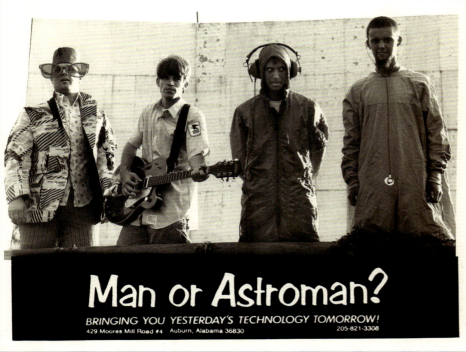

Man or Astro-Man? **FROM TOP:** T-shirt logo, 1994, design Devlin Thompson; Dr. Deleto promotional tongue depressor, 1993; sticker, 1994, design Brian Teasley; promotional photo, 1993 **OPPOSITE TOP:** Man or Astro-Man? 1993, photo Michael Galinsky **BOTTOM:** Man or Astro-Man? 1994

100% APESHIT DISCOGRAPHY

FELLS

THE FELLS
THE FELLS (ES1237), 1997
ROB YAZZIE (The Fells): The album cover has this sorta old punk flyer aspect to it—cut and paste; like, literally cut and paste. I really loved how stripped down it was.

JEFF GLAVE (The Fells): We all wanted a simple cover like MC5's *Back in the USA* or The Real Kids' first album. I remember vehemently not wanting a monster, a hot rod, a surfboard, or a cartoon woman with giant boobs. And I know at that point the label was moving away from that sorta stuff too; but we thought as part of the Estrus family we wanted to move away from the shag coupe—the stereotype that had sorta been a part of it.

Design: Art Chantry

Photo: Bianca Finley

GASOLINE
GASOLINE (ES1243), 1997
TIM KERR: The thing that's so amazing about Gasoline was that they could all play really good, and they all played lead on their instruments the whole fucking time. [I just watched and thought] "who leads?"

GAN CHAN (Gasoline): Recording at the Egg was like a miracle. [The] engineers there knew exactly where the microphones needed to be to get the particular sound, and we worked so fast that it was like magic. I couldn't believe we finished recording the whole album in a day and a half.

CLOCKWISE (from top left): Man or Astro-Man? promotional photo, 1994; Man or Astro-Man? promotional pin, 1995, design Brian Teasley; Man or Astro-Man? Cliffs Notes, 1995; Man or Astro-Man?, Lounge Axe, Chicago, IL, 1994, photo Marty Perez

CLOCKWISE (from left): Carl and Traci, Estrus warehouse, 1996; Carl and friends, 3-B Tavern, Bellingham, WA, 1998, photo Francisco Santalices; Carl and Nick Vahlberg (The Nomads), 1999, photo unknown

BOOKMAN GOES TO BELLINGHAM

In the summer of 1997, University of Auburn undergrad and Ron Asheton look-alike Carl "Bookman" Ratliff left Birmingham for Bellingham[30] to work for Dave full-time; he was key in Estrus' life after the fire (see pages 168–177). Carl and Dave had established a rapport while the former was serving as Man Or Astro-Man?'s roadie, and this eventually led to Carl doing promotional work for Estrus and helping Dave network in the South.

Ratliff's work ethic synced well with the operation; he went full force, whether it was mindless tasks like stuffing records or multifaceted undertakings like coordinating several tours simultaneously. But Ratliff was also an ambassador of the label in many respects. For an outsider trying to reach Estrus, he was typically the first point of contact. And as for the roster, he had a "band first" mentality that helped alleviate stress for veterans and newbies alike while on the road.

"Carl was the friend of the band [so they] don't have to deal with the bullshit," said Man or Astro-Man?'s Brian Teasley. "I mean, touring with Man or Astro Man? was a fucking disaster. We thought carrying a TV on stage or putting stickers on telephone poles was just as important as writing a song. So Carl was in the band, really."

---

[30] "Birmingham for Bellingham"—you'd think he was part of a fucking traveling cavalry for Henry V.

IS IT MAN OR ASTRO-MAN? (ES129), 1993

ART CHANTRY: One of the things we always enjoyed doing was hiring "Old Forgotten Masters" to work on Estrus Records covers whenever we could. A great example of that is Man or Astro-Man?'s first LP. I'd been collecting old sci-fi novels just because I liked the covers, and one day I was admiring my collection when I noticed that all the cover art was actually done by the same guy—Richard M. Powers.

Powers' styles changed from watercolors to oils to collage to surrealism to portraits. He could do ANYTHING—and it always looked like his work. Really quite astonishing. It turns out Powers was THE paperback cover artist of choice for all the "new wave" of sci-fi writers in the 1950s. He became the artist who switched the visual *look* of sci-fi from Flash Gordon/Buck Rogers rayguns and rockets to actual Surrealist floating cities and swirling dreamscapes.

I researched Powers and found out he was living mainly in Spain, where he was a popular gallery artist. I asked him if he'd do an image for our record cover, and he was thrilled that anybody under 30 even knew who he was! I sent him a tape of the band, and he sent me the image we used on the cover. He was a really cool guy.

Along the way, we also tried to hire Ron Cobb (he replied, "I don't do monster stuff anymore.") We also tried to find Harry Chester (designer of Warren Publications and of *MAD* magazine) and Bill Ward (infamous men's magazine illustrator). Sadly, both men passed away before they were able to do their artwork.

Another time we attempted to hire Steve Ditko (the creator of Spiderman), but he literally slammed the door in our face (no joke). Turns out he was a virtual hermit and wanted to be left alone. So, it didn't always work out very well.

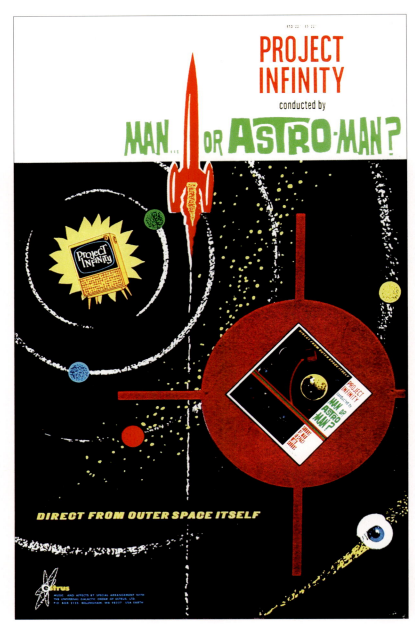

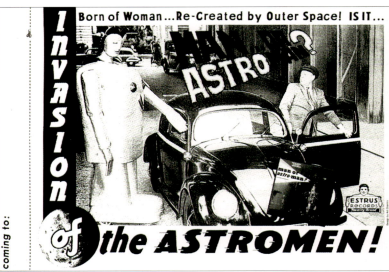

Man or Astro-Man? **CLOCKWISE (from top left):** *Project Infinity* promotional poster, 1995, design Art Chantry; Unused promotional photo, 1994, photo Marty Perez; Unused promotional photo, 1994; Coco and Cap'n Zeno (Jason Russell), Garage Shock '95, photo Jilayne Jordan; *Invasion of the Astromen!* promotional poster, 1993, design Art Chantry

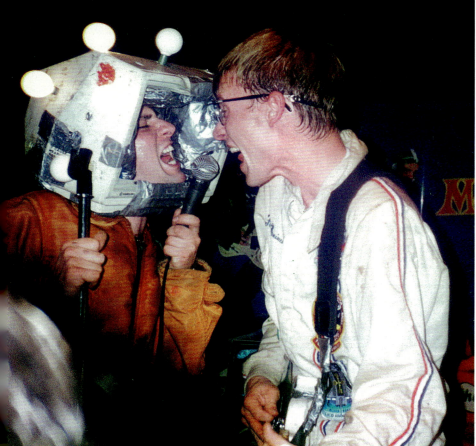

Accolades aside, Man or Astro-Man?'s presence on Estrus struck a chord with the legion of geek-punks, further expatiating the Estrus family of freaks.

The Mono Men toured the west coast of the US in 1992, and all four stayed at the Mummies/Phantom Surfers house in Daly City. Dave was enamored by the setup; the Budget Rock™'ers had a recording studio in the basement filled with vintage gear—most of which had been purchased on the cheap at thrift stores in the Bay Area. In some cases, equipment was even yanked from dumpsters.

The stop in Northern California was also when Trent (Ruane) played Dave the debut Supercharger LP, the self-titled collection of lo-fi hoppers on Radio X Records.[32]

"I shat myself," Crider said of the time he first heard Supercharger. Needless to say, it didn't take him long to reel in the short-lived South San Francisco trio for *Goes Way Out*, a record Crider said was a definitive offering of "'90s lo-fi, trash budget rock." Soon after the record came out, Supercharger and the Mummies toured Europe, further fanning the scent of Estrus… and then both bands broke up, and everyone lived happily ever after.

EXTRA! EXTRA! READ ALL ABOUT (SH)IT!
THE IN-HOUSE ZINE TO SATISFY FIENDS

Meanwhile, the Crust Club members increased, and the mail-order customer base continued to grow. This new level of popularity had Crider turn the label's newsletter into the *Sir Estrus Quarterly* after 19 editions. The in-house fanzine model was a shift away from being confined to a mail-order catalog format.

Articles, information on Estrus-related tours, columns by bands, and exclusive artwork were mainstays in the *Quarterly*. The Makers' manager, Vic Mostly, also had a hand in the publication by contributing "Vic's Picks"—dark humor gossip—as well as other editorial roles.

Estrus also began offering subscriptions to the *Quarterly* separate from the Crust Club. Plus, about 500 extra copies were sent to Mordam, who distributed them to "Estrus-friendly" stores (included with their orders). Twenty-five issues of the *Quarterly* were released between 1993 and 2005.

TOP LEFT: Supercharger promo photo, 1993 **BOTTOM:** Supercharger *Goes Way Out!* promotional poster, 1993 **OPPOSITE:** Howse of Estrus advertisement, 1998, design Art Chantry

---

[32] Estrus would re-issue the album in 1997 (ES1240).

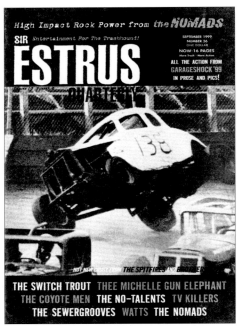

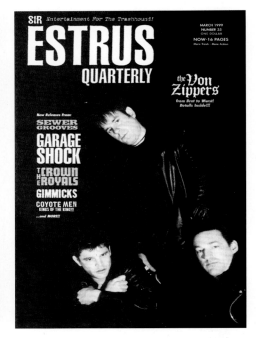

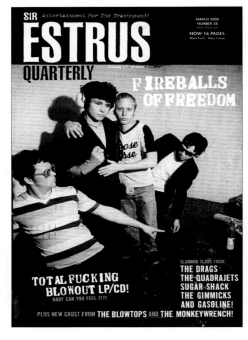

ESTRUS: SHOVELIN' THE SHIT SINCE '87   137

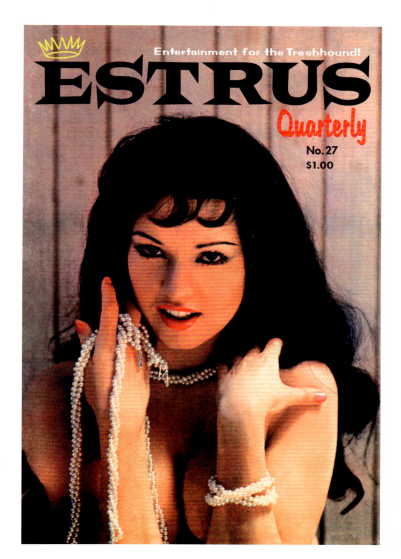

Sir Estrus Quarterly **CLOCKWISE (from top left):** Number 27, June 1996; February 1996; *Sir Estrus Quarterly* interior pages, Vol. 6, Number 3, 1995, designs Dave Crider **OPPOSITE FIRST ROW:** Vol. 5, Number 3, 1994; Vol. 6, Number 3, 1995; Vol. 6, Number 1, 1995 **SECOND ROW:** Number 36, September 1999; Number 41, February 2001; Number 35, March 1999 **THIRD ROW:** Number 34, October 1998; Number 32 (Vol. 9, Number 1), February 1998; Number 38, March 2000

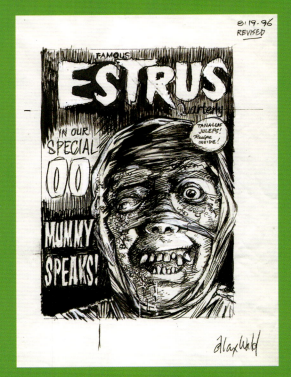

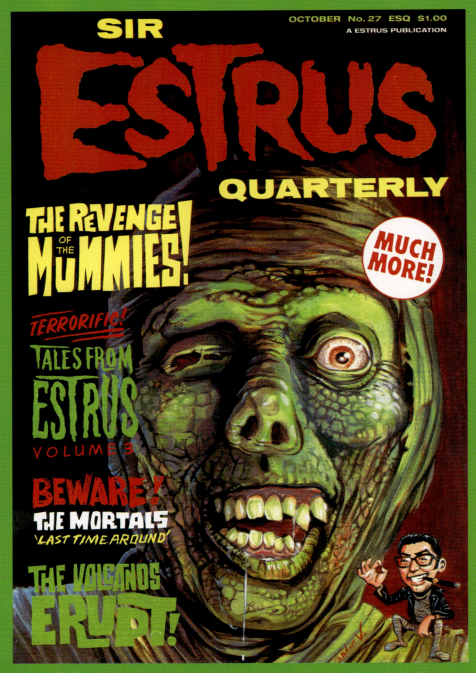

ALEX WALD (Artist): Unlike most Estrus bands, the Mummies supplied their own covers, photography, and graphics, so there were few opportunities for Estrus High Command to delegate an ink-slinger to glorify their cheezy garage-gauze fabulosity in Technicolor and 3D. I was thus understandably honored and excited when Dave assigned me a Mummies gig, albeit for the *Sir Estrus Quarterly*. Art Chantry's design concept was a tribute to a specific *Famous Monsters* cover, issue 40, brilliantly illustrated with in-your-face style by Ron Cobb, an artistic influence for whom Art and I possess a mutual reverence. Art would render the hand-made typographic elements, and I'd paint the illustration.

This is one of those rare works that bears a historical lineage. If you compare the original FM 40 cover art with the US one-sheet poster for *Horror Hotel* (aka *City of the Dead*, UK 1960), you'll see the identical vile visage monstrously multiplied. For many years I believed that Cobb revised his own pre-existing poster art to create the cover—why waste a good riff, right? But it turns out that the horrific one-sheet movie poster that Cobb copped is by Jack Davis. For my part, I knew I'd need to keep Cobb's sense of presence but style the subject with the band's badass bandaging. The gratuitously missing eye and crackled skin are my nods to Cobb, while the shoulder sprite is a nod to *Famous Monsters* covers 6, 7, and 8, where artist Albert Neutzell inserted a tiny Lon Chaney Phantom [of the Opera] as a mascot. The mascot on the *Sir Estrus* cover is Dave Crider, his own bad self. I confess at last that the Mummies cover painting is by my hand, signed with the nom de plume "Zandor Vorkov."

A curious postscript to this episode… I put the original acrylic painting up on eBay during lean times, where it sold (for the minimum bid) to a buyer who claimed it was to be a present for his brother, a big Mummies fan. Some years later, I received a call from a puzzled gent who had just moved into a new apartment and found this painting lying on the floor in a bedroom closet; my name, address, and phone number were on the back. I gave the caller some background about its creation, which seemed to be all he wanted. I've become very fond of this sold-and-then-abandoned piece and wonder who might have it now, and whether the current owner appreciates this little slice of garage rock/monster history. If anyone reading this is in possession of the little Mummies painting, please contact me through the publisher of this book. I'll make it worth your while.

the makers

ESTRUS

Entertainment for Trashounds Worldwide

Garage Shock in 1993 was the first to have a silk-screened poster—one of two made by Chris "COOP" Cooper—to promote the festival in record shops several months in advance of the weekend. The tradition was continued for every Garage Shock thereafter.

Another Garage Shock custom was hosting mind-blowing bands from the Far East. "Japan Night" in 1993 featured Supersnazz, Jackie & The Cedrics, The 5.6.7.8's, Teengenerate, and Guitar Wolf.

November of the same year marked the beginning of another fruitful and lasting relationship between Estrus and one of its bands. Crider released "Here Comes Trouble" from Spokane's honey-badger-of-a-band, The Makers. The 7" EP would serve as a three-song tease ahead of *Howl*, the band's blistering debut LP.

"A cassette was dropped into my guitar case at some point at a [Mono Men] show, and it was by a band called The Haymakers," Crider said. "There was no contact information on it or anything. So I listened to it. I really liked it. I said, 'this is great,' but I'd no way of reaching these people. This was pre-Internet, so you couldn't hop on your computer and search for 'The Haymakers.' So, I thought maybe our paths will cross at some point. I believe it was at least a year later, maybe longer, that the Mono Men were recording down at Egg and somehow [The Haymakers] got brought up. Scott McCaughey was there and he said, 'Oh, I know those guys!'"[32]

OPPPOSITE: The Makers *Here Comes Trouble* EP interior cover, 1993, design Art Chantry **ABOVE:** Discos Estrus logo, 1996, design Alex Wald

---

[32] Coyle, C.A; 'We've Always Been Trouble: An oral history of The Makers, 25 years after their debut LP *Howl*.' (*The Inlander,* October 4, 2018).

FIRST ROW: The Makers, live 1993, photos John Maker (John Gunsaulis) **SECOND ROW:** The Makers show posters 1992–93 (note the Makers' previous name, the Haymakers); The Makers portraits, illustration Mike Maker **THIRD ROW:** The Makers *The Devil's Nine Questions* unedited cover photo, 1994, Vic Mostly; The Makers "hair" merchandise, 1993, design Mike Maker

CLOCKWISE (from top left): The Makers *Here Comes Trouble* EP photo sessions, 1993, photo Vic Mostly; The Makers (as The Haymakers) cassette j-card, design/illustration Mike Maker; The Makers *Howl* LP unedited cover photo, 1993, photo Vic Mostly; The Makers promotional matchbook, 1993, design Art Chantry

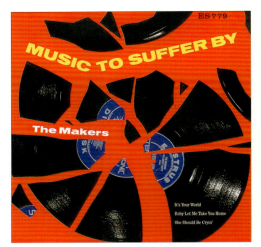  

TOP: The Makers promotional photo, 1995, photo Vic Mostly **MIDDLE:** The Makers *Music To Suffer By* EP (ES779), 1995; "Long Love" single (ES7112), 1997; *Here Comes Trouble* EP (ES744), 1993, design Art Chantry **BOTTOM:** The Makers comb logo, design Art Chantry **OPPOSITE:** *All-Night Riot!* LP promotional poster, design Art Chantry

Along with The Makers' *Howl* Estrus' movers and shakers of 1993–94 included singles from Jackie & The Cedrics and the 5.6.7.8's, as well as a generous collection of rare and unreleased recordings from smart-man's-slacker-punk trio the Fall-Outs.

Crider had also reconnected with Tim Kerr earlier in 1993 when the Mono Men did a handful of shows in Texas[33]—one of which was with Kerr's "non-existent" raw-soul/blues quartet Jack O'Fire. "I get a call from Emo's sayin' 'Hey, the Mono Men are comin'. Dave wants to play with your band,'" Kerr said. "I tried to explain to him that there wasn't a band, but [he insisted]. So we got [Jack O'Fire] all back together. They flew Josh down from D.C., which was pretty fucking nuts for this kinda thing."

"Literally, the last note's finishing, and Dave is already up on stage hugging me saying, 'Do you wanna play Garage Shock? Do you wanna put something out?' And I was like, 'This is fuckin' nuts.'" And soon, Jack O'Fire's 10-inch *Six Super Shock Soul Songs* hit the shelves running.

At the end of the year, the Mono Men returned to Texas, this time with The Makers in tow. Though the Spokane pack had met Kerr briefly at the Spook'n'Bowl,[34] this trip was particularly auspicious. The group bonded and made plans to record together, which led to the explosive self-titled Makers record—also known as the "Middle Finger album." This powwow took place either before or after The Makers were escorted by police from a gig in Houston.

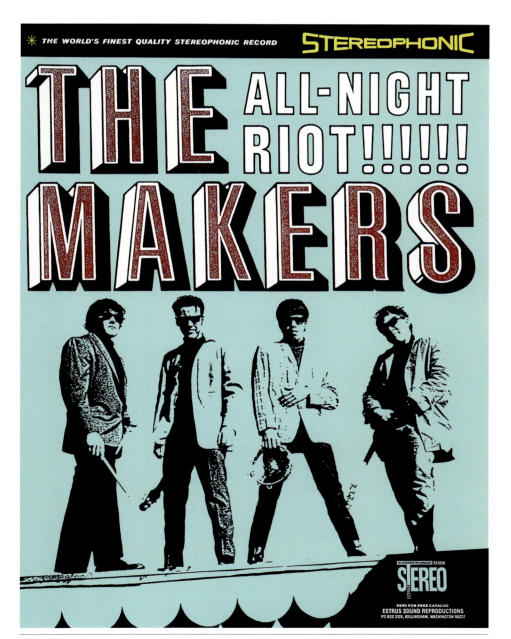

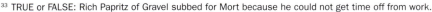

[33] TRUE or FALSE: Rich Papritz of Gravel subbed for Mort because he could not get time off from work.
[34] See Oral History Lesson: Garage Shock, pages 66–92.

100% APESHIT DISCOGRAPHY

MADAME X
MADAME X (ES115), 1998
DIANA YOUNG-BLANCHARD (Madame X/the Dt's): I'd been singing some soul and jazz in Yakima and in Seattle, and [Dave] decided I should do a project. He thought an Estrus band at that time, Impala, would be the perfect band for me to do this project with. Dave got me in contact with the Impala guys—Johnny Stivers in particular—and we started collaborating and writing songs together. And since I was still in Seattle, we were mailing cassette tapes back and forth [between Memphis and Seattle]—pre-Internet stuff. So we wrote five or six songs in that fashion with the plan that I'd fly to Memphis when we were ready and rehearse in preparation for recording.

Dave had arranged for us to record at Phillips Studio. ...So, they—Impala plus my friend John McRandle—recorded at the studio, but I didn't get to record any vocals because we ran out of time. It really sucked [laughs]. It was heartbreaking. Anyway, after the music tracks were down, I flew to Austin a couple of months after that and recorded the vocal tracks with Tim Kerr at a place he was working at the time called Sweatbox—a big-time punk rock space. So I end up recording these jazzy, sultry, smooth vocal things in a broom closet at one of the most notorious punk rock studios. I was surrounded by brooms, mops, and cleansers. Not exactly as elegant as I'd have wanted it.

Design: Jamie Sheehan; Director of Photography: Susan Mckeever; Photo: Lori Albertson

Chantry's pre-press paste-up of the Spook'n'Bowl poster, 1994

100% APESHIT DISCOGRAPHY

THE SPLASH FOUR
FILTH CITY (ES117), 1998
WALTER DOOLEY (Wally Dü & The Butter Cutter Five): Me and the But-Cut Five were supposed to open for the Splash Four when they came through Eugene in '98 or '99. However, two days before the gig, Mikey, our second rhythm guitar player, busted his paw while nailing a mailbox to his house. Wouldn't ya know it, he missed the nail completely and swung right into his right thumb. The bastard smashed it real bad. There was blood everywhere—and he's hootin' and hollerin', lettin' all the cuss words fly. Heck, I bet half of the U of O campus could hear ol' Mikey screaming things like, "MOTHERFUCKING PIG-FUCK DICK SALAD!! AHH!! MY FUCKING THUMB! I SMASHED MY FUCKING THUMB!! OH MY GOD!! SON OF A FUCK RABBIT, I SEE THE BONE!! OH MY FUCKING GOD! I CAN SEE MY BONE! SOMEBODY DRIVE ME TO THE HOSPITAL!!"

Needless to say, the But-Cut Five would be in no shape to play the gig without Mikey's foundational licks in our 90-minute repertoire. We were all bummed we couldn't do the gig. The Splash Four seemed like they knew their rock'n'roll. It woulda been a good show. Heard they were from France?

DESIGN: Art Chantry

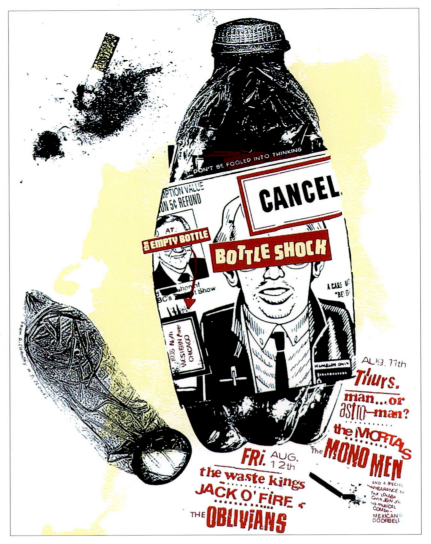

TOP: Bottle Shock poster, 1994, design Art Chantry, illustration Dan Clowes **BOTTOM:** *Sensational Sounds of the 1995 Estrus Invitationals* EP (ES3233), 1995, design Art Chantry **OPPOSITE:** The Galaxy Trio, *Saucers over Vegas*; inside CD booklet artwork, 1994, design Art Chantry

Tim Kerr's presence in Austin made the liberal oasis feel like a second home for the label. And roughly 1,200 miles to the northeast was Chicago, Illinois, another second home to Estrus.

In 1993, the Mono Men were invited to play at the wedding reception of friend Brendan Burke and his wife Sheila in the Windy City. Brendan was behind booking the first Mono Men show at the legendary club the Empty Bottle, as the normal go-to spot, the Lounge Act, was occupied. Nevertheless, the gig initiated a long-standing relationship between the Empty Bottle and both the Mono Men and Estrus. In fact, the Mono Men, who typically hold the record for bar sales for venues they played regularly, were able to run the Empty Bottle completely out of beer.

The E.B.—as I'm sure no one calls it —hosted "Bottle Shock" in 1994. The shitshow featured Man or Astro-Man?, the Mortals, the Mono Men, the Waste Kings, Jack O'Fire and the Oblivians. Tagged onto that weekend was Tom Sparrow's bachelor party at a bowling alley in Normal, Illinois.[35] The Mono Men paired up with the Mortals and took part in the festivities before doing a string of shows with the Oblivians in the South.

Dave said the Illinois gauntlet of debauchery weekend was when he first really partied with Carl "Bookman" Ratliff, music director for Auburn's radio station, roadie for Man or Astro-Man? and doer-of-all-the-things at Bust Out Promotions. It was also when he met the gracious, soft-spoken Chet Weise.

"Carl and I were talking about him doing promotions for the label while he finished school in Auburn," Crider said. "And he came up to Chicago so we could work out details. Though Carl denies it, he and I made a drunken 'agreement' to shave our heads before meeting at the Empty Bottle. I wandered off after load-in and found a Supercuts. I got the full-on 'Moon Pie' head. When I showed up at the bar and met Carl, he had a full head of hair and had a pretty good laugh. So, I got to make my first sojourn to the deep South looking like a fucking skinhead... thanks, Carl!"

All four Mono Men confirmed that Crider's heinous appearance warranted a ban on him sitting in the front seat for the entire tour.

An Empty Bottle connection helped get *Speed Kills* magazine to sponsor 1995's Estrus Invitationals: Midwest Divisions. Bands who were part of the traveling circus included the Mono Men; Memphis brass-heavy instrumental combo Impala; lo-fi raunch-spewing trio the Drags; Tim Kerr and Mike Carroll's post-Poison 13 effort Lord High Fixers; and power pop kingpins the Insomniacs. Estrus dished out a promotional 45 to coincide with the string of shows called Sensational Sounds of the 1995 Estrus Invitationals. The following year the Nomads and The Makers would sub in for the "West Coast" division of the Invitationals.

New sounds continued to burst from the Estrus headquarters, as did the tangible goodies that came with the music. Crider and Chantry continued to push the envelope in oddities. Some examples include the Drags' *Dragsploitatation…Now!* 10-inch, which came with a custom barf bag; the Insomniacs' *Wake Up!* CD, which came with a little black address book; and The Untamed Youth's *Live in Vegas* LP, which came with an escort service card.

Popularity for Estrus specialty items and unique packaging grew. Local wizard Lance Thingmaker and his wife Beth took over the bulk of those types of projects—ones that included duties Crider said "could have never been realized without Lance's ingenuity and printing skills."

Garage Shock's popularity had, unfortunately, gotten too big for its own good. Crider was faced with having to turn people away at the door who had traveled thousands of miles or even continents. The bummer-shock was felt around the garage circuit when the news broke that there would be no Garage Shock in 1996 due to Crider and Bekki simply needing a break from the asses-to-the-wall, 3–4-day hullabaloo inside a dive bar—and hosting a small country inside a house.

It was ok to take a break, Dave thought. Things were looking good…

---

[35] The Mono Men ended up releasing a live recording of the show the following year as the 10-inch *Live at Tom's Strip-N-Bowl*.

the INSOMNIACS

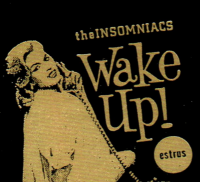

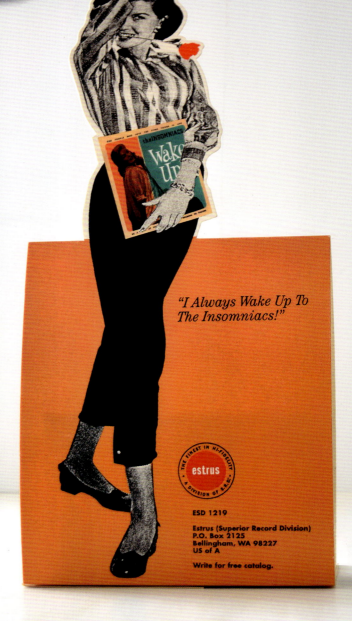

THINGS YOU'LL NEVER KNOW
INTO THE MIRROR
NOTHING IS REAL
UP TO ME
I DON'T THINK SHE'S COMING HOME
WHAT A GIRL CAN'T DO
STOP PRETENDING
TIME TICKS BY
I'VE BEEN AROUND
SILVIA GREY
~~YOU CAN BE MY BABY~~
THAT'S WHAT I WANT
THE ME
LITTLE GIRL
WAITING FOR THE WORLD...
IT'S AS IF
I'M GONE
FAVE
MILKCOW
YOU CAN BE MY BABY

The Insomniacs **CLOCKWISE (from top left):** Logo, 2000; *Out Of It* LP (ES1233), 1996; *Wake Up!* LP promotional address book; Vampira promotional bookmark; *Wake Up!* LP promotional stand-up, designs Art Chantry; promotional photo, 1998, Marty Perez

THE APEMEN
PERCOLATOR STOMP (ES748), 1994

ALEX WALD: Sometime in the early '90s, I'd been laid off from my straight job as a comic book art director in Chicago and was looking for freelance work. I put together a selection of my most arresting art on xeroxes, stuffed the flimsy excuse for a portfolio into envelopes, and mailed them to dozens of magazines and record labels. Though personal computers had become a Thing, the likelihood of my owning one was still many years away. And the Internet? It was a handful of geeks on bulletin boards feuding with each other via America Online. Not for me. Of the dozens of would-be markets, Estrus was one of the few that replied—and by phone! A personal call conveyed a sense of urgency. I was impressed. After the first few minutes, I knew I was communing with a kindred soul: Someone who loved monster movies, comics, and loud, greasy, trashy rock'n'roll that was the antithesis of the SPIN-approved music of the day. I knew I'd look forward to every call from Dave Crider. The Apemen sleeve was my first assignment, and I was told that this Dutch surf rock band performed wearing ape masks. Shades of The Nairobi Trio! It seemed only natural to me that *all* the figures, band, and audience should be apes! The whole artboard was less than 8 inches square, and the challenge was painting guitars that small: It's really hard to detail guitar strings when the object in the image is less than an inch long. I also appreciated that every graphic element was being left to me: the logo and the typography, front, back, and labels. There was no budget to hire others; if I didn't do it, it wasn't getting done. The Apemen gig set the pattern for all the Estrus assignments to come. The compensation was modest. There was no illusion of working for a Major Label with extravagant budgets. I couldn't yet pay the rent, but I'd arrived.

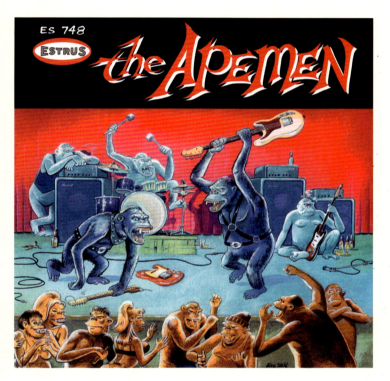

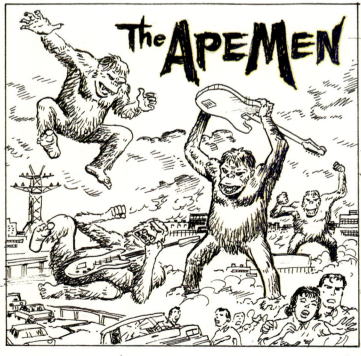

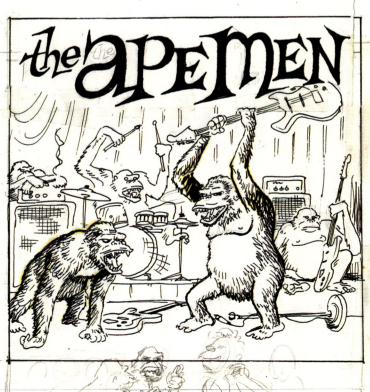

INSTRUMENTAL ROLES

DAVE CRIDER: I've always been a fan of instrumental rock. The first record I remember making me want to totally fuck shit up as a young kid was a scratchy 45 of Link Wray's "Rumble" from my parents' record collection. When I started the label, instrumental stuff was decidedly uncool, especially in garage-punk circles. That might still be the case. However, instrumental releases were a large portion of the label's output and I think it'd be fair to say that Estrus played a major part in kickstarting the '90s instro revival.

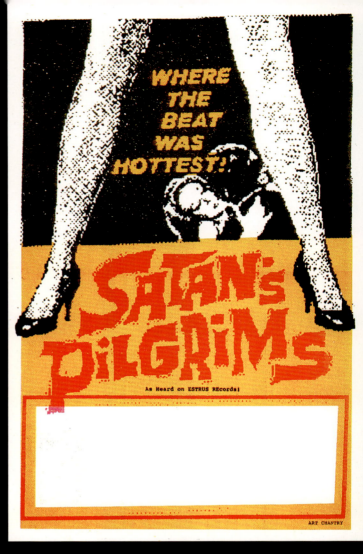

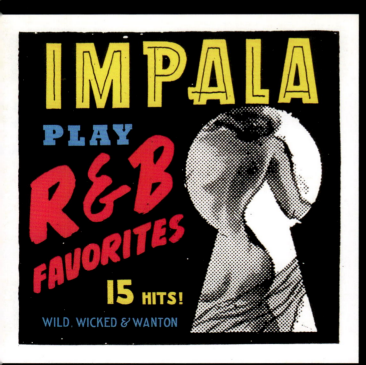

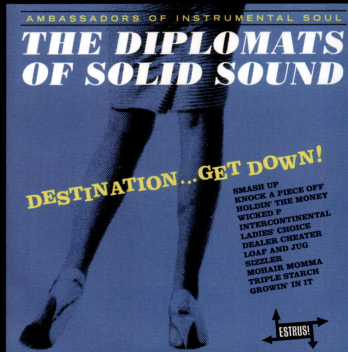

CLOCKWISE (from top left): The Galaxy Trio *Saucers Over Vegas* mini-LP (ESD105), 1994; Satan's Pilgrims tour poster blank, 1996; The Diplomats of Solid Sound *Destination... Get Down!* LP (ES2110D), 2004, design Johnny Bartlett; Impala *Play R&B Favorites* LP (ES1245), 1998, design Art Chantry

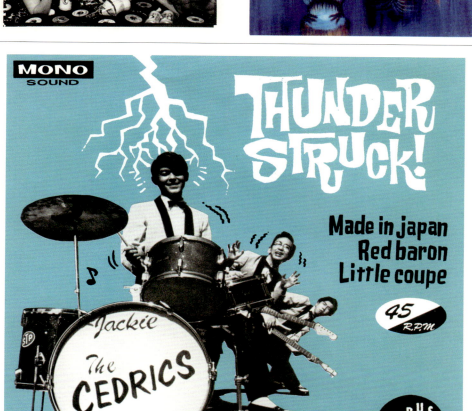
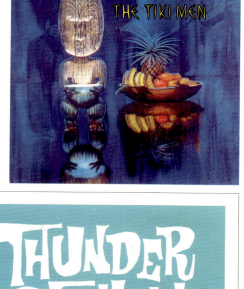

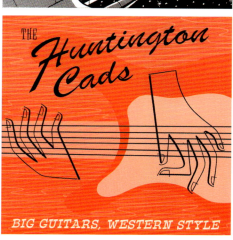
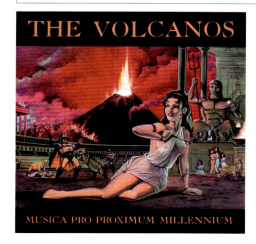

FIRST ROW: The Trashwomen "Bird Dance Beat" promotional single (ESP9), 1994, design Art Chantry; The Tiki Men *The Good Life* EP (ES766), 1995, design Art Chantry; The Galaxy Trio "Sheriff-Boy-R-Dee" single (ES790), 1996, design/illustration Alex Wald **SECOND ROW:** Jackie & The Cedrics *Thunderstruck!* EP (ES737), 1993, design Rockin' Jelly Bean, photo Ya-Mummy; Huevos Rancheros *Rocket To Nowhere* EP (ES722), 1991, design/illustration Tom Bagley; The Huntington Cads *Big Guitars, Western Style* EP (ES7108), 1997, design/illustration Shag **THIRD ROW:** The Volcanos *Musica Pro Proximum Millenium* EP (ES7107), 1997, design/Illustration Alex Wald; Switch Trout *Under The Wire* EP (ES7147), 2000, design Johnny Bartlett; The Crown Royals *Funky-Do* CD (ESD1255) 1999, design Art Chantry

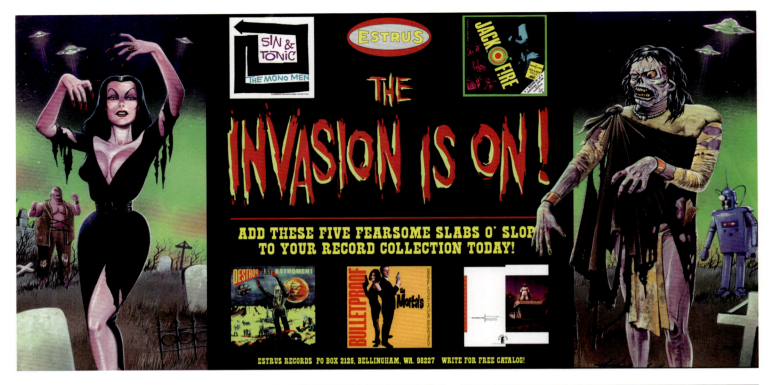

CLOCKWISE (from top): Estrus Invasion promotional poster, 1995, design Dave Crider, illustration Alex Wald; Original Vampira sketch for proposed Mono Men "Mystery Girl" single; Wald's sketches for Estrus Invasion poster

ESTRUS: SHOVELIN' THE SHIT SINCE '87 155

ALEX WALD: Dave called to ask for a cover for a new Mono Men single to be titled Mystery Girl—and it's possible he suggested working Vampira into the design. OK, twist my arm, Dave! Even though I was a Chicagoan and a mere five years old when Miss Nurmi held her all-too-brief reign over Angeleno airwaves, I was quite familiar with the legendary and lethal charms of the Dark Goddess of KABC-TV. The first sketches were laid out to suggest a *Playboy* centerfold, allowing maximum exposure of Vampira's slinky silhouette. The first rough shows Vampira on set surrounded by her chaise longue and clunky TV camera; the second sketch has her posing outside LA's famous Googie's Diner, offsetting James Dean's crumpled Porsche 550. Within days, Dave told me the single had been scrapped. Still, he had a brainstorm to salvage the work in progress—an homage to the Aurora Plastics Corporation poster flogging their insanely popular monster model kits. He even lifted the original poster's tagline: The Invasion is On! The first poster rough adds El Brainiac, the Baron of Terror, which was vetoed in favor of The Aztec Mummy! The amendment was further amended to employ the iconic Topstone Shock Monster visage, which had been appearing on various Estrus swag. Really! How's a guy supposed to paint with all that arm-twisting going on?

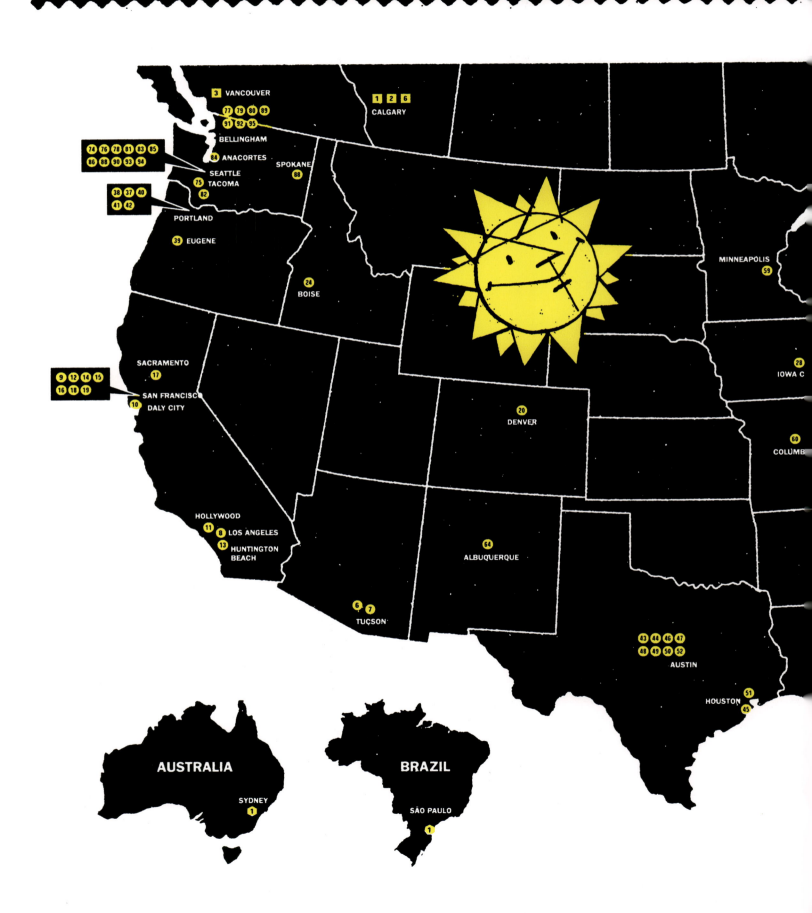

THE WIDE WORLD OF ESTRUS

ALABAMA
1. The Dexateens: Tuscaloosa
2. The Immortal Lee County Killers: Lee County
3. Man Or Astro-Man?: Auburn
4. The Quadrajets: Auburn
5. The Wednesdays: Florence

ARIZONA
6. The Fells: Tucson
7. The Knockout Pills: Tucson

CALIFORNIA
8. The Beguiled: Los Angeles
9. The Bobbyteens: San Francisco
10. The Brentwoods: Daly City
11. Deke Dickerson: Hollywood
12. The Go-Nuts: San Francisco
13. The Huntington Cads: Huntington Beach
14. The Mummies: San Francisco
15. The Phantom Surfers: San Francisco
16. Supercharger: San Francisco
17. The Tiki Men: Sacramento
18. The Trashwomen: San Francisco
19. Zen Guerrilla: San Francisco

COLORADO
20. The Ray-Ons: Denver

DELAWARE
21. The Rocket Scientists: Wilmington

DISTRICT OF COLUMBIA
22. Go To Blazes: Washington, DC

GEORGIA
23. The Woggles: Athens

IDAHO
24. The Pills: Boise

ILLINOIS
25. The Crown Royals: Chicago
26. The Nerves: Chicago
27. The Waste Kings: Chicago

IOWA
28. The Diplomats Of Solid Sound: Iowa City
29. Los Marauders: Iowa City

LOUISIANA
30. Famous Monsters: New Orleans

OHIO
31. Cheater Slicks: Columbus
32. The Cowslingers: Cleveland
33. The Cybermen: Cincinnati
34. The Mortals: Cincinnati
35. Prisonshake: Cleveland
36. The Soledad Brothers: Maumee

OREGON
37. Fireballs Of Freedom: Portland
38. The Galaxy Trio: Portland
39. Marble Orchard: Eugene
40. New Wave Hookers: Portland
41. Satan's Pilgrims: Portland
42. Screamin Furys: Portland

TEXAS
43. The 1-4-5s: Austin
44. Death Valley: Austin
45. The Fatal Flyin' Guilloteens: Houston
46. The Inhalants: Austin
47. Jack O'Fire: Austin
48. King Sound Quartet: Austin
49. Lord High Fixers: Austin
50. Poison 13: Austin
51. Sugar Shack: Houston
52. Total Sound Group Direct Action Committee: Austin

MAINE
53. The Brood: Portland

MICHIGAN
54. Bantam Rooster: Detroit
55. The Gories: Detroit
56. The Hentchmen: Detroit
57. The Monarchs: Detroit
58. The Volcanos: Detroit

MINNESOTA
59. The Midnight Evils: Minneapolis

MISSOURI
60. The Untamed Youth: Columbia

NEW JERSEY
61. Electric Frankenstein: Whippany
62. The Insomniacs: Englishtown
63. The Swingin' Neckbreakers: Trenton

NEW MEXICO
64. The Drags: Albuquerque

NEW YORK
65. The A-Bones: New York City
66. The Blowtops: Buffalo
67. The Baseball Furies: Buffalo
68. The Mooney Suzuki: New York City

NORTH CAROLINA
69. The Cherry Valence: Raleigh
70. Southern Culture On The Skids: Chapel Hill

PENNSYLVANIA
71. Gas Money: Philadelphia

TENNESSEE
72. Impala: Memphis
73. The Oblivians: Memphis

WASHINGTON
74. The Blow Up: Seattle
75. The Boss Martians: Tacoma
76. The Del Lagunas: Seattle
77. The Dt's: Bellingham
78. The Fall-Outs: Seattle
79. Federation X: Bellingham
80. Game For Vultures: Bellingham
81. Gas Huffer: Seattle
82. Girl Trouble: Tacoma
83. The Gimmicks: Seattle
84. Gravel: Anacortes
85. The Invisible Men: Seattle
86. Madame X: Seattle

87. The Makers: Spokane
88. The Monkeywrench: Seattle
89. The Mono Men: Bellingham
90. Nightcaps: Seattle
91. The Roofdogs: Bellingham
92. The Star Spangled Bastards: Bellingham
93. The Statics: Seattle
94. Stumpy Joe: Seattle
95. Watts: Bellingham

VIRGINIA
96. The M-80's: Norfolk

WISCONSIN
97. The Mistreaters: Milwaukee

AUSTRALIA
1. Brother Brick: Sydney

CANADA
1. Huevos Rancheros: Calgary
2. The Mants: Calgary
3. The Spitfires: Vancouver
4. Shadowy Men On A Shadowy Planet: Toronto
5. Tricky Woo: Montreal
6. The Von Zippers: Calgary

FINLAND
1. The Flaming Sideburns: Helsinki

FRANCE
2. The No-Talents: Montrouge
3. The Splash Four: Paris
4. Thundercrack: Nancy
5. T.V. Killers: Bordeaux

NETHERLANDS
6. The Apemen: Tilburg

NORWAY
7. The Lust-O-Rama: Oslo

SWEDEN
8. Dee Rangers: Stockholm
9. The Hellacopters: Stockholm
10. The Nomads: Stockholm
11. The Sewergrooves: Stockholm

UNITED KINGDOM
12. The Coyote Men: Newcastle
13. Golden Guineas: Newcastle
14. Thee Headcoats: Chatham

BRAZIL
1. Thee Butcher's Orchestra: São Paulo

JAPAN
1. The 5.6.7.8's: Tokyo
2. DMBQ: Tokyo
3. Estrella 20/20: Tokyo
4. Gasoline: Yokkaichi
5. The Goners: Tokyo
6. Jackie & The Cedrics: Tokyo
7. Mad3: Tokyo
8. Thee Michelle Gun Elephant: Tokyo
9. The Royal Fingers: Tokyo
10. The Switch Trout: Tokyo
11. Supersnazz: Tokyo
12. Teengenerate: Tokyo

The Nomads *Big Sound* 2000, promotional photo

SUGAR SHACK
YOU DON'T MEAN SHIT TO ME (ES770), 1995

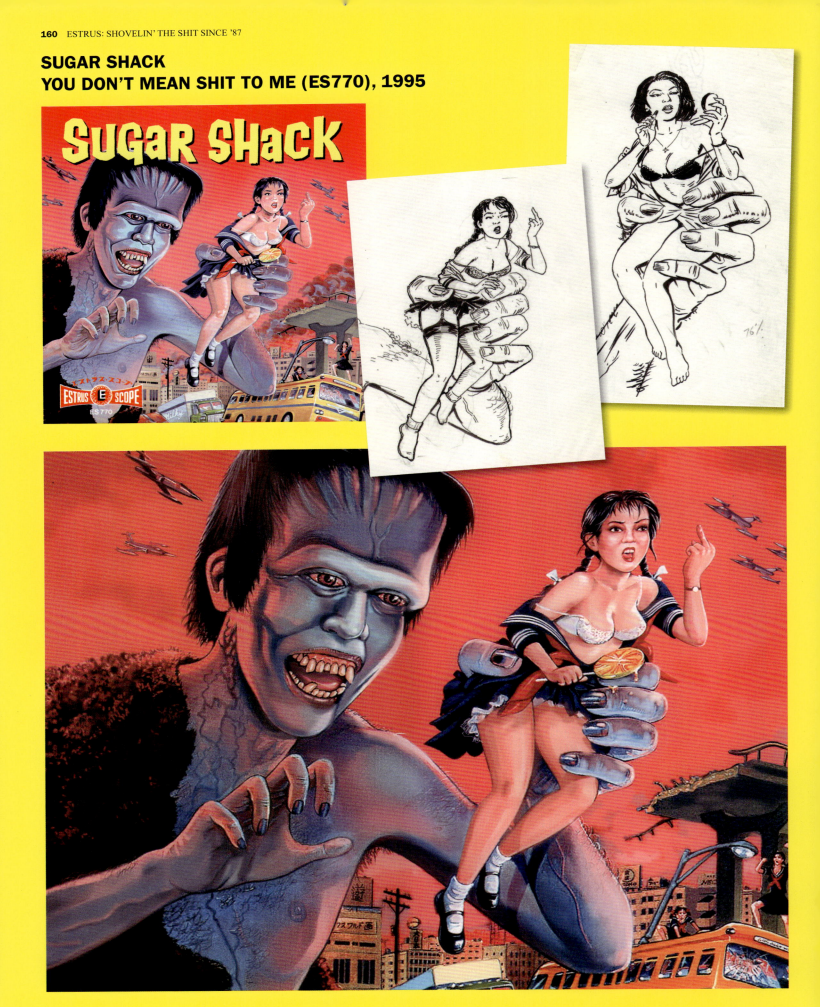

TOP LEFT: Sugar Shack "You Don't Mean Shit to Me" single (ES770), 1995, design/illustration Alex Wald **RIGHT:** Original and alternate sketches
BOTTOM: "You Don't Mean Shit to Me" original painting

SOUTHERN CULTURE ON THE SKIDS
SANTO SWINGS (ES7967), 1996

TOP LEFT: Southern Culture on the Skids *Santo Swings* EP (ES7967), 1996, design/illustration Alex Wald **RIGHT:** Wald's notes to Crider regarding SCOTS stand-ups for insert; original sketches and concepts for *Santo Swings* cover **BOTTOM LEFT:** Original painting for *Santo Swings* insert

ORAL HISTORY LESSON: INTERNATIONAL STAGE WORLDWIDE NOISE-MAKING

ESTRUS RELEASES SPROUT UP INTERNATIONALLY

DAVE CRIDER: Once you were sorta able to tap into these [regional] scenes, it was pretty amazing to see how much else was out there.

Twelve and a half countries have been represented through Estrus releases—13 if you count Canada. The nature in which connections on the international front were made varied, of course. In some cases, it was the Mono Men's overseas travels netting a batch of new buds. Other times it was fellow label head honchos and bands reaching out to Crider.

Three pockets that had significant traction included ones in Scandinavia, France, and most notably, Japan. And for Canada, there was not necessarily a cool pocket of trash but a remarkable pizza joint in Calgary called Tom's House of Pizza.

AL VON ZIPPER (The Von Zippers): They've been around since 1963. Great pizza.

Unfortunately for Dave, signing a 12" pie to put out a record wasn't a realistic option. The Von Zippers, however, were available.

AL VON ZIPPER: The first time I met Dave would've been when the Mono Men toured through Calgary in the early '90s. My first impression? Straight-up dude, maybe a cross between Weird Al and a porn star whose name I can't remember. …I think the VZ's were a pretty good fit with Estrus. Geographically, Bellingham is relatively close to Calgary, or at least not on the other side of the world, so we were able to do a few other shows there too. …Timelines considered, you could say we were part of something wider in terms of Estrus bands and releases [internationally speaking]. But Huevos Rancheros were the first Canadian—and Calgarian—band to put out an Estrus record, if I'm not mistaken.[37]

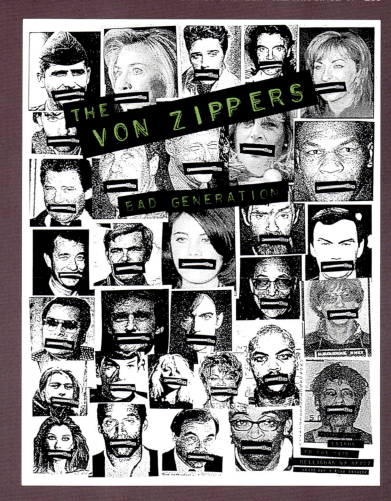

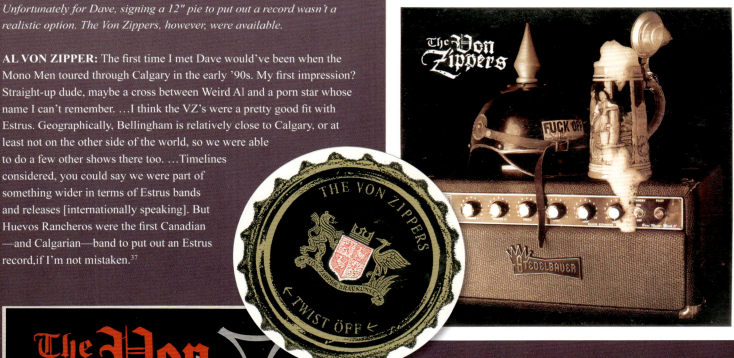

The Von Zippers **CLOCKWISE (from top right):** *Bad Generation* LP (ES1247), 1998, design Art Chantry; *Würms* EP (ES7989), 1997, design Art Chantry, lettering Jamie Sheehan, photo Jason Stanhe; "Twist Off" single (ES7131), 1998, design Art Chantry; promotional sticker, design Al Charlton

---

[37] Al is not mistaken.

THE QUADRAJETS
PAY THE DEUCE (ES1242), 1998
CARL RATLIFF (Bookman): With the Quadrajets, Tim [Kerr] came to Auburn and recorded *Pay the Deuce*. Dave had agreed [to do the record] after he saw them live. He hadn't really liked their Sympathy for the Record Industry records, but he liked the guys and wanted to see them live. The Mono Men were doing some shows in the Midwest and the Quadrajets came up and did one of the shows. And that's when he decided he wanted to put out the record.

CHET WEISE (The Quadrajets/Immortal Lee County Killers): *Pay the Deuce* was the first time we let someone into our circle. At Dave's suggestion, we asked Tim Kerr to produce. Tim did an amazing job. That's the record for me. The songs. How it was recorded. Where it was recorded. The name. Artwork. It all came together. *When the World's on Fire* has some of my favorite tunes and performances, but *Deuce* had everything come together at the right time.

Jason Russell and I were also hanging out, living together and continually bouncing ideas and riffs off each other. That's probably the most I've ever collaborated with someone like that. Just two guitars and riffs. It really showed in the songs. The 'Jets and the Killers both hammered out songs in the rehearsal room, but at that time, Jason and I actually spent time on riffs and choruses before going to rehearsal. Of course, it was always about the riffs. Neither of us concentrated on vocals as much. We just screamed.

Design: Art Chantry

The Mono Men had a strong following in France, which is how Dave was led to discover the slew of relentless, no-bullshit Frenchies to dish out a handful of les releases. The No-Talents, Splash Four, T.V. Killers, and Thundercrack provided a healthy supply of Euro-trash to Estrus' catalog.

For Scandinavia, the seed was planted very early on.

NIKLAS VALBERG (The Nomads): It all started back in '89 when Dave got in touch with our record company. We obviously hadn't heard anything about Estrus or the Mono Men [at that time], but we were pretty excited that an American band would do a cover of one of our songs. It was really interesting to finally meet Dave and the Mono Men when they came to Copenhagen [in 1993]. To finally sit down and have dinner together, drinks together—and to see that Dave was someone with a lot of drive; it seemed like he was the kind of person who could make things happen…. It was so cool to get together with people like Tim Kerr from Poison 13 and the Lord High Fixers. And to meet up with Mike Carroll and hear him say that the Nomads were an inspiration for Poison 13?! To hear things from people like that was very cool for us.

Aside from the Nomads, Estrus unleashed wax and compact discs for Sweden's Dee Rangers, Hellacopters, and Sewergrooves, as well as Finland's Flaming Sideburns.

TOP: The Flaming Sideburns, photo Jay Burnside **BOTTOM:** Thundercrack, photo C. Zerling **OPPOSITE:** The Nomads, photo Jacob Covey

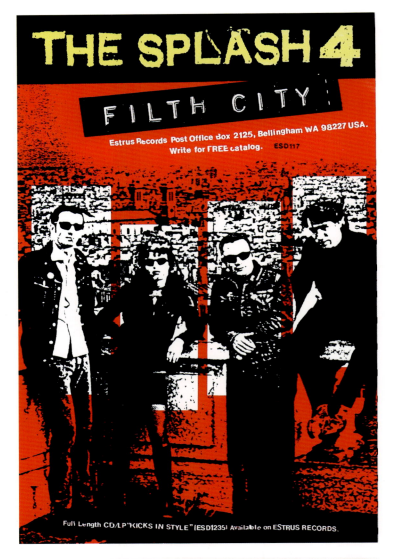

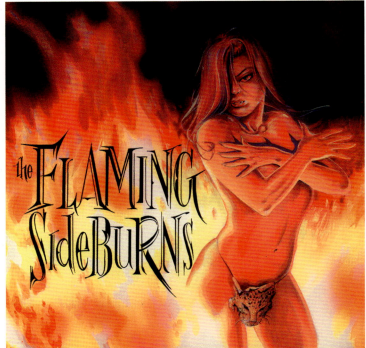

CLOCKWISE (from top left): Sewergrooves *Three Time Losers* promotional poster, 1999, design Art Chantry; The Splash Four *Filth City* promotional poster, 1998, design Art Chantry; The Flaming Sideburns "Jaguar Girls" single (ES7134), 1999, design/illustration Alex Wald; T.V. Killers *You Kill Me* EP (ES7116), 1998, design Art Chantry **OPPOSITE TOP:** The Coyote Men **LEFT:** The Splash Four **RIGHT:** Thundercrack

THE ESTRUSSIAL SOUNDS FROM THE FAR EAST

DAVE CRIDER: I set up a couple of shows for the American Soul Spiders (Japan) when they came out to the Northwest, and I drummed up a friendship with Fink while they were here. So when he told me about his new band, Teengenerate, I asked him if they could come over and play Garage Shock. That kickstarted the Japanese night that year, which was purely selfish because I wanted to see all those bands.

The Japanese night at Garage Shock 1993 proved to be momentous for both the label and the garage'n'punk rock circuits in Japan. Following the event, Estrus would go on to work with The 5.6.7.8's, DMBQ, Estrella 20/20, Gasoline, The Goners, Jackie & The Cedrics, Mad3, Thee Michelle Gun Elephant, The Royal Fingers, Supersnazz, Switch Trout, and, of course, Teengenerate.

(Note: The majority of the commentary from participants in Japan was translated by Mari Tamura.)

ROCKIN' THUNDERBOLT ENOCKY (Jackie & The Cedrics): I came to know about Estrus through Barnhomes Records, an import record store in Shinjuku, Tokyo. The owner, Mr. Yoshiwara, also had his own independent label called 1+ 2 Records, which released the Mono Men records in Japan. …We first met Dave in November 1992 when Jackie & The Cedrics opened for the Mono Men in Seattle. Our bass player, Rockin' Jellybean, realized at the last minute that he couldn't travel to Seattle, so Yoshiko of The 5.6.7.8's filled in on bass. She was already coming along for the fun of it anyway. If her performance on the night was an audition, she definitely didn't make the cut, but Dave thought it was good. After the show, we followed Dave's car to Bellingham to stay at his house. I remember eating a burrito at a convenience store late at night. Dave played some hard-to-find vinyl and cult B-movies for us. He also had a beautiful blue Stratocaster that he let me play on. … I still have the postcard that Dave sent me in February 1992, when he offered to put out a Jackie & The Cedrics record on Estrus. Shortly after, I bought a fax machine, which became my main communication tool until I bought an iMac in 1999.

TOMOKO BUTANE (Supersnazz): I'd always wanted to work with Estrus. I viewed it as my dream label run by someone in the Mono Men. I used to be a garage punk record buyer at Disk Union, an import record shop in Japan. I thought labels like Estrus, Sympathy, and Norton were hands down the coolest and that one day, I'd love to be on one. Everybody in my music community more or less shared my feelings.

SEIJI (Guitar Wolf): In the early '90s, nobody in the Japanese punk and garage community dreamed about going overseas to play. Nobody thought it was an option. But Estrus shone a light on Japanese bands when it featured us, Teengenerate, and The 5.6.7.8's on Japan night during the Garage Shock weekend in 1993. It was monumental because we were never the focus of attention outside of Japan. …The same year we played Garage Shock, Guitar Wolf got to release our first album on Goner and then later signed with Matador. Because of our releases on those labels, we played all over the world, including Europe, Australia, New Zealand, Brazil, Argentina, Thailand, Korea, and China. We owe all of this to Garage Shock.

ABOVE: DMBQ, photo Chris Fuller **OPPOSITE TOP:** The 5.6.7.8's, photo Masao Nakagami **BOTTOM:** Rockin' Enocky in front of Crider's house, 1993

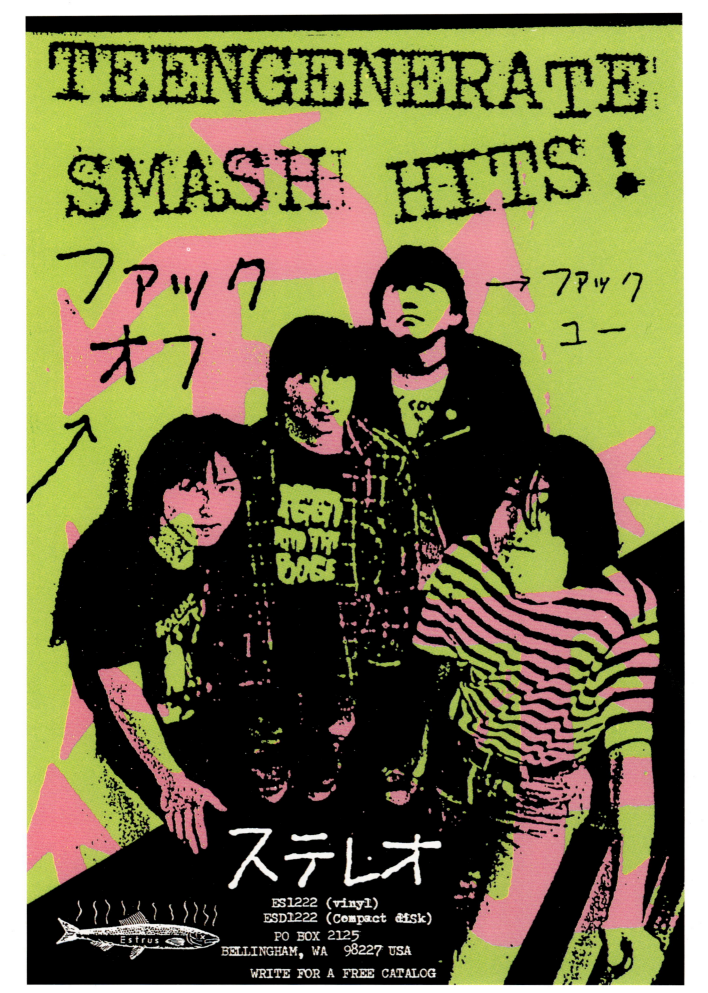

Teengenerate *Smash Hits!* promotional poster, 1995, design Art Chantry

DAVE CRIDER: We were playing with The Makers down at EJ's,[37] and they'd just gotten back from Japan. They were all raving about Gasoline and told me that "their demo is on the way, and you gotta check it out." At some point I got the package, and of course, I loved it.

GAN CHAN (Gasoline): We sent a demo to Dave that Fink (Teengenerate) had recorded for us. Dave wrote back in Sharpie on a fax, saying "fucking amazing!" and that was how we started working together. …After we had our first release on Estrus, we received many offers from different countries, English-speaking and non-English-speaking. I couldn't understand some of them, so I'm pretty sure I missed out on a few opportunities.

NAOHITO TROUT (The Switch Trout): Estrus dropped some killer tunes that more than matched the level of destruction I was craving. Those definitely set a standard in the music community I was a part of, something I kept going back to in order to stay true to myself.ABusive's involvement and excitement with our releases were beyond what we expected. It was as if we were working together, even though we were separated by the ocean. It brought me almost to tears every time I received the finished product.

HIRO (Estrella 20/20): Dave had just come back from Japan, and when we first went to his place and met him, he showed us some pictures of Japan as well as pictures of himself wearing a Godzilla costume! When he talked about the Toho studio in Japan—the Godzilla studio—he smiled like a child.

DAVE CRIDER: The first time The 5.6.7.8's and Jackie & The Cedrics came out here, they stayed at the house for a week, or a week and a half, doing American stuff. …We're having a party here after a show, it's late, they're not speaking a lot of English. They're all really hungry but still being polite. I opened the freezer and they saw the corndogs and were into it, so I said, "Yeah, I'll make some corn dogs." The next thing I know, Jackie is walking around eating a frozen corn dog. Hiro (Estrella 20/20) did the same thing at a completely different time. I guess it's a thing?

ABOVE: Estrella 20/20, photo Eri Sekiguchi

---

[37] Staple club in the punk rock circuit owned by Etta James (not *that* Etta James).

100% APESHIT DISCOGRAPHY

THUNDERCRACK
OWN SHIT HOME (ES1249), 1998
ESTRUS SALES PITCH: What do you get when you combine the slop-raunch groove of the legendary Slim Harpo with the back-alley brontch of a three-legged junkyard dog? Answer: All hail Thundercrack!! From the ashes of Frogland's mighty Squares (dig out their swivel-hipped "Trapped in a Square" LP on Hangman for the dope on that combo, Jack)…Thundercrack kickup a tire-slashin', teeth-gnashin', punk/blues beat rumble in the bad blood tradition of Bo Diddley, Billy Childish, and Jack O' Fire. Estrus Records proudly presents their full-length debut, the "Own Shit Home" LP/CD!—12 sweat-caked screamers guaranteed to set yer hoof a' tappin' and get that tailfeather waggin.' Lowdown n' raunchy trash-a-boogie deluxe, baby! So don't delay, Porky, get yer ass some Thundercrack!! Watch for THUNDERCRACK on tour in the USA this winter!!

Design: Art Chantry

ABOVE: Guitar Wolf, photo Keith Marlowe **OPPOSITE TOP:** Jackie & The Cedrics, Garage Shock '94 **LEFT:** Crider meets Ultra Man, Tokyo, Japan, 1993, photo Brian Teasley **RIGHT:** Supersnazz, 3-B Tavern, Bellingham, WA, 1993, photo Dave Crider

LEFT: Promotional photos for The 5.6.7.8's

BELOW: The Switch Trout, promotional "magic fish," design Art Chantry

CENTER: Original photograph of Jackie & The Cedrics from the "Thunderstruck" single. A surviving artifact of the warehouse fire, photo Ya-Mummy

TEENGENERATE
PEARL HARBOR DAY POSTER

ART CHANTRY: This was for a concert at the 3-B Tavern on Pearl Harbor Day. Teengenerate is/was a Japanese garage rock band and somehow that seemed funny to me at the time, so I did a "rising sun" motif (Japanese flag). The typeface is the one used in the NRA logo (that's the National Recovery Act of World War II and NOT the National Rifle Association of today, but the confusion is intentional).

To finish off the posters, we silk-screened them on some metal I stole from Grant Alden. Then we took a collection of SERIOUS weapons from my old pal Michael Decker, drove out to the boonies, and blew the metal posters full of holes. Note that we shot them from the BACK side, so it looks like the bullets are coming TOWARD YOU! I'm sure we spent more money on ammo than on making the things.

SUPERSNAZZ
I GOTTA GO NOW/I AM A CLICHE! (ES774), 1996

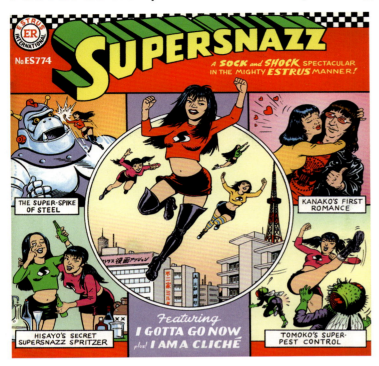

ALEX WALD: I fell in love with Supersnazz before (once again) ever hearing their music. How can you not love a band named after a Flamin' Groovies album? What's not to love about a Ramones-flavored cover of the Ronettes classic "I Wonder?" (on Diode City). To answer a question with a question, I shall have to quote Oscar Hammerstein, "Oh, why should I have spring fever—When it isn't even spring?"

In retrospect, I must have been languishing from an excess of schoolboy crush, for I believe I volunteered to expand the parameters of the usual cover deal to a full eight-page comic plus deluxe covers package. For sheer labor alone, this was the most complex of all my Estrus gigs. Dave was generally relaxed about deadlines… Yet I think it took at least three months to write, pencil, ink, and letter the comic and create the covers. There isn't room to footnote every influence that went into this dish, but the '60s-style DC Giant cover, complete with Go-Go Checks behind the logo, the Justice League-like clubhouse and oath of allegiance, the Toho nod for a robot ape, and the Joey Ramone cameo all lent spice. And there must still be fanboys today devastated that the Faster Pussycat model kit ad was a cruel hoax! My guess is that when the dust settled, I ended up making a whopping $0.29 an hour—maybe. But I had fun doing it.

> "We were just handed the finished product, which made us go, 'Wow! Great!' We became cartoon characters!"
>
> **TOMOKO BUTANE** (Supersnazz)

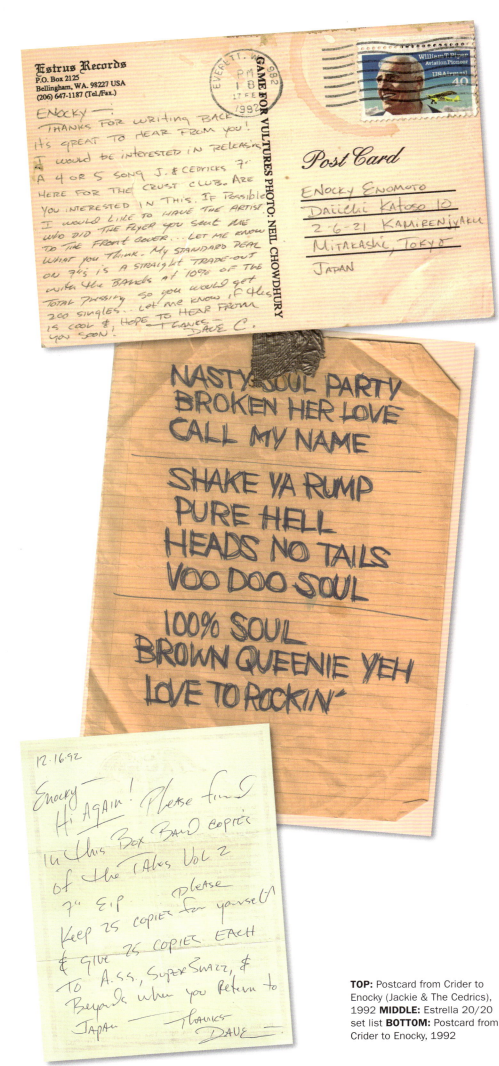

100% APESHIT DISCOGRAPHY

ELECTRIC FRANKENSTEIN
I WAS A TEENAGE SHUTDOWN
(ES1251), 1998

ART CHANTRY: Sal Canzonieri [Electric Frankenstein] is a collector. He set about trying to get as many different artists and labels as he could muster to design a different cover for him. In the end, Electric Frankenstein must have released near 100 records—all with the coolest covers you've ever seen. ... I did two EF record covers; one was a 45 cover, and the other was *I Was a Teenage Shutdown* for Estrus. I tried to make it look like a cheesy lobby card for "I Was a Teenage Frankenstein." Sal later told me he especially liked my cover because it was maybe the only one that used Teenage Frankenstein on it. Virtually every other one had the Universal Studios version.

Design: Art Chantry

ESTRELLA 20/20
AFRO MEXICANA (ES1020), 1999
ATSUSHI MORIKAWA (Estrella 20/20): The artwork on *Afro Mexicana* is perfect! I was a big fan of Art Chantry's artwork. All of the artwork on Estrus is amazing, and I'm honored to be one of them.

DAVE CRIDER: I love that record, and I love that band, but that was definitely a more dividing [release]. The people who liked them, liked them—and the people who didn't were just like, "What the fuck?" I remember they were playing at Garage Shock, and Mike LaVella came up to me and yelled, "Why?!" I was just laughing…

TOP: Postcard from Crider to Enocky (Jackie & The Cedrics), 1992 **MIDDLE:** Estrella 20/20 set list **BOTTOM:** Postcard from Crider to Enocky, 1992

SEIJI ON MEETING MAN OR ASTRO-MAN?

"We played together at a show that Eric (Friedl) booked in Memphis. Summers there are super hot. I warned Man or Astro-Man? that they were gonna die because they were all costumed up in air-tight space suits. They took one look at us—clad in leather—and said we were no better. We had a good laugh at each other."

TOMOKO BUTANE'S APPRECIATION FOR THE MONO MEN'S STYLE

"The Mono Men were a great band and had a big influence on Supersnazz's sound and style. We wore flannel shirts and jeans on stage, a style idea we borrowed from them. I love the Mono Men."

CLOCKWISE (from top right): Supersnazz/Teengenerate; DMBQ, photo Chris Fuller; Fink, photo Masao Nakagami; Crider, American Soul Spiders, Supersnazz; The Switch Trout

GAN REVEALS HOW CHICAGO'S EMPTY BOTTLE STILL LIVES WITH HIM

"Just before our show at the Empty Bottle, Dave sent me a fax saying, "You better get in touch with your girlfriend in Japan. She has something important to tell you." She told me on the phone that she was pregnant, so we got engaged over the phone. On my way to the club, I ran into Kelly from Fireballs of Freedom, so I told him what had just happened. Kelly dashed to the club to have the whole place congratulate me, and we had a party. Kelly is such a goofball, and I love him. My daughter is 19 now.

TOP: Teengenerate, photo Masao Nakagami **BOTTOM:** Estrella 20/20, photo Jacob Covey

WATTS
WATTS (ES1258), 1999
JEFF BRAIMES (Watts): I do actually remember coming up with the vocal phrasing for "The Kings of Jackin' You Around." I thought the raw song was laid out a bit like Thin Lizzy's "Jailbreak," and I started singing that over it. Since no one else could hear what I was singing, it didn't matter—and I could work it out a bit. If you listen to it with that ear, I think you can still hear that verse in there. Great song, either way...

One super funny memory I have is that after the record came out, Aaron said that he really liked my vocals. We'd been playing these songs for a year by this time. He goes, "I never knew what you were singing." I don't think that meant just lyrics—I think he couldn't even hear pitch or inflection or anything; like he wouldn't even have known I was singing unless he could see my lips moving.

DAVE CRIDER: I'm really proud of that record.

Design: Art Chantry

Gasoline
photo Keith Marlowe

> "Hey Carl, this is Dave. Please give me a call. Something's going on."

ORAL HISTORY LESSON: THE FIRE

"FREEZER FULL OF TURKEYS"
ELECTRICAL FIRE DECIMATES LABEL'S WAREHOUSE

LARRY HARDY (In The Red Records): I was devastated. It was awful. I'd been [to the space], so I'd seen his setup, and, yeah, he lost it all. Not only did he take this gut punch to his label—a label run by a really great guy—but he lost his record collection. I don't know if you collect records, but I always have—that's why I did a label—and the idea that you'd lose all that in a fire just makes my head spin. It just bummed me out really bad. Like, on every level.

On January 16, 1997, the Criders, Estrus, and the punk rock community suffered a tragic blow. Because of an adjacent tenant's recklessness—

shoddy wiring on a freezer full of turkeys—an electrical fire decimated the label's warehouse. As a result, Estrus lost its archives and mail order; the Mono Men lost most of their equipment; and Dave lost his personal record collection, including his own copies of the label's output over the previous decade. On top of that, numerous master tapes and equipment for the planned Estrus Studio were total losses.

Though several components of the label were spared, such as financial records and inventory, the devastation was unlike anything Dave and Bekki could have prepared for.

ESTRUS WAREHOUSE BURNS

Equipment, mail-order and studio lost. By S. Duda

Bellingham, WA—Fire destroyed a warehouse owned by Estrus Records owner Dave Crider on January 16. The blaze devastated the space, destroying much of its contents. The fire claimed the beginnings of an on-site studio Crider was building as well as the Estrus mail order operation. Also lost in the blaze was the gear of Crider's band, the Mono Men, as well as Crider's personal record collection and other archival material. Prelimi-

Total losses may reach upwards of $250,000.

nary reports suggest that total losses in the fire may reach upwards of $250,000 on the building and its contents, both of which were uninsured. Though Crider declined direct comment, he did say that Estrus, one of the world's pre-eminent distributors of garage rock, planned to stick to its regular release schedule. All the news isn't completly tragic, Crider reports that the majority of Estrus material is warehoused in San Francisco.⦿

OPPOSITE: Estrus warehouse fire, January 16, 1997, photos Art Chantry/Jamie Sheehan
ABOVE: Article from *The Stranger*, 1997

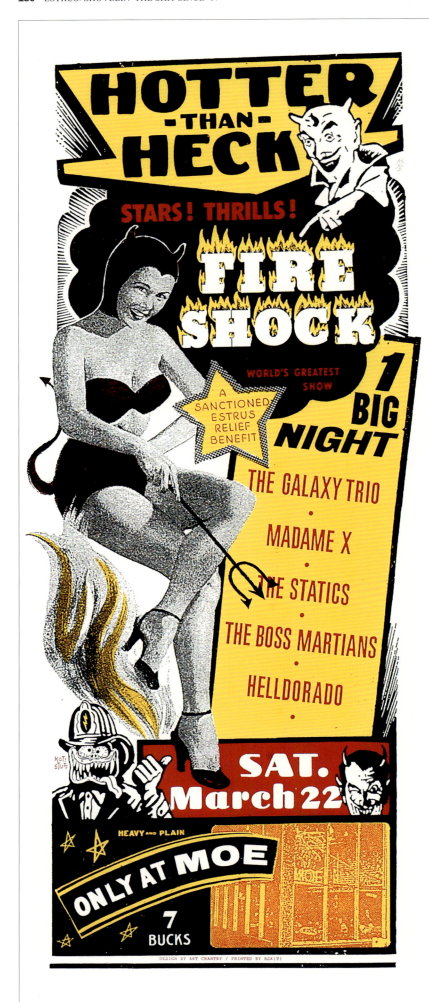

CARL RATLIFF (Estrus): I remember waking up, and there was a message on my answering machine. It was from Dave. He sounded tired and depressed. He said, "Hey Carl, this is Dave. Please give me a call. Something's going on." I was like, "Oh shit!" So I called him back immediately, and he told me the warehouse had just burned down. At that point, I hadn't made the final decision [to move to Bellingham]—and Dave had encouraged me to stay [at Auburn] to finish school —but the fire sorta changed everything. Estrus was planning on getting a new building and having offices, with maybe Art [Chantry] moving up, and with Tim and Beth [Kerr] planning on moving up. That just sorta threw a wrench into everything.

In December 1996, it looked as though Estrus could soon be operating with an in-house producer (Kerr) working in a regional studio, an in-house designer (Chantry), and a house inside of a house to create a true in-house house…

The community's response to the Estrus disaster was nothing short of world-class. A handful of satellite benefit shows titled "Fireshock" took place in Portland, Chicago and Tokyo. Donations, gifts, and other items from fellow label heads came in and humbled Dave; these were people he hardly knew, from independent labels of all sizes. Several other benefits tied to Estrus' restart popped up in a dozen other cities. Because Crider's focus in the fire's aftermath was on rebuilding and reassessing Estrus' future, he was completely caught off guard by the communal generosity and floored by the support.

On the home front, newly acquired label help Carl "Bookman" Ratliff teamed with Frank Kozik, famed designer and owner of Man's Ruins Records, to make Flaming Burnout: An Estrus Benefit Comp. *One friend in Bellingham made a quilt out of T-shirts burned in the fire; and Aaron Roeder's 3-B Tavern hung dozens of burned records from its ceiling.*

The response to the Estrus warehouse fire proved to be more than a collective effort to help refill a small business's lost inventory. It was a case of family helping family. While the loss of irreplaceable personal items was a proverbial kick in the dick from a donkey to Crider, he remains grateful that no one was hurt. Had he or Bekki been inside the warehouse at the time, there was little chance they would have escaped.

ABOVE: Seattle Fireshock poster, Moe, Seattle, WA, 1997, design Art Chantry **OPPOSITE:** Portland Fireshock, Mercury Room, Portland, OR, 1997, design Nancy Kimball

READ THESE FACTS

ON THURSDAY, JANUARY 16TH, 1997 the Bellingham warehouse which housed Estrus mail order inventory and Estrus archives burned to the ground. The building was a total loss. All color vinyl and other items sold thru the Estrus Quarterly were destroyed in the fire, so mail order will be temporarily closed. We are hoping to be up and running again within 6 months. The majority of our regular inventory is stored at our wholesale distributor's warehouse in California and is unaffected. Stores can still get Estrus releases from Mordam Records: (415) 642-6800 (wholesale orders). The Estrus business offices and computer data files were unaffected by the fire, but we'll be closed temporarily until we sort things out. If you had a pending order, we will either issue you a refund, a credit voucher or return your order unopened. Crust Club and Estrus Quarterly mailings will be delayed. We would like to express our appreciation to you, our friends and music fans who've helped and supported the label over the past 10 years, and we look forward to hearing from you in the future. Thanks for your patience and understanding.

"If it's HOT, it's ESTRUS"
P.O. Box 2125, Bellingham, WA 98227, USA
Phone: (360) 647-1187

TOP: Estrus warehouse fire advertisement, 1997, design Dave Crider **BOTTOM:** Tokyo Fireshock flier, Club251, Tokyo, Japan, 1997 **OPPOSITE:** Chicago Fireshock poster, The Empty Bottle, Chicago, IL 1997, design/illustration Alex Wald

ABOVE: Tokyo Fireshock, Club251, June 1, 1997, featuring Teengenerate, The 5.6.7.8's, Mad3, and Jackie & The Cedrics, photos Eri Sekiguchi

ESTRUS: SHOVELIN' THE SHIT SINCE '87 191

CLOCKWISE (from top left): Estrus Fireshock T-shirt, 1997, design Art Chantry, printing Jim Sorenson; Flaming Burn Out! benefit compilation CD, 1997, design Coco Shinomiya, typography Art Chantry, illustration Jaime Hernandez, colorizing and production Jamie Sheehan; Fireshock benefit show poster blanks, 1997 (these posters were sent on request to cities hosting their own Fireshock shows), design Art Chantry; Fireshock sticker, 1997, design Art Chantry; Fireshock Survivor CD jacket, 1997 (generic CD covers printed up to house compact discs that survived the fire. Each jacket had a hand-written title), design Art Chantry; Estrus Combustibles logo, 1997, design Jamie Sheehan

Fireshock Fire Sale, 1997, design Art Chantry

THE DRAGS
DRAGSPLOITATION...NOW! (ES110), 1995

ART CHANTRY: This record is a good case study for how much actual THINKING and ideas can go into a single cover. Most people assume we just do any stupid thing that comes into our heads on these covers (like exploding hot rods and naked ladies). Not true at ALL! Honest! I swear!

When I was told about the name of this record ("Dragsploitation...NOW!"), my initial thoughts went directly to cheezy 1950s thru 1970s exploitation films, naturally. For some reason, I was drawn to the old headliner typeface "Interlock." It was designed in the late 1950s and featured free-form drawn letterforms that actually "interlock" into and around each other. It was used to DEATH in the early 1960s beatnik revolution. Usually, I avoid using it, but this title SCREAMED out for it.

Then I cut out the grid, assuming I could put a naked lady or an exploding hot rod "behind" that grid, peeking out. But Dave Crider had other thoughts about the image and personality of this band. They were a little weirder than that, so the search began for the PERFECT image to "dragsploit" on that cover. The examples here are the ideas I liked enough to keep around (largely for laughs). A couple of them were jokes that weren't intended to be used (obviously). I began trying to shock Dave with what I came up with.

The image that Dave and I chose was from a bizarre, then-obscure Japanese horror movie advert. It seemed to fit the band best of all. We printed that sticker to inform the casual consumer that if they bought this record, they would likely need to run for their lives if they actually PLAYED it. We even created a promotional BARF BAG for individuals with weaker stomachs.

Just to make things exceedingly annoying, we printed a nice poster on the INSIDE of the record sleeve, so that if you wanted to look at it (or hang it up), you'd have to tear open the record cover and destroy it. The PLUS side would be that you'd probably have to buy a second copy of the record because you'd wrecked your original. That meant more money for us!!!

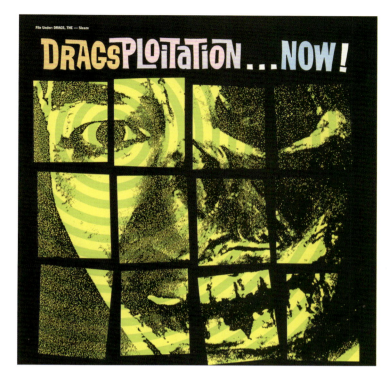

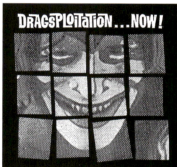

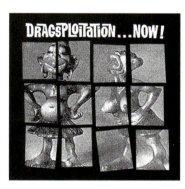

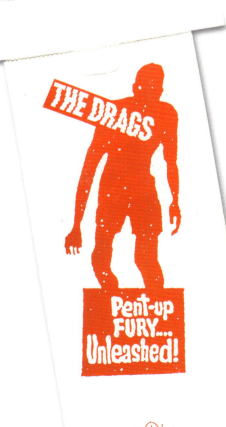

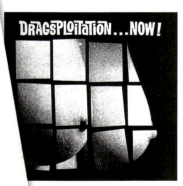

ABOVE: The Drags *Dragsploitation...Now!* (ES110), 1995; *Dragsploitation...Now!* cover sketches, designs Art Chantry; The Drags promotional barf bag, printing Thingmaker

5 More Creatures to Feature

A moat of devastation surrounded the label in the days after Crider had to watch some of his life's most prized possessions burn to a crisp. Few can fathom what it's like to try and take the first step in the "restart" process after something so crippling.

One positive thing that did happen in 1997—whether intentional or not—was a few of the label's mainstays cranking out some of their most raw, balls-out material. The Makers' *Hunger* LP had the insanity of its predecessor, yet it was somehow tighter and faster. The Drags' *Stop Rock And Roll* LP demonstrated the band's genius beyond strict lo-fi limitations. Plus, new groups entered the mix with full-lengths for Estrus, including Gasoline, the Quadrajets, the Von Zippers, and Sugar Shack. Tim Kerr continued to bring out the animal in bands at both Egg and Austin's Sweatbox.

Ol' Bookman (Carl Ratliff) moved to Bellingham and began working full-time for the label doing promotions, tour help, booking, assembling, and so forth. And as the Internet became a household phenomenon, Ratliff helped build and manage Estrus.com. The website obviously streamlined getting out information about bands, releases, and shows, as well as providing an unexpected upgrade to the mail order.

Bekki continued to run the mail order and attended to whatever Estrus or Estrus-adjacent bands passing through town needed.

ABOVE: Estrus Gasoline logo, 1997, design Art Chantry
OPPOSITE: Tomb of Estrus advertisement, 1998, design Art Chantry

On Planet Mono, Mort would part ways with the band to spend more time with family. And rather than replace him (as the trio did with Marx), Crider, Morrisette, and Roeder chose to move forward as a three-piece. After multiple recording sessions, the Mort-less Monos unleashed the aptly titled *Have a Nice Day, Motherfucker!* LP. Further external issues led the band to pull the plug entirely, and the Mono Men played their "last show"[38] in December 1997.

As the '90s came to a close, Estrus had a new breed of front-running filth. The garage rock that had helped shape the label's identity in the previous few years was still healthy through bands like Thundercrack, the Fells, The Mooney Suzuki, and the Coyote Men, but a herd of new bulls came running in with an explosiveness that the label had not yet hosted. All-out psychos like Fatal Flying Guiloteens and Estrella 20/20 turned off some in the bowling shirt crowd, but overall they excited a contingency of pagans hungry for new sounds.

And while a garage rock explosion was happening in Detroit, the Soledad Brothers, sons of Maumee, Ohio, offered a unique take on haunted blues.

Dave Crider, of course, could not stay idle for long in the guitar department and he formed a four-piece band called Watts with Roeder, Chris Degon, and Jeff Braimes—Patti Bell's husband. Watts picked up right where the Mono Men left off with all fucks thrown out and all levels at maximum volume.

The guitar-heavy stuff wasn't the only alternative to the garage grind. Ken Vandermark's soul-jazz combo The Crown Royals' *All Night Burner* and Madame X's (Di Young) EP shone a light into the hidden corners of Crider's non-rock brain. Crider credits Vandermark with introducing him to some of the most challenging music he's ever heard.

Choosing not to repeat what everybody expected, The Makers injected glam, upped musicianship, and gave the middle finger to their Middle Finger-album-and-earlier days with the *Psychopathia Sexualis* record. It was unmistakably the same Makers, but they had evolved and grown up too much to make another album that largely resembled the one before.

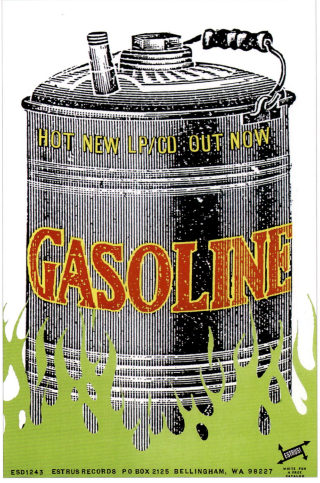

CLOCKWISE (from top left): Splash Four T-shirt; *Gasoline* LP postcard, 1997; Fatal Flying Guiloteens *Ask Marie Antoinette* EP (ES7140), 1999, design Art Chantry; The Fells "She's Alright" single (ES7110), 1997 **OPPOSITE TOP:** The Fells promotional photo, 1997 **BOTTOM:** Fireballs of Freedom, photo Jenny Ankeny

---

[38] Sneaky fucks came back in 2006 and in 2013.

THE DRAGS
SET RIGHT FIT TO BLOW CLEAN UP
(ES1263), 1999

C.J. STRITZEL (The Drags): *Set Right Fit to Blow Clean Up* was definitely a different thing. I think that direction had to do with Scott [Derr] joining the band. That album is a lot looser and larger than anything we'd done before. When I think of things I regret, one is that we didn't make a record after that one, because I think that was a very transitional record that ended up being the last—which, really, still kinda makes me sad. We learned so much and did things in a really different way on that record [so] I wish we could have made another, having digested those lessons. ...We learned to be more improvisational and to just let things be large. I think that our earlier stuff—[although] I loved it—sometimes felt too tight for me; it didn't open up.

Design: Art Chantry

THE VON ZIPPERS
NOT WORTH PAYIN' FOR E.P.
(ESP 11), 1999

C.A. COYLE: Which Von Zippers release are you most proud of?

AL VON ZIPPER: I'm most proud of our *Not Worth Payin' For E.P.* I'd never miked up a women's bathroom before, especially not for an internationally distributed record release. Absolutely stellar artwork to boot.

C.A. COYLE: Which Von Zippers release are you most ashamed of?

AL VON ZIPPER: I'm most ashamed of our *Not Worth Payin' For E.P.* The musical performance on the stage outside that women's bathroom was probably our most heinous ever.

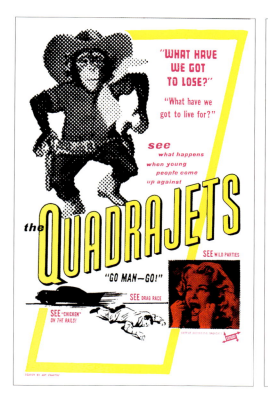
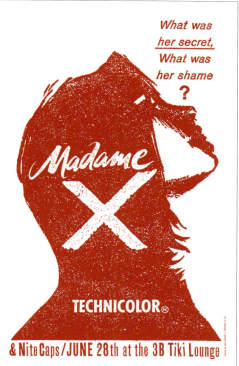

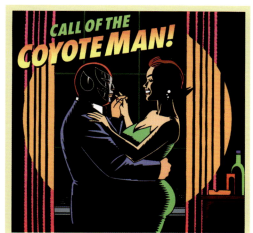

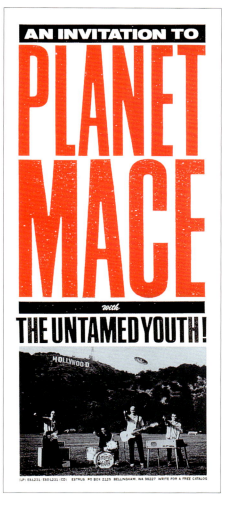

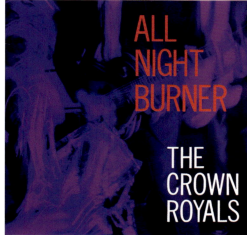

FIRST ROW: Quadrajets tour poster blank, 1997; Madame X/Nite Caps, 3-B "Tiki Lounge," Bellingham, WA, 1998; Gasoline tour poster blank, 1997, designs Art Chantry **SECOND ROW:** The Coyote Men *Call of the Coyote Man!* EP (ES7125/6), 1999, design Coco Shinomiya, illustration Jaime Hernandez **THIRD ROW:** The Screamin' Furys *Why* EP (ES7102), 1997; The Crown Royals *All Night Burner* (ES1236), 1997, design Jeff BBQ Cohn; The Untamed Youth *Planet Mace* LP promotional poster, design Art Chantry

OPPOSITE CLOCKWISE (from top): The Soledad Brothers, photo Chris Fuller; The Mants, photo Bob Groin; Fatal Flying Guiloteens, photo Leningradskoje Optiko Mechanitscheskoje Objedinenie; Sugar Shack, photo Jeanette Huddleston

ORAL HISTORY LESSON: TIM KERR

TIM KERR'S CELEBRATION OF "RIGHT NOW"
LIFELONG PUNK'S SPIRIT BRINGS ESTRUS TO A NEW LEVEL

Caveman humor and charming sleaze were undoubtedly celebrated in the early years of the label—some of those Mono Men album covers may have tipped you off. Anyway, that tradition continued through to Estrus' "peak." However, an ingredient was added to the concoction that expanded the label's identity and prestige far beyond Crider's dreams: Tim Kerr.

Kerr and Crider immediately connected after meeting for the first time in Seattle in 1992. The Mono Men had a release show for Wrecker *at the Crocodile Cafe with The Fall-Outs and Del Lagunas (Gas Huffer in Hawaiian shirts, playing surf music). Tim was in town recording the debut Monkeywrench LP for Sub Pop and therefore was present to see his 'wrench-mate Tom Price at the show.*

As many Pacific Northwesterners did upon introducing themselves to Kerr, Crider was quick to gush over and praise the sounds of Poison 13, Kerr's "too blues for punk, too punk for blues" ensemble—underground heroes among many circles in Seattle, Portland, and Mayne Island in the '80s.[40] Soon after the initial meeting, Mono Men would play a string of shows in Texas, including Kerr's hometown of Austin. And while the other Monos stayed with Frank Kozik after the Austin gig, Kerr and Crider sat up all night geeking out over shared avocations like Thelonius Monk and Japanese action figures of the 1960s.

Kerr, whose background was mostly born out of the ethos of hardcore punk, soon saw himself drawn to a sector of the punk community he'd largely been watching from afar. Despite Estrus' smut, gimmicks, and absurdity, which may have been at odds with his appreciation of hardcore culture, Kerr saw freedom of expression used as it was meant to be used. He saw an opportunity.

---

[40] Mayne Island is an island in the southern Gulf Islands chain of British Columbia. In the late '80s, early '90s, there was a ravenous DIY punk scene centered around all-ages cabin shows. One of the more well-known bands to come out of Mayne Island was The Sippy Couples, whose fame is centered around being the only band to have ever been banned from Portland's Sunrise Village Retirement Home.

BELOW: The Monkeywrench, photo Jacob Covey
OPPOSITE: The Estrus Invitationals poster, 1996, design Art Chantry

FIREBALLS OF FREEDOM
TOTAL FUCKING BLOWOUT (ES1265), 2000

JOHNNY SANGSTER (Producer): One of the more memorable sessions was with Fireballs of Freedom. Those guys had just come off tour and were truly on fire. Of course, it was the kind of tour where one's personal hygiene suffers. Let's just say they were ripe. Conrad had a spray can of "Smells-B-Gone" which he'd come down and attempt to freshen the place up with. It quickly got relabeled "Balls-B-Gone." That became the Total Fucking Blowout record.

ART CHANTRY: The Fireballs were one of those amazing, great live acts that had difficulty transferring over to recordings—Zen Guerrilla was another. This band was so intense and pushing at you the whole time that you never forgot how you felt—and that's really hard to capture on tape. When I started to work on this cover, I felt that the title should be complemented by the way the band performs: IN YOUR FACE and MELTING IT. WHAM!!

The actual cover used—B&W with Day-Glo orange type done with a Japanese rubber stamp kit—has a photo of a badly damaged mannequin wearing headphones having just been TOTALLY FUCKING BLOWN OUT. That works, too.

Design: Art Chantry

Photo: Chelsea Mosher

TIM KERR: That's what was so great about the garage stuff. It was independent of the "alternative nation," "college rock" kinda stuff. …When Big Boys were playing, you had Big Boys who didn't sound anything at all like Really Red, who didn't sound anything at all like Butthole Surfers, who didn't sound anything at all like the Dicks. We didn't have that uniform formula. So here comes garage: You've got the Motards, you've got all these crazy bands—it was this "other thing" that was going on. It was just a neater thing. I gravitated more toward that.

DAVE CRIDER: If bands didn't already have an arrangement [to record with Tim], I'd just present it as an option. As more and more releases came out, it was pretty obvious Tim was doing a lot of stuff, and so many bands hoped that would be a possibility. But it was never a mandate.

Tim's Touch™ may not have been as obvious in the first round of Estrus releases with Kerr behind the soundboard. Recordings from The Inhalants, Sugar Shack, Death Valley—or noise from the several bands of which Kerr was a member (Lord High Fixers, Jack O'Fire)—were consistent in sound; he'd recorded those groups many times over the course of several years. And the sessions were predominantly held at Austin's Sweatbox Studio.

The first indication that something special happens to bands when they record with Tim may have been The Makers' self-titled LP (ES1227), also known as "the Middle Finger album." The Makers, one of the crown jewels of the Estrus family and the bigger acts corrupting the garage punk circuit, saw their raw angst amplified beyond the limitations of a proverbial lo-fi cage with Kerr conducting. The rampage tied with The Makers' reputation on stage was captured in a two-day recording session at Egg Studios. What was secured on tape allowed the world to see there could be more to the garage formula that had been nearing ad nauseam status.

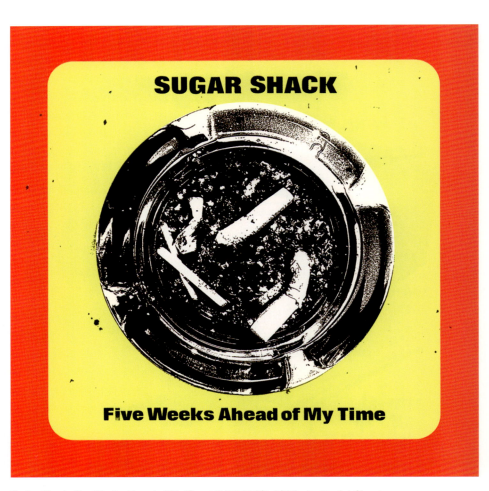

Sugar Shack *Five Weeks Ahead of My Time* LP (ES1238) 1997, design Art Chantry, photo Arthur S. Aubry

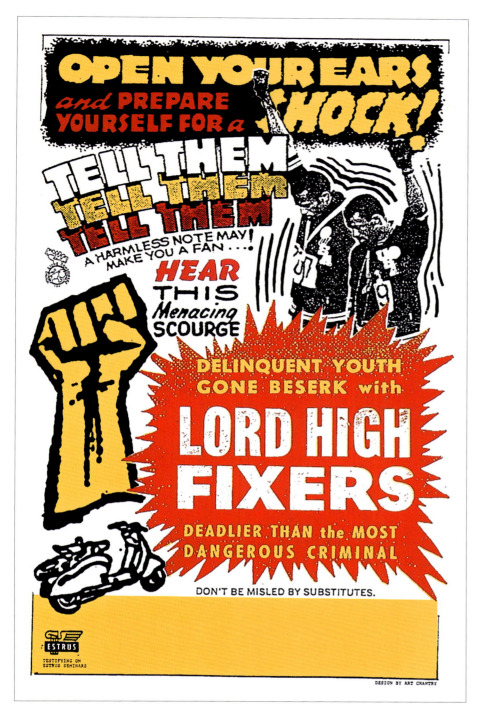

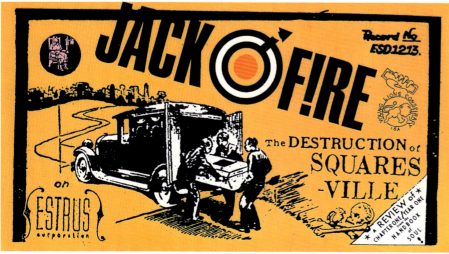

CLOCKWISE (from top): Lord High Fixers tour poster blank, 1996; Fireballs of Freedom *Welcome to The Octagon* promotional poster, 2001, photo Scott Pellet; Jack O'Fire *The Destruction of Squaresville* promotional postcard, design Art Chantry

THE MONKEYWRENCH
ELECTRIC CHILDREN, (ES1269), 2000

TOM PRICE (...too many bands): [We] released our second album on Estrus. It was quite a bit different from the first album, which had been re-workings of Poison 13 songs. Now we were mainly doing originals in a more psychedelic vein. The Seattle World Trade Organization (WTO) protests were going on. We could smell the smoke and tear gas while driving home from late-night sessions. There were some differences of opinion about how to approach the recording, and things got fairly intense. *Electric Children* came out with '60s-ish cover art by Art Chantry and, I think, it captured some of the transitory confusion and friction of those times.

DAVE CRIDER: The Makers had canceled Garage Shock '99 kinda at the last minute, so I just offhandedly, in a smart-ass way, mentioned to Tim [Kerr], "Why don't Monkeywrench fill in?" And then he called me the next day and said, "Yeah, we'll do it." And I don't think they had played in like seven years. So, they couldn't have practiced or rehearsed—or whatever you wanna call it—more than a couple of times before they did Garage Shock. So then afterward, it was sort of organic; they had a good time playing, they played some more shows and decided they wanted to do a record—so they asked me if I wanted to put it out. And, of course, I said, "Well, let me think about it. I'll have to get back to you."

Design: Art Chantry

Photo: Charles Peterson

The Monkeywrench
photo Charles Peterson

Tim Kerr, Crider, Mike Carroll

CARDBOARD HEARTS

The Makers weren't the only band to watch their sound expand thanks to Tim—and the producer's special touch didn't always translate into wild, batshit-crazy feedback orgies. When asked which band he thought he saw the biggest change in after his involvement with them, Kerr said it was the Dexateens, the twang-rock'n'rollers from Tuscaloosa, Alabama.

TIM KERR: The very first time they brought me, Craig "Sweet Dog" Pickering [Dexateens] got me to come; I'm not sure if any of the other guys knew who I was, but they knew that I'd done the Quadrajets records. And Sweet Dog thought I smoked a bunch of pot because I had dreadlocks, and they were trying to find some pot for me before I got there [laughs]. When I got there, we were basically recording Quadrajets number three. That was what was going on. And I was like, "Why? There's already a Quadrajets. Why are we doing this?" And I kinda raised the question a couple of times and still kinda played [with] some stuff. And then they played "Cardboard Hearts." And when they played that I went, "Holy shit. That's fucking great. You got more stuff like that?" And one of them asked, "You like that?" So they sent me home, and when I came back, that's when we started the record. …Those first two Dexateens records are still some of my favorite things I've done.

The Dexateens *Red Dust Rising* (ES2107), 2005, design Jason Willis

The Dexateens
photo Michael Palmer

WHO IS "NOISEMASTER?"

JOHNNY SANGSTER (Producer): I started engineering whenever Tim Kerr came to town. Crider was sometimes around; usually, if there was a show, we'd see him, but otherwise, he'd leave Tim and me to it. At first, Tim's method confused me. It was obvious that all who came to work with him revered him. A lot of time would be spent telling stories about a show where the wheels had come off—guitar strings breaking and amps falling over, players in the audience; the audience on the stage; not knowing what was coming next but playing on until the room was sated. The stories provided inspiration, and the message was, "Go for it like you're in that hot, sweaty club. Play it for real and play it for keeps. Shout and scream and make mayhem."

TIM KERR: My whole thing was the feel. It can be recorded on a ghetto blaster, but if it's making you move when you hear it… that's just the fucking greatest thing. [The feel] is what I've always been more interested in. It's a celebration of right now. Right here. You and your friends. This may be the last time you get to do this. Let's do something so that when you put the needle down 20 years from now, you just start laughing or say, 'Man, that was such a great time."

DAVE CRIDER: One of Tim's strengths in the studio is getting you to think a little differently and look at things a little differently. Because recording can be intimidating, especially for bands who haven't recorded that much before, or are feeling a lot of pressure.

KELLY GATELY (Fireballs of Freedom): We'd already built a solid relationship with Tim while working on *The New Professionals* LP on Empty Records. When Crider suggested Tim as a producer we were naturally way into it. We'd always been huge fans of his bands, and he'd recently worked with The Makers and Quadrajets. Tim is a really laid-back dude. He encouraged us to cut loose and just go fuckin' bananas, capturing more of that live vibe—a dynamic of insanity and noise. Growing out of a pretty isolated scene in Montana, we didn't really have a clue how to harness that energy in the studio. Being a very energy forward band, he helped us tie together a wall of insanity and our attempt at deconstructing rock and punk. We were trying to do something that was 180 degrees from everyone else, and Tim understood that. He's from Austin, and we loved all the weird bands from there, like the Butthole Surfers and Big Boys. We were freaks of the scene. So was Tim.

ABOVE: Fireballs of Freedom promotional photo, 1997 **OPPOSITE:** Estrella 20/20 Brown Queenie Yeh Yeh EP (ES7135), 1999, design Art Chantry

BIG NOISE FROM THE EAST

Tim had a proclivity for working with bands that were willing to experiment, embrace feedback, fuck shit up, let it all out, and so forth. Therefore, it was no surprise when he was tapped to record bands like Estrella 20/20 and Gasoline; a new standard had been realized.

TIM KERR: With the Japanese bands, the very first note of the very first song is the grand finale, and we go up from there. That's how it should be…You go and see the Cramps. The Cramps are great. Lux stands on his amp at the end of the set, but why didn't he do that on the first song?

HIRO/20 (Estrella 20/20): It's hard to tell exactly how Tim changed our sound, our groove—the way we think or feel to make or play our music. He gave us advice [about] the parts of playing that we didn't know about. The most important thing was that he showed us how to make noise real. We were inspired by his attitude to making noise and playing music. …I think I was so influenced by Tim about life; the way to think, how to live, how to enjoy music and art. The first time I saw Lord High Fixers I was really blown away by Tim. He gave his guitar to the people who stood in front of him. [That's how] Tim started the show. I was so surprised. It seems to me that Tim wants everyone [to be involved in the show]. There's no border [between] player and audience. He wanted to tell everyone they can be the player. At every show, he's always smiling.

MIKE MAKER: Tim was so dedicated to toys back in the day. We'd be on tour and he'd always be wanting to go to toy stores, and he'd be trading other people in other bands for toys. He especially loved the Japanese bands because they'd just give him toys from Japan. He'd see these toys and go, "Oh my God!" And we all really admired him; he was everyone's elder, so everyone would just give him stuff—and he loved it. But now, you can see he's kept growing and doesn't need to have stuff.

GAN CHAN: Tim taught the young me everything about rock'n'roll. That is, (1) play it loud, and scream into your microphone! (2) Don't hesitate to record your jokes, and (3) stand up to play your guitar, even in the studio. I'm so glad I met him when I was young.

TIM KERR: I was constantly trying to get Dave to not put "producer" [on the records]. I'd tell him to put "guidance counselor" or "coach" or anything else. "Producer" has so much fucking baggage to it that has nothing to do with me.[41]

---

[41] *Shovelin' the Shit* intern Morty Cabbage could not find any Estrus release that lists Kerr as a producer.

THE MOONEY SUZUKI
THE MOONEY SUZUKI (ES1273), 2000

DAVE CRIDER: Sam [Buonaugurio] was sending me postcards. He sent me the first CD they released on their own, the black album. That was their demo, basically. I wrote him a postcard back saying, "I dig it. If you're ever out this way, I'd love to see you live." So they fucking set up a show at the 3-B and drove from New York to Bellingham to play a goddamn show. I mean, it worked out [laughs]… And they did it again! They were huge Monkeywrench fans, and I think Tim mentioned offhand that Monkeywrench was playing at the 3-B—they fucking drove from New York to Bellingham to play one show with fucking Monkeywrench!… They worked their fucking asses off. They were on the road all the time—Sam and those guys… they were just a very hard-working motherfucking band.

Design: Art Chantry

Photo: Jessica Arp

> "Tim was my American father and a teacher. From him, I learned everything about how to record rock'n'roll. I'm still making records based on that. …'Noisemaster' will be on Kerr's tombstone…"
>
> GAN CHAN (Gasoline)

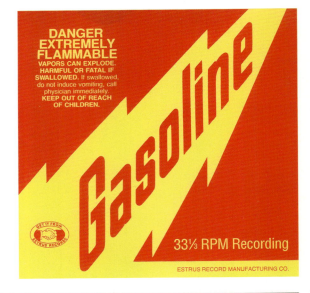

BECOMING NOISEMASTER

Tim Kerr's wish to not be listed as "producer" worked out. During a session at Egg with Gasoline in October 1997, Kerr's holiness got Eastern praise. He could sense something was lacking with guitarist/singer Gan Chan's mojo…

TIM KERR: The Makers are there, Dave's there, and we're sitting in the control room. I go into the live room because I want to see the band and make sure they're hearing what I'm saying and to see if they're ok. I don't do the "button thing" or any of that kind of shit. I come around the corner, and [Gan's] holding his guitar like a Samurai sword. I start to say something to him, but [he interjects with], "No. No. You please. You Noisemaster. Please." And, of course, Dave and all of them are rolling around on the floor. So from then on, Dave listed me on the records as "Noisemaster."

GAN CHAN: Tim was my American father and a teacher. From him, I learned everything about how to record rock'n'roll. I'm still making records based on that. …"Noisemaster" will be on Kerr's tombstone, but he was also known by some as the "Wizard."

TIM KERR: When the Quadrajets recorded *Pay the Deuce*, they were trying to figure out what to do for the record cover. They thought they were playing Southern Rock, but it's like the most fucked-up Southern Rock you've ever heard— it was great. I probably wouldn't have been into it if it was Southern Rock. So I told them to get somebody from junior high to draw that classic mountain with a wizard [drawing] and have that be the cover because Dave would love it. He'd put out eight tracks of it and stuff. And then, all of a sudden, I became the wizard on the mountain.

TOP: Gasoline *I Just Low* EP (ES7103), 1997, design Art Chantry **MIDDLE:** Diana Young-Blanchard (Madame X), Tim Kerr, Rowland Janes, Memphis, TN, 1998 **BOTTOM:** Gasoline, photo Chris Fuller

SWITCH TROUT
PSYCHODESTRUCT SOUND FROM TOKYO (ES7127/8), 1998

ALEX WALD: My tendency to "bloody simple-mindedness" is a liability I'm painfully aware of. So, no surprise that on hearing the band name, I instantly flashed on an electro-mecha-piscine behemoth. What to do with that and enlarge the scope of the narrative became my challenge. At first, I envisioned "Switch Trout" as a magazine cover mashup, somewhere between *Popular Science* and *Field and Stream*— a lone angler in hip waders hauling a 10,000-ton battle-beast out of a river. I was only told that Switch Trout was a Japanese surf band; I'd never heard them play. I should add that in every case, I'd never heard ANY of the Estrus bands whose covers I was assigned. It wasn't until well after the discs were manufactured and the product distributed that I became familiar with the recorded works of the many brain-shaking combos curated by The Pompatus of Platters, Dave Crider. In many ways, the paradigm of my method was based on that of American International Pictures, the apex of exploitation cinema of the 1950s and '60s: That is, a sensational title first, something which, once heard, would echo forever in the crustiest of cerebellums; and second, a poster image to set the senses aflame. Only then was a story crafted for a narrative frame. In this case, I decided that the ichthyic descendants of lost Lagonia had crafted an oceanic super-sub to traverse the globe in search of flounder for their hibachis. The world-building was kept to a modest scale. I just needed to draft a diagram of the mechanical juggernaut, a trusty crew, and the beautiful Atlantean princess whom they served. After that, the rest just writes itself.

VARIOUS
ESTRUS 100% APESHIT ROCK SAMPLER VOL. 2 (ES1275D), 2000

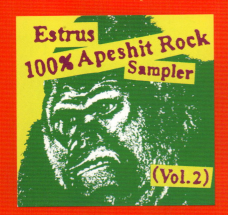

DAVE CRIDER: I sequenced songs alphabetically on all the compilations because I didn't want to call attention to one band over another. There may have been some minor jockeying around for time purposes, but I think I was able to make it work alphabetically pretty much every time.

I don't think anyone really gave a shit.

Design: Art Chantry

THE FATAL FLYING GUILLOTEENS
THE NOW HUSTLE FOR NEW DIABOLIKS (ES1276), 2000

DAVE CRIDER: Tim turned me on to those guys. He recorded them and sent me their stuff. I guess they were a little oddball for what most people would expect, but they were just always looking to fuck shit up. And not in a bad way! Well, sometimes it was bad. But that wasn't the intention. The intention was just to fuck shit up, and I think they succeeded.

Design: Art Chantry

MORE FROM BEHIND THE 'BOARD...

TIM KERR: When we were recording Fireballs of Freedom, Conrad came down from upstairs because it was so loud that stuff in his kitchen was rattling. And in a real nice way, he was like, "Is this gonna take a lot longer?"

JOHNNY SANGSTER: Tim and I would tag team the mixes. Once I had levels and a basic balance Tim would join me and fine-tune things. He learned from working on records at Sweatbox in Austin to pan elements so that they don't quite sit exactly on top of each other. A lot of folks pan kick, snare, bass, and lead vocal right up the center, but Tim would always spread these things out. Not hard panning, but just so nothing sat exactly on another thing. It's a technique that helps to let things through a dense and raucous mix, and it also made his productions stand out from others.

TIM KERR: I kinda come from the school of SPOT,[42] who did the SST stuff. Basically, I'm working for the band. They asked me to come do this. I'm not one of those people who says, "Alright, y'all go away while I mix this." It's an honor to be asked to record a band. It already cost them a whole bunch of money to rent the studio and get everyone together… I would never really charge. And that kinda drove a lot of people crazy. When it got to the point where I was doing a lot of stuff for Estrus bands, or whoever would pay for my transportation, I didn't mind sleeping on the floor.

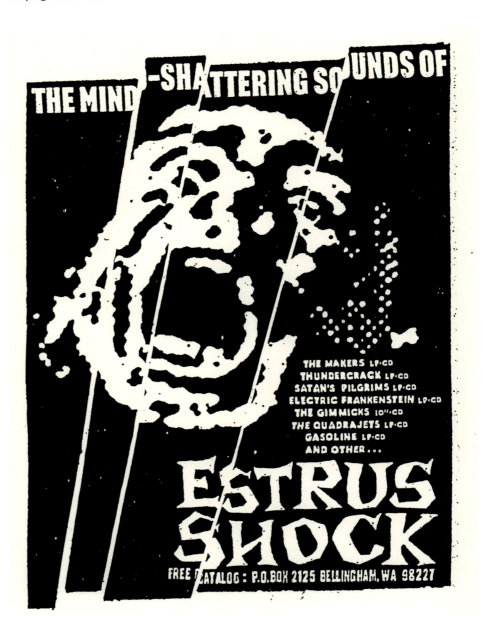

ESTRUS: SHOVELIN' THE SHIT SINCE '87   211

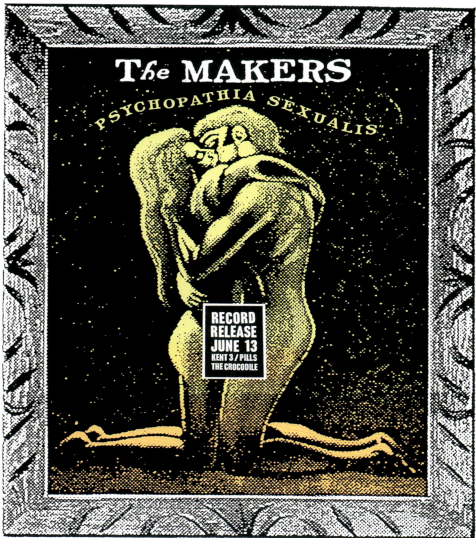

LEFT: Lord High Fixers *Is Your Club a Secret Weapon?* promo poster, 1997, design Art Chantry **RIGHT:** The Makers *Psychopathia Sexualis* record release show poster, 1998, design Art Chantry **OPPOSITE:** Estrus house advertisement, 1997, design Art Chantry

JOHNNY SANGSTER: When we started working on the Earaches' LP *Fist Fights, Hot Love,* Tim brought a sketchbook to the studio and told us he was getting back into drawing and painting. The pieces were kind of crude, but the blueprint for what he's gone on to do all over the world was there. Portraits of Tim's heroes, accompanied by a quote. Usually revolving around a DIY ethos or the power of following your own path.

TIM KERR: You'd have to be fairly vain to think that you've had anything to do with something or that you're gonna have an influence on somebody. But I don't give a fuck—I think I probably did. A lot of the bands were different after they recorded with me.

MIKE MAKER: I feel like Tim Kerr is more powerful now, and he's not even in the garage rock scene. He just floats around. He whispers in your ears [laughs]. But, I'll have a Tim Kerr skateboard or something lying around [at the store], and young dudes have asked me, "Is that a Tim Kerr board?" and I'm like, "Whoa! How come this guy?" He was old when he hit the scene! Like somehow, he's the most relevant guy from that scene. When I see him now, his performance is him playing banjo with like three or four other old guys on a porch at a gallery opening. And I'm like, "That's just beautiful." He looks the part.

DONNY MAKER: Tim Kerr came with Dave and us on our journey. We were absolute savages. But Tim tamed us and showed a kindness that we never knew could exist in that world. We'd always fight, due to Spokane, but we learned to be better from Tim. He taught us a lot —teachings that I still use to this day.

TIM KERR: [The jazz influence] is probably why Estrus ended up being where it didn't have any boundaries on it anymore. It's like, "Do you like it? Are you smiling? Cool. Let's go."…There were so many bands that weren't "garage," like in the sense of that San Francisco-type stuff. Fireballs of Freedom? That's absolutely not "garage." The Quadrajets think they're playing Southern Rock, but it's the most fucked-up, crazy thing. Lord High Fixers didn't fit [into the "garage" label] either. We were playing jazz mixed with soul. There wasn't that formula kinda thing going on, which was great. It's probably why Dave and I are family.

---

[42] Producer and engineer known for work with Black Flag, Minutemen, and other quintessential '80s punk acts; later became a photographer.

LORD HIGH FIXERS!

```
stefanie paige friedman - drums
robbie becklund    - bass
andy wright - guitar
mike carroll - vocals
tim kerr  - guitar
```

WHAT ARE YOU DOING TO PARTICIPATE?!

WHAT'S THAT FEELING?

"When we rehearsed, we'd actually play things pretty straight," said Andy Wright, Tim Kerr's guitar counterpart in Austin's Lord High Fixers. "Then we'd get on stage, and it would just go a totally different direction."

Wright and Kerr—along with drummer Stefanie Friedman, bassist Robbie Becklund, and frontman Mike Carroll—quickly established a reputation for spending their LHF set flinging themselves across the stage (mostly Tim), throwing instruments into the crowd (mostly Tim), and charming the feedback out of amplifiers destined to die young (still mostly Tim).

But the Fixers' sonic assault was more than a noise contest. It was a band of lifelong friends lionizing their time together and making the most of every opportunity thrown their way. Five members of a unique family were creating something bigger than they'd ever expected.

TIM KERR: [Being in] the Lord High Fixers was pretty crazy. People would hear about these shows, but we didn't play that much. I mean, it was pretty over the top, but we weren't trying to be the Who or any kinda shit like that. When Mike [Carroll] came back, we realized, "This could be the last time." Lord High Fixers shows were having a bunch of fun with your friends…. We didn't care about somebody being there thinking, "They can't play!" I don't need to prove anything to you at all—none of us do—in order to celebrate.

Lord High Fixers logo, design Art Chantry; Young Lions Conspiracy logo, design Big Daddy Soul; Tim Kerr and Mike Carrol, The Empty Bottle, Chicago, IL, 1995

LANCE THINGMAKER

ART CHANTRY: Many Estrus releases had rather exotic and sometimes insane production efforts. A great deal of that creative work has to be credited to Lance Webber (aka THINGMAKER), a marvelously talented and hard-working printer of the arcane. He always put the "real shit" into "SHOVELIN' THE SHIT" at Estrus.

Lance made too many amazing things for Estrus to list them all here, but here are a couple that I've chosen because they show off just how far he was willing to go. Much of this work was literally put together by hand.

THE MONO MEN
Another Way (ES782), 1996

ART CHANTRY: This little record was printed on metal-flake paper. I designed the cover, and Lance made it real. The purple flames and the golden background were printed with transparent offset inks. The pinstriping was printed using silk-screened opaque inks. "THE MONO MEN" was hot-foil stamped using a shimmering red metal foil (to further denote flames) on a letterpress.

The back was printed separately in black and white on a piece of adhesive paper. The whole thing was then folded and sandwiched together, then glued into place utilizing that adhesive paper (using a slip-sheet technique).

POISON 13
Ain't Superstitious (ES773), 1995

ART CHANTRY: The gatefold sleeve was printed in black and white and then folded and glued by hand. The "stand-up" ghoul was first printed in black and white and then coated with PHOSPHORESCENT ink to make it "glow-in-the-dark." Then it was glued in by hand again. As you open the gatefold sleeve the little ghoul pops up and glows in a ghostly hue. VERY scary!

To top it off, Lance designed and printed the "ribbon" (known as an obi strip in Japan). He added a bunch more scary monsters to it (there are three or four different sets of monsters on the ribbons) and then had the ribbon translated into Japanese. I *think* it says "POISON 13" in kanji, but I don't know. It could say anything, and I wouldn't know: I can't read Japanese.

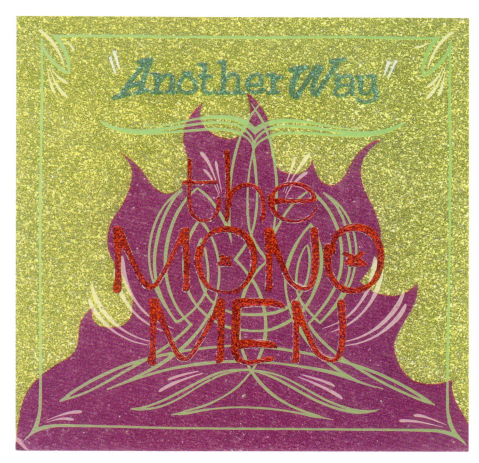

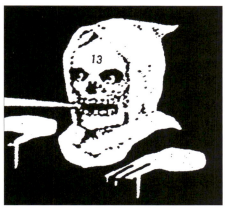

6. Punkinheaded Motherfuckers

"What I loved about Estrus is that you had Beatle boot garage rockers, mods, classic rock dudes like the [Quadrajets], noise bands, surf, jazz, soul," Chet Weise said when asked about Estrus at the time of the Quadrajets' and Immortal Lee County Killers' entry into the family. "The term 'garage' was almost a misnomer or contradiction when describing that label."

A further inflation of Estrus' musical vocabulary came with Fireballs of Freedom's *Total Fucking Blowout*, Fatal Flying Gilloteens' *The Now Hustle for New Diaboliks*, and the Quadrajets' *When the World's on Fire*. If Estrus had built an undeserved reputation for being the number one source for punk centered on hot rods, pinups, and other smut, the onslaught of anything-but-garage rock that came in the 21st century demonstrated it was not a genre-based label.

The cast of established bands on Estrus had their LPs to promote on tours, but a lot of the smaller bands who were given a "let's do a single"-type deal from Dave made waves immediately in rags across the globe and in the CMJ (College Music Journal).

Dave also got the opportunity to do one-off 45s with some of his favorite bands who already had deals with other labels. Tricky Woo offered up "Trouble," Zen Guerrilla gave "Dirty Mile," and Bantam Rooster flung "I, Gemini."

ABOVE: Estrus Enron logo, design Art Chantry
OPPPOSITE: The Quadrajets, photo Keith Marlowe

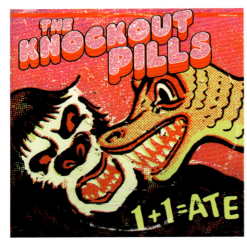
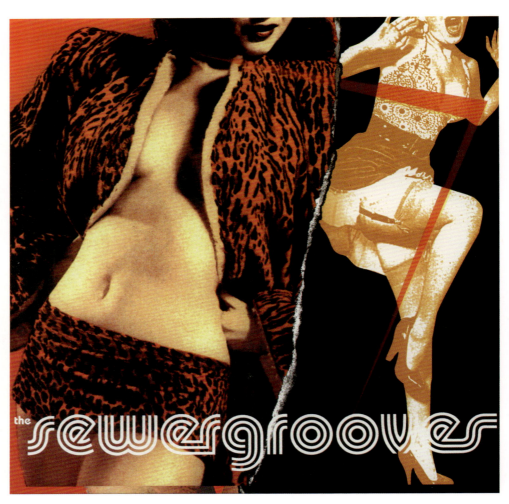

CLOCKWISE (from top left): The Knockout Pills *1 + 1 = ATE* LP (ES2106), 2004, design Jason Willis; The Sewergrooves "7th Floor" single (ES7148), 2000, design Amy Marchegiani; Golden Guineas *Shit or Bust* EP (ES7150), 2000

Meantime, Crider struck a deal with Chicago-based Touch & Go Records for distribution. The change coincided with the drop-off in vinyl sales and an increase in CD production. Not only was Estrus starting to sell more CDs for each release, but a handful of releases were CD-only.

In 2001, Garage Shock was held in Austin's Emo's instead of Bellingham and featured a lineup that looked nothing like the first one held in 1992. The new breed was on display, with thundering performances by Cherry Valance, Zen Guerrilla, and Total Sound Group Direct Action Committee —the latest Kerr & Carroll ensemble.

Crider and sister of a different mister Di Young started the "Hard Soul" combo the Dt's, first as a three-piece featuring only Crider on guitar, Phil Carter on drums, and Young's gritty-Tina howling. After getting an offer to play in Spain, the band grabbed fellow "Hambilly" Scott Greene.[43]

On paper, the Dt's may have seemed like a pivot in a different direction. And although the main ingredient for the combo was '60s soul, sonically, the live show was just shy of Crider's previous endeavors Watts and the Mono Men. Madame X, who had gently massaged eardrums through rhythms of jazzy lounge, was now shattering windows and windshields with a Tina-Turner-meets-an-angry-Bruce-Banner.

The Dt's were Crider's ticket into uncharted territory. "For me personally, it's the most freedom I've had in a band as far as not feeling tethered and not feeling that if I do go out, or go off, that the show is gonna stop and I'm gonna lose everyone else in the band," he said in August 2003. "…There's a certain attitude that you want to convey. Where did the hard soul come from? Well, duh! Hard rock and soul music! Those are the influences that we share as a group. But we also want people to be proactive at shows and proactive in their lives by thinking and reacting to their surroundings rather than just being a part of the MTV generation."[44]

Following the Dt's' *Filthy Habits* album, the lineup gained a new rhythm section featuring Spokane-bred bassist Matt "Zed" Zielfelder and Mike "Snare-Destroyer" VanBuskirk—and when she was available, Patti "now Braimes" Bell lent keys.

---

[43] The offer from abroad assumed the Dt's had a bass player. Greene was handed a ticket to Spain and brought in as the new bass player just a few weeks before the tour.
[44] An Interview with Dave Crider and Diana Young-Blanchard (*The Odyssey*, August 2003).

The new chapter with the Dt's also featured the growth of a relationship between Dave and Seattle-based producer/engineer/original-set-of-grunge-ears Jack Endino. The two had worked together on a handful of projects over the years—notably, the Mono Men's firestorm of an LP *Have A Nice Day, Motherfucker*—and shared a deep appreciation for loud-ass music and the scientific aspects of recording. Endino was a Univeristy of Washington graduate with a degree in electrical engineering who could casually talk shop with NASA-types.

Understandably, the Mono Men is the band most people associate with Dave; the Men etched themselves in three-chord history. But, the Dt's' steady output of releases, mini-tours, and international shows spanned more than 17 years. Since 2010, the Dt's have knocked out three LPs, a live album, six singles, and an EP for a half-dozen different labels.

TOP/BOTTOM: The Dt's, Dave Crider and Diana Young-Blanchard, 3-B Tavern, Bellingham, WA, 2000, photos Chris Fuller
PAGES 202–203: Estrus T-shirts 1987–2003

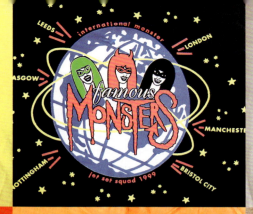

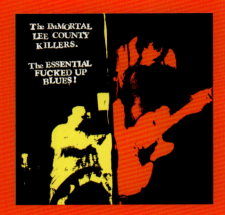

THE IMMORTAL LEE COUNTY KILLERS
THE ESSENTIAL FUCKED UP BLUES!
(ES1277), 2000

CHET WEISE (Quadrajets/Immortal Lee County Killers): As much as I like collaborating with Jason—or seeing how the Quadrajets would take riffs and turn them into songs during our rehearsals—or working with Tim, by the time Immortal Lee County Killers started, I did have a vision, so to speak, of what that duo should be. It was heavily based toward blues. So I wanted the recording to be as fucked-up and organic as the music. Our first record was recorded in a shed where we ran one extension cord to the neighbor's kitchen outlet. I duct-taped mics to stands and bought an MD8 minidisc recorder. It looked a lot like a four-track, but with eight tracks and mini discs, and we recorded the record. I dubbed vocals in my bedroom after the tracks were all recorded. I can't believe my roommates tolerated the screaming, but they were all old-school metal heads, and no one loves music like that generation of metal heads.

DAVE CRIDER: The only time I went down to South By Southwest to do an Estrus showcase, we had an Estrus party. Chet said he was gonna be there, and so I thought, "Fuck, let's get your band on for the party." And he played with the Mooney Suzuki and the Nomads, if I remember correctly. And, fuck, of course they blew me the fuck away. Right after that, I was like, "Yep. Let's do a record." I think he was surprised that I liked it.

It didn't sound like the Quadrajets—and that's good, ya know, because why would you leave that band and then do the same thing? It was totally something different.

Design: Art Chantry

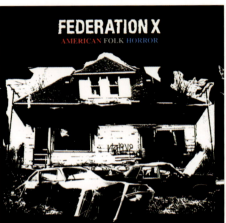

FIRST ROW: The Sewergrooves *Songs From the Sewer* LP (ES1264), 1999, design Orson & Co., photo Dirty Harry Välimäki; Total Sound Direct Action Committee *Party Platform…Our Schedule is Change!* LP (ES1283), 2002, design Damon Locks **SECOND ROW:** The Immortal Lee County Killers II *Love is a Charm of Powerful Trouble* LP (ES1285), 2003, design Dave Crider & ILCK, photo Daniel Coston; Federation X *American Folk Horror* LP (ES1282) 2001, design Federation X & John Cope, photo Beau Boyd **THIRD ROW:** The Blow Up "Microscope" single (ES7157), 2001, design Dave Bessenhoffer; The Quadracopters/Hellajets "Think It Over" single (ES7144), 1999, design Ink Spot & Design Co. **BOTTOM:** The Mooney Suzuki promotional poster, 1999, design Art Chantry, photo Jessica Arp

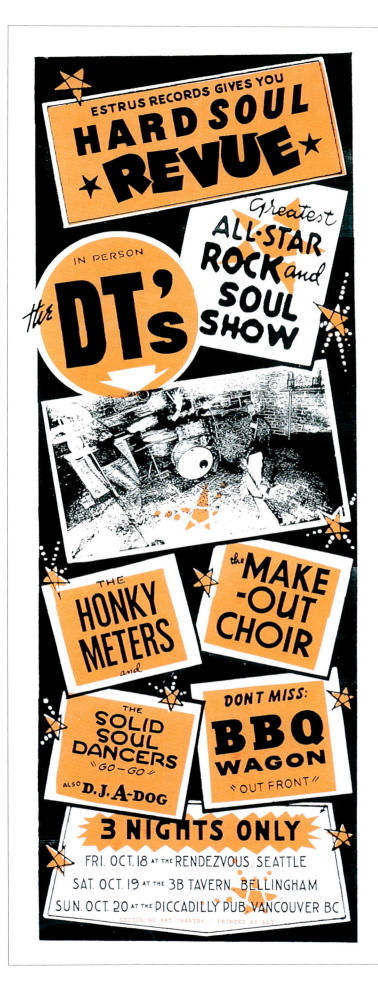
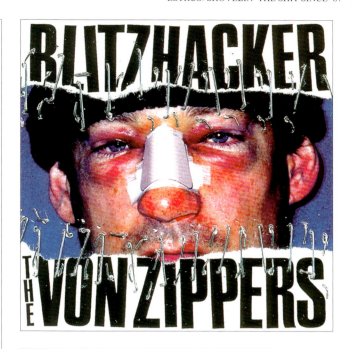

CLOCKWISE (from top left): The Dt's show poster, 2001; The Von Zippers *Blitzhacker* LP (ES1270D), 2000; The Immortal Lee County Killers *The Essential Fucked Up Blues* promotional poster, 2000, designs Art Chantry, ILCK photo, Photobooth

ESTRUS MERCH

ART CHANTRY: Dave and I always enjoyed coming up with fun SWAG (aka "promo items") to help promote the releases. The usual package was the LP/CD, a single, a poster, and some fun novelty swag idea. Dave always kept his eyes open for inexpensive SOMETHINGS to send out into the world. Some of the early Estrus bands (Man or Astro-Man? The Makers) did their own homemade promo items—which were often ridiculous (Man or Astro-Man? toothpaste; Makers hair combs.)

Some of the things we managed to whip together (often with the assistance of people like THINGMAKER) were lotsa matchbooks (fun to design); T-shirts (sort of expensive to just give away); and postcards (reliable promo). We also designed things like temptoos, bookmarks, swizzle sticks, buttons, decals, stickers, car fresheners, key rings, coasters, guitar picks, frisbees, "little black books," and other fun but useless junk.

But as Dave and I went deeper into weirdness, we came up with a professional "advertising novelty" catalog and began to mine that for stuff that was cheap to produce. We made a couple of cool things (like an "Indian headdress" for Satan's Pilgrims (Why? It seemed dumb and fun.) But that company proved difficult to work with, so we quit that approach.

A couple of the more fantastic ideas were a Zippo lighter (promoting the label, not a band) and the cream of the crop—the Man or Astro-man? "ASTRO-GLASSES." These were printed up by Thingmaker, and I designed them to look like those classic "X-Ray Spex" you saw advertised in old comic books. In the lens holes were differently colored pieces of cellophane—often with as many as four sections! They allowed you to see the cosmos exactly like Man or Astro-Man? saw it.

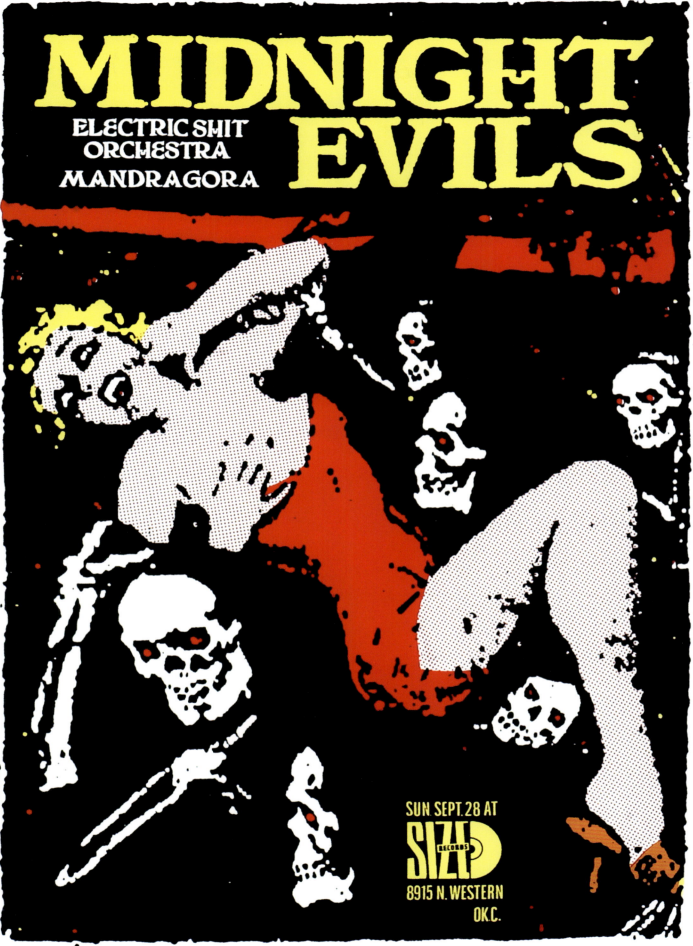

The Midnight Evils/Electric Shit Orchestra/Mandragora poster, Sized Record, Oklahoma City, OK, 2003, design Art Chantry

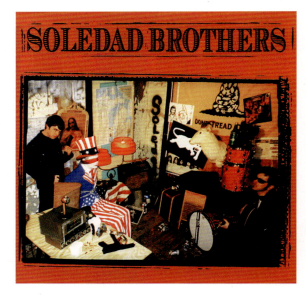

CLOCKWISE (from top left): The Spitfires "Cut Me Some Slack" single (ES 7138), 1999, design Art Chantry; *Estrus Kamikaze Ass Chomp N' Stomp* CD sampler Vol. 4 CD (ES2115), 2005, design Jason Willis; The Insomniacs *Switched On!* LP (ES1294), 2004, design William Grapes/PopArt Productions; *The Soledad Brothers* LP (ES1271), 2000, design RankArt & Cholomite; Fatal Flying Guiloteens *Get Knifed* LP (ES1295D), 2003 **OPPOSITE TOP:** Federation X, photo Keith Marlowe **BOTTOM:** Fatal Flying Guiloteens, photo unknown

100% APESHIT DISCOGRAPHY

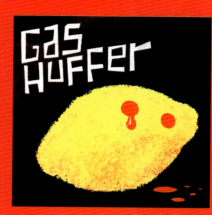

GAS HUFFER
LEMONADE FOR VAMPIRES (ES2111D), 2005

JOHNNY SANGSTER (Producer): I remember Tim Kerr saying that we needed to capture Tom while he could still play, as his Parkinson's was really coming on, and his doctors were still trying to figure out which drugs worked on him. Joe was soon headed to New York to work for *Rolling Stone*, so it was a farewell record. Some days were a challenge for Tom, and he'd get frustrated, but then he'd come back and try it again. He's somewhat unstoppable. Tom is like the heart of the Seattle scene. I have so much respect for him.

TOM PRICE (...too many bands): Our previous LPs had been on Empty and Epitaph records, so it seemed only natural to sign with another 'E' label! But the real reason was that Dave Crider had always been totally straight-up with us, and meticulous in his record-keeping. He might've appreciated that we'd played a benefit when the Estrus warehouse was destroyed in a fire. Mostly, I think, we just enjoyed each other's company.

ROUND 45s

ART CHANTRY: When I designed the 45 cover for the Estrus release of the Jack O'Fire tune "Punkin'" (w/vocals by Mike Carroll of Poison 13), the obvious design choice was a jack-o'-lantern pumpkin (that's what a "jack o'fire" actually is). To create the look, we die-cut holes in the eyes and mouth and used glow-in-the-dark vinyl to make the thing actually light up when you turned off the lights—like a REAL jack-o'-lantern!

To further enhance the "round" shape of a pumpkin, I had the printer trim off the corners. After it came out, Dave Crider thought it would have been cooler if it'd actually been round. We talked it over, and I designed a cutting ring to create a REAL, honest-to-god ROUND 45 sleeve. It worked perfectly, too. In fact, it worked so well we tried to make as many "round idea" covers as we could. We were (and still are, I think) the ONLY record company in the world to release ROUND 45 sleeves.

TOP: Jack O'Fire *Punkin'* EP (ES755), 1994 **FIRST ROW:** Death Valley *Apollo XIII* EP (ES795), 1996; The Mono Men *Cross Alley Stomp* EP (ES788), 1996; The Screamin' Furys "383" single (ES7118), 1998 **SECOND ROW:** The Nomads "Pack of Lies" single (ES7104), 1997; The Quadrajets "Super Double Buzz" single (ES7119), 1997; The Quadrajets "My Car, My Spaceship" single (ES7136), 1999, design Art Chantry
OPPOSITE TOP: The Quadrajets **BOTTOM:** Watts, photo Chris Fuller

DIPLOMATS OF SOLID SOUND
LET'S COOL ONE (ES2101D), 2003

ART CHANTRY: My initial ideas were a sort of garage rock "James Bond" look: suave, debonair, and fucked-up. I thought my little sketch was cool, but Dave and the band both had other ideas in mind. They were [envisioning] something that was more of an old school easy-listening/percussion jazz/stereo effects record cover—sorta like [something from] Command Records. So, I did this design instead.

Design: Art Chantry

CHERRY VALENCE
RIFFIN' (ES1286), 2002

HELEN O'DONNELL (somebody's aunt): This record is a cocaine hullabaloo without comparison—it took five years off my life. "Get Wild Tonight!" Are you fucking kidding me?! I wanna eat flesh when this comes on!

Cover illustration: Lana Rebel

No Reason To Stay Quiet

Running a label in the digital music age never seemed to click with Dave, although ironically, he's one of the most tech-savvy people you'll talk to. When individual songs began to be sold, shared, and stolen digitally, the world of physical/tangible releases started to fall. Some contemporary labels jumped on board and were able to transform operations to accommodate the new digital landscape. Dave saw that the way he wanted to run a label wouldn't be optimal, moving forward.

However, Estrus never technically closed up shop or made a declarative statement that it would no longer be releasing new music. The website is relatively up to date, and you can still order plenty of items from the extensive catalog.[45]

After a brief reunion with the Mono Men in 2013, Crider's main squeeze, the Dt's, saw their pace slow to doing clumps of shows just 2–3 times each year. As a result, Crider's desire to lay assault via guitar led to the formation of Machine Animal, a four-piece "Bonehead Rock" band, in mid-2015. The quartet amplified bad-pub-meets-bad-psych-meets-bad-proto-metal with as much fun and humor as any of the bands that had won over the 3-B during a set at Garage Shock years earlier. They have a song called "Hail Farner."

Machine Animal take the same approach that the Mono Men did—simple riffs and playing as loud as possible—but this time there's no debate about whether "garage" has an influence on the overall package. The band blatantly embrace the stupidity of rejected 1970s monster-guitar anthems and the type of lyrics cavemen would scribble out if tasked with writing a poem about Mark Farner [the original lead singer and guitarist of Grand Funk Railroad]. If the band were to choose between playing a small tavern where the sound person lets Crider play his guitar as loud as he wants or a well-paying gig with volume limits, Crider & Co. would always go with whatever option has better beer and access to Mark Farner clips on YouTube.

The Dt's *Hard Fixed* LP (ES2102), 2005, design/illustration Jim Blanchard

---

[45] I was not paid to write that.

Crider probably isn't much different than the last time you saw him. The hair has gotten a little bat-shit crazy, and his enthusiasm for attending shows with more than three bands has died. But other than that, you'll still find the lanky Mono Man wandering about downtown Bellingham, trying new craft beers weekly, and discovering cool lamps in thrift stores.

Now he's an elder statesman, Crider can admit to having had a phase of "Angry Dave." The vast majority of people who had (or still have) a problem with Dave encountered his alter ego before meeting the real deal.

Shedding the "Angry Dave" layer of skin has benefitted the low-key lifestyle Crider has adopted in the years of Estrus inactivity. Days spent stressing over accommodations for bands, pressing plant issues, or postal price fluctuations have been replaced by hanging out with the usual suspects of the "Hambilly" contingency on the back porch of Crider's humble Bellingham charmer. "Porchin'," is how he refers to it.

TOP: The Bobbyteens *Fast Livin' & Rock n Roll* LP (ES1266D), 1999, design C.J. Carter **BOTTOM:** Crider's infamous "You Suck Shit" postcard to Seattle club RK Candy, 1992

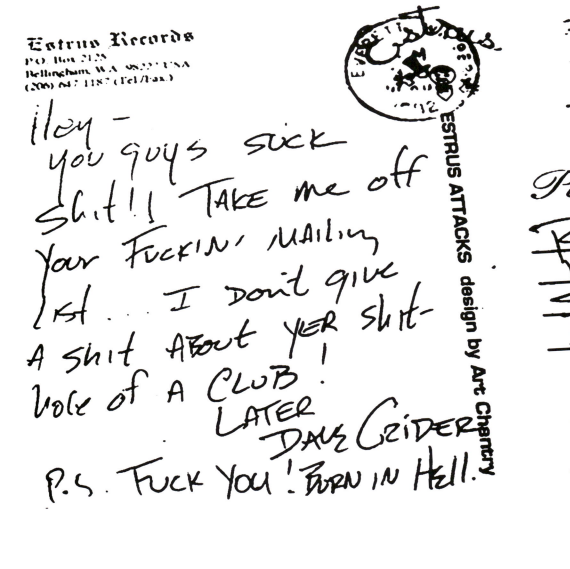

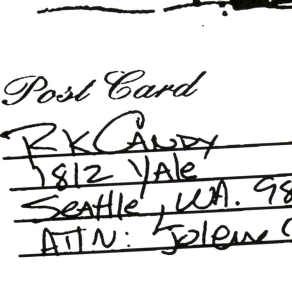

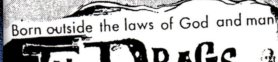
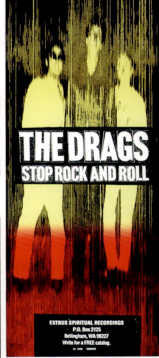

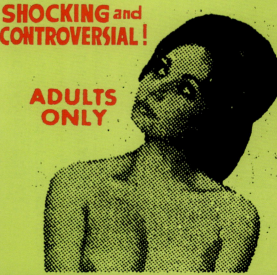

The Drags **CLOCKWISE (from top left):** Logo, 1995; tour poster blank, 1997; *Stop Rock and Roll* promotional poster, 1997; "Shocking and Controversial!" *Dragsploitation...Now!* inside cover, 1995, designs Art Chantry; C.J. Pretzel and Lorca Wood, photos courtesy Chris Hedlund; *Dragsploitation...Now!* sticker, 1995; *Stop Rock and Roll* LP (ES1239) 1997

26 Excellent Estrus Spicy Sizzlers sampler ad, 1999, design Art Chantry

ORAL HISTORY LESSON: PEACE, LOVE, BULLFUCK

ESTRUS' LEGACY IS WHATEVER YOU WANT IT TO BE, BUT THE FAMILY BORN OUT OF THE LABEL IS GENUINE, HIGH-END, UNCUT AFFECTION

TIM KERR: It was a family. It was a big family. That's how we always [approached] stuff. And that's how Corey [Rusk] did stuff with Touch and Go. It was the same sorta attitude of, "You're helping me? Sure! C'mon, I'll help you when you need it."

ART CHANTRY: The records I did with Estrus were always a collaboration. It wasn't a situation where I sat down, got to follow my muse, and did a piece of art. No, this was a collaborative art form. And I collaborated with the band. Mostly, I collaborated with Dave, and Dave would do a lot of the interpretation of [the band] to me. He was, in a way, like [a band's] best interpreter.

MIKE LAVELLA (Gearhead/ex-Gearhead Records): Dave was along for everything [with] Gearhead. We were in no way financially connected, just friends. He always took ads in the mag, which was hugely helpful, and I'd review his records and everything. We're all taking care of each other, and it was unspoken.

TOP: Comet Tavern, photo Matt Johnston
BOTTOM: The Cherry Valence, photo Chris Fuller

MESSAGE MACHINE MAN

"Sending a demo" to a "label" today is worlds different than sending a demo to a label in the pre-Internet era. Yes, emailing an MP3 can be quite the titillating experience, but it lacks the magic that the old standard practice had.

BRIAN TEASLEY (Man Or Astro-Man?): We'd recorded demos on an old MCI 4-track machine and sent that to Dave. I remember Dave left a message that said, "This is Dave Crider from Estrus Records, and I was calling because of the demo you sent"—or whatever he'd say at that point—and we were like, "What?! Really?! Why?!" We were literally jumping up in the air like we'd won the lottery. We were just these stupid fucking redneck kids from Alabama, and this guy from a record label is calling us on our answering machine! …We went on to do what people would consider "bigger" things, like selling out the Filmore, but honestly, the two biggest moments in my music career were us being played on college radio for the first time […] and when Dave called us that first time. That was a fucking huge moment.

C.J. STRITZEL (The Drags): We sent [our stuff] to everybody, but we were really hoping to get on Estrus. I thought it would be so cool to get on Estrus. And so one day I came home, and there was a really long message on my machine saying, "Hey, this is Dave from Estrus, and I really fucking love your record. I really wanna sell it in the catalog, and I think you guys are really cool, and you should come and play Garage Shock," and whatever. I listened to the message but I didn't think it was really him; I thought it was Keith, who was our drummer at the time. I thought it was Keith fucking with me [laughs]! So I didn't call him back. I was just like, "fuckin' Keith." Like, Dave left a number in the message, but I just thought it was a number Keith had made up. …Then, a week later, we're at practice, and I'm not even thinking about it at this point. And Keith was like, "Have you heard from anyone?" And I was like, "Oh yeah, that was fucking funny the other day when you called. That was a good one." And he's like, "I don't know what you're talking about." [Laughs] Then it just sorta went from there. Soon, all three of us were like, "Oh, wait, what the fuck?! It was him?!"

CURAN FOLSOM (The Midnight Evils): I sent out about 100 CDs to any label I was familiar with that might be able to help us out. The funny thing about it was we got one reply back, and it was from Dave Crider. And it wasn't even an offer to do anything. It was just a little note that said something like, "Hey, thanks for sending the CD in. It would be cool to see you guys live some time." Literally the next day, I was on the phone trying to book a tour [laughs]. For me, it was a hole in one. Of all the labels to get back to me, Estrus? …We ended up playing Bellingham and Dave came down to see us. Afterward, he thanked us for coming out [from Minneapolis] and stuff—he hung with us for a little bit. And then it wasn't until we got back that he reached out and said he'd like to do a single for the Crust Club. …We were excited to get the opportunity to go record with Tim Kerr at Sweatbox. We thought of recording two songs for the 7-inch, but if we were going to Austin, we might as well record every tune we had. …We did an entire record's worth, and I sent it to Dave. About a week later, I was working and my girlfriend at the time called me to say Dave had called and left a message. I asked her, "What did he say?" And she said, "All he said was, 'Fuck it. Let's do an album.'"

JOHN SZYMANSKI (The Hentchmen): It was great when Norton signed us, and they invited us to play New York on New Year's Eve 1993 with the Lyres, Swinging Neckbreakers, John Felice, and many, many more. But! When Dave Crider called me saying he wanted to do a single and have us play Garage Shock, I remember deciding I was finally going to drop out of Washtenaw Community College!

THE FALL-OUTS
SUMMERTIME (ES2104), 2004

JOHNNY SANGSTER (Producer): The Fall-Outs' *Summertime* was an amazing record to work on. I remember it going really fast and then also going really slow. I really got Dave's Brian Wilson arranger brain, and I loved how he was stretching out. He really knew what he was hearing and how it should go, but it took some experimenting to get it there. At the time, I'd just put together my first portable recording rig. At Egg we were on 16 track, but for records that needed more tracks, we'd sync up a Tascam DA88 and have it chase the 16 track reel to reel. I took the next step and had a Motu hard disc system that could also chase the 16 track. I went to Dave's house a few times to record some things. Mostly, he just wanted to talk about TV shows or '60s records, but we did record his piano and maybe a melodica.

C.A. COYLE: What was it about Estrus or Super Electro that made you want to release stuff on those labels? Was it more like you're friends with these guys, or was it like you believed in the "brand" or shit like that?

DAVE HOLMES (The Fall-Outs): It was more that no one else was really asking us.

Design: Rick Reinert
Illustration: Dave Holmes

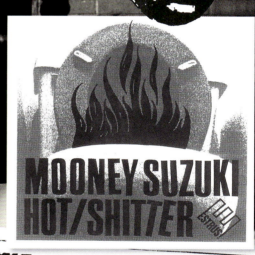

The Mooney Suzuki **CLOCKWISE (from top left):** Logos, 1999, designs Sammy James, Jr.; "Hot/Shitter" single (ES7162), 2002, design Art Chantry, photo Charles Peterson; *People Get Ready* tour postcard, 2000; Postcard from Crider to The Mooney Suzuki, 1999; 3-B Tavern, Bellingham, WA, 2000, photo Chris Fuller; *People Get Ready* photoshoot, photo Jessica

MICHAEL MAKER: Now, I get [Dave's] train of thought [for signing bands]. His reasoning was more about people. Because there were some bands, I remember thinking, "God, this is so fucking lame." It seemed like a parody of real rock'n'roll. …The good thing about Dave is also the thing that's perhaps seemed like his weakness, you know: his human relationship with everybody. You might have looked at him as being very small. Like, Estrus seemed small because you were camped out at his house having a barbecue.

MICHAEL NICHOLS (Former Love Battery, Gits tour manager/Comet Tavern booze-slinger): We always feel welcome to join the carousels going on over there—and have often joined in. But for every legendary event, there are just as many smaller neighborly interactions that are important, if not as dramatic or provocative. Once, my car broke down, and I was late to work—Bekki dropped everything and drove me across town. When Dave found out we shared an appreciation for the Kings of Rhythm, he gifted me a collection of their entire catalog. When my beloved dog died, they sent lilies and a card so lovely it still makes me tear up. These are just a few of the countless generosities shared with us over the 20 years we've been neighbors. …Mainlining anti-freeze is too hardcore for me, personally, but overall, the Criders are good neighbors and great friends.

CHET WEISE (The Quadrajets/Immortal Lee County Killers): Personally, I got along with Dave really well. He was a straight shooter. We might not have always agreed on everything, but I knew I'd receive a royalty statement, and he wasn't going to make me change the way I sounded or take me to the cleaners. I was young and green, and I needed someone I could trust. And even though the label didn't have money, it did feel like a sort of family, with Dave sitting at the end of the table. That proved a real plus for road bands like the Quadrajets and [the Immortal Lee County] Killers. Dave would help us connect with bands to play with in different cities and hook us up with the right promoter. He even lent me a Gibson SG for a spell!

JEFF BRAIMES (Watts): Honestly, Dave hasn't changed that much that I've noticed. He still loves High Voltage and Tarantino. He still loves Bekki and his dogs and a hardy IPA. He still likes to talk business, and he's still stubborn A.F. when it comes to how it's conducted. He still believes in scheduled rehearsals, even if the guitars never get out of their cases and it just turns into drinking practice. Dave is fiercely loyal and much more sentimental than I bet a lot of people realize. He'll do anything for you and often does.

PATTI BELL (The Roofdogs/the Dt's): He's gotten so much gentler over the years. Definitely not as intense—though he still can be. He's like a big teddy bear now! And I'd trust him and Bekki with my life. When our kids were young, we actually put [Dave and Bekki] down as emergency contacts at their school. That always gave us a little giggle, but we could count on them.

ABOVE: Watts/MQN posters, Seattle, Bellingham, Glacier, WA, 2000, design Art Chantry **OPPOSITE TOP:** Fireballs of Freedom **BOTTOM:** The Makers, photo Keith Marlowe

TOP LEFT: The Mooney Suzuki **RIGHT:** The Soledad Brothers **BOTTOM:** The Immortal Lee County Killers, photos Chris Fuller
OPPOSITE TOP: Fatal Flying Guiloteens, photo Keith Marlowe **OPPOSITE BOTTOM:** The Mistreaters

The IMMORTAL LEE COUNTY KILLERS.

CHET WEISE: We toured the UK and Europe so much we had a back line in London and a tour manager ready to go whenever we came over. We also played two John Peel Sessions. When I walked into our first Peel Session, John looked at my leather pants and said, "Last time I saw leather trousers like those was Jimi Hendrix and Jim Morrison. Morrison's smelled like dead babies." That might be the moment that I felt clearly a part of rock'n'roll. Moments of clarity are few and far between. When you have them, jump in the deep end and swim. As meager as Immortal Lee County Killers might be in the big picture, I stood in the BBC studios and realized we were a very legit rock'n'roll group.

Immortal Lee County Killers: Logo, 2000; "Let's Get Killed" single (ES7156), 2000, designs Art Chantry; top photo by Marty Perez

TOP LEFT: The Gimmicks **RIGHT:** The Von Zippers, photo Bob Groin **BOTTOM:** Watts

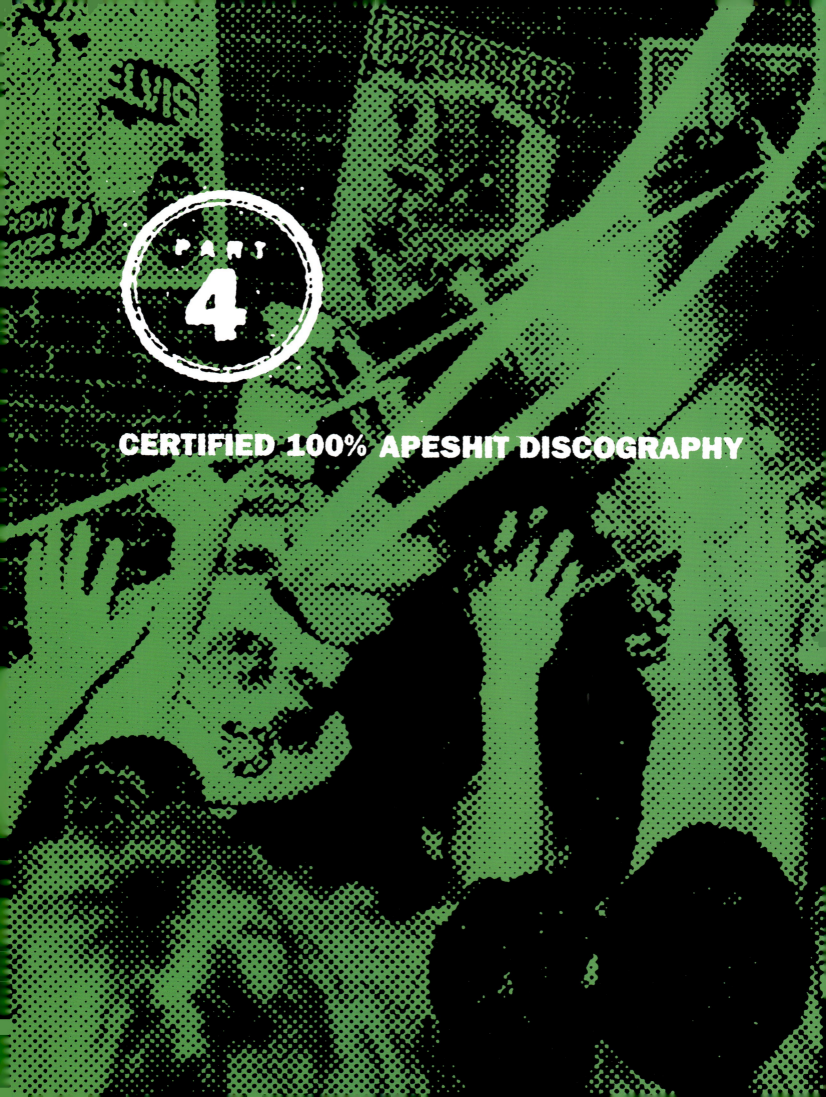

PART 4

CERTIFIED 100% APESHIT DISCOGRAPHY

CERTIFIED 100% APESHIT DISCOGRAPHY

Catalog No.	Artist	TITLE	FORMAT
7" Releases			
ES71	THE MONO MEN	Burning Bush	7"
ES72	STUMPY JOE	Daydreams	7"
ES73	GAME FOR VULTURES	Goin' my way	7"
ES74	THE MONO MEN	I don't care	7"
ES75	MARBLE ORCHARD	Something Happens	7"
ES76	V/A	The Estrus Lunch Bucket	3x7"
ES77	V/A	The Estrus Lunch Bucket	3x7"
ES78	V/A	The Estrus Lunch Bucket	3x7"
ES79 (Crust #1)	THE MUMMIES	Out of Our Tree	7"
ES710	V/A	Tales from Estrus	7" EP
ES711 (Crust #3)	PRISONSHAKE	Spoo	7" EP
ES712 (Crust #2)	V/A	On the Rocks	7" EP
ES713 (Crust #4)	THE PHANTOM SURFERS	Orbitron	7" EP
ES714 (crust #5)	THE ROOFDOGS	Havin' A Rave Up	7" EP
ES715	V/A	The Estrus Half Rack	3x7"
ES716	V/A	The Estrus Half Rack	3x7"
ES717	V/A	The Estrus Half Rack	3x7"
ES718 (Crust #8)	THE MONO MEN	Booze	7" EP
ES719 (Crust #6)	THE MORTALS	Disintegration	7" EP
ES720 (Crust #7)	ROCKET SCIENTISTS	Pithe Helmet	7"
ES721 (Crust #11)	THE WOGGLES	I Got Your Number	7" EP
ES722 (Crust #9)	HUEVOS RANCHEROS	Rocket to Nowhere	7" EP
ES723 (Crust #10)	THE FALL-OUTS	Don't Want the Sun	7" EP
ES724 (Crust #12)	THE GORIES	Baby Say Unh!	7"
ES725	The M-80's	Seeing Things	7" EP
ES726	THEE HEADCOATS	My Dear Watson	7"
ES727	V/A	Tales From Estrus Vol. 2	7" EP
ES728	CHEATER SLICKS	84 Ford 79	7"
ES729	SHADOWY MEN ON A SHADOWY PLANET	Dog & Squeegie	7"EP
ES730	V/A	Gearbox	7"
ES731	V/A	Gearbox	7"
ES732	V/A	Gearbox	7"
ES733	GRAVEL	As for Tomorrow	7"

Design/Illustration Sam Leyja

Design Art Chantry

CERTIFIED 100% APESHIT DISCOGRAPHY

Catalog No.	Artist	TITLE	FORMAT
ES734	THE MORTALS	Come and Get It	7"
ES735	THE BROOD	I'll Come Again	7"
ES736	MARBLE ORCHARD	It's My Time	7"
ES737	JACKIE & THE CEDRICS	Thunder Struck!	7" EP
ES738	LUST-O-RAMA	The Dark Side	7" EP
ES739	THE UNTAMED YOUTH	Sophisticated International Playboys	7"
ES740	THE A-BONES	Here They Come!	7"
ES741	GO TO BLAZES	Got It Made!	7" EP
ES742	THE BEGUILED	Black Gloves	7" EP
ES743	JACK O'FIRE	Clothes Make The Man	7"
ES744	THE MAKERS	Here Comes Trouble	7" EP
ES745	THE WASTE KINGS	Garden of My Mind	7"
ES746	THE COWSLINGERS	Hogtied	7"
ES747	THE SWINGING NECKBREAKERS	Workin' & Jerkin'	7"
ES748	THE APEMEN	El Tortura	7"
ES749	TEENGENERATE	Sex Cow	7"
ES750	THE 5,6,7,8'S	I Walk Like Jane Mansfield	7"
ES751	MAN OR ASTRO-MAN?	Astro Launch	7" EP
ES752	THE MONO MEN	Mystery Girl	7"
ES753	THE GO-NUTS	Flight Of the Go-Nuts	7"
ES754	THE NOMADS	(I'm) Out of It	7"
ES755	JACK O'FIRE	Punkin'	7" EP
ES756	OBLIVIANS	Blow Their Cool	7" EP
ES757	THE INHALANTS	Alright, Hit It!	7"
ES758	SATAN'S PILGRIMS	Haunted House of Rock	7"
ES759	LOS MARAUDERS	Wild Women	7"
ES760	THE DEL LAGUNAS	Time Tunnel	7"
ES761	V/A	The Estrus Cocktail Companion	3x7"
ES762	V/A	The Estrus Cocktail Companion	3x7"
ES763	V/A	The Estrus Cocktail Companion	3x7"
ES764	THE MONARCHS	Heads Up	7"
ES765	MAN OR ASTRO-MAN?	Inside the Head of Mr. Atom	7" EP
ES766	THE TIKI MEN	The Good Life	7" EP
ES767	MAD 3	The Space Legend	7"
ES768	THE HENTCHMEN	Ypsilanti's Newest Hitmakers!	7" EP
ES769	MAN OR ASTRO-MAN?	World Out of Mind	7" EP w/die cut

Design Art Chantry

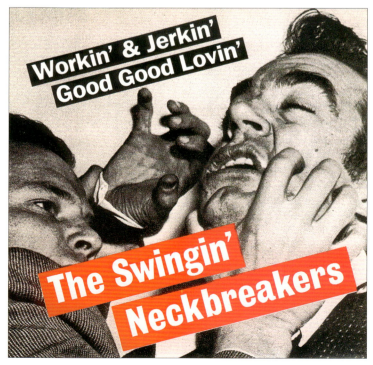

Design Art Chantry

CERTIFIED 100% APESHIT DISCOGRAPHY

Catalog No.	Artist	TITLE	FORMAT
ES770	SUGAR SHACK	You Don't Mean Shit to Me	7"
ES771	FAMOUS MONSTERS	Famous Monsters…are GO!	7" EP
ES772	DEKE DICKERSON	Asphalt Aisle	7"
ES773	POISON 13	Ain't Superstitious	2x7" w/gatefold
ES774	SUPERSNAZZ	I Gotta Go Now b/w I Am A Cliché	7"
ES775	LORD HIGH FIXERS	Take Me Home	7"
ES776	THE BRENTWOODS	You Broke My Heart	7"
ES777	THE 1-4-5S	Planetary Annihilation!	7" EP
ES778	THE INVISIBLE MEN	Hunt You Down	7" EP
ES779	THE MAKERS	Music to Suffer By	7" EP
ES780	THE VOLCANOS	Deora	7"
ES781	THE FELLS	What I Got	7"
ES782	THE MONO MEN	Another Way	7"
ES783	MAN OR ASTRO-MAN?	The Sounds Of Tomorrow	7"
ES784	V/A	Tales From Estrus Volume 3	7" EP
ES785	THE INSOMNIACS	Already Down	7"
ES786	MADAME X	Madame X	7"
ES787	KING SOUND QUARTET	Annihilate This Week b/w Memphis Train	7"
ES788	THE MONO MEN	Cross Alley Stomp	7" EP
ES789	GIRL TROUBLE	The Track b/w Scorpio 9	7"
ES790	THE GALAXY TRIO	Sheriff Boy-R-Dee	7"
ES791	THE GALAXY TRIO	Cocktails with Gravity Girl	7"
ES792	THE SATANS	Satan's Surf b/w Surf Rat	7"
ES793	IMPALA	Play R&B Favorites	7" EP
ES794	GAS MONEY	Two Women	7"
ES795	DEATH VALLEY	Have Rocket, Will Travel	7" EP
ES796	SOUTHERN CULTURE ON THE SKIDS	Santo Swings	2x7"
ES797	SOUTHERN CULTURE ON THE SKIDS	Santo Swings	2x7"
ES798	THE VON ZIPPERS	Würms 2x7" Set ES7989	2x7"
ES799	THE VON ZIPPERS	Würms 2x7" Set ES7989	2x7"
ES7100	THE MAKERS	Tear Your World Apart	2x7"
ES7101	THE MAKERS	Tear Your World Apart	2x7"
ES7102	THE SCREAMIN' FURYS	Why	7"
ES7103	GASOLINE	I Just Low	7"
ES7104	THE NOMADS	Pack of Lies	7"
ES7105	DEE RANGERS	This is Not the Modern World	7" EP

Design Sean Yseult

Design Art Chantry

CERTIFIED 100% APESHIT DISCOGRAPHY

Catalog No.	Artist	TITLE	FORMAT
ES7106	THE MANTS	I Smell…Woman!	7" EP
ES7107	THE VOLCANOS	Pompeii	7" EP
ES7108	THE HUNTINGTON CADS	Big Guitars, Western Style	7" EP
ES7109	THE RAY-ON'S	Lipstick Pickup Lines	7" EP
ES7110	THE FELLS	She's Alright	7"
ES7111	THE SWITCH TROUT	Rod Action!	7"
ES7112	THE MAKERS	Supa Low Fly	7"
ES7113	THE GONERS	Hide Out	7" EP
ES7114	LORD HIGH FIXERS/GASOLINE	Young Man Blues	7"
ES7115	THE NIGHTCAPS	You Lied	7" EP
ES7116	T.V. KILLERS	You Kill Me	7"
ES7117	THE PILLS	Don't Blues	7"
ES7118	THE SCREAMIN' FURYS	383	7"
ES7119	THE QUADRAJETS	Super Double Buzz	7" w/die cut
ES7120	THE BOSS MARTIANS	Boss-O-Nova	7" EP
ES7121	NEW WAVE HOOKERS	Crystal Bullet	7"
ES7122	THE HELLACOPTERS	Looking At Me	7"
ES7123	ELECTRIC FRANKENSTEIN	You're So Fake	7"
ES7124	DEE RANGERS	Don't!/Hot Ice	7"
ES7125	THE COYOTEMEN	Call Of The Coyote Man!	2x7"
ES7126	THE COYOTEMEN	Call Of The Coyote Man!	2x7"
ES7127	THE SWITCH TROUT	Psychodestruct	2x7" EP
ES7128	THE SWITCH TROUT	Psychodestruct	2x7" EP
ES7129	SATAN'S PILGRIMS	Play Ghoulash for You!	7"
ES7130	FAMOUS MONSTERS	Knock Knock Halloween	7"
ES7131	THE VON ZIPPERS	Twist Off	7" EP
ES7132	THE INSOMNIACS	Guilt Free	7"
ES7133	THE BOBBYTEENS	Rock-n-Roll Show	7"
ES7134	FLAMING SIDEBURNS	Jaguar Girls	7"
ES7135	ESTRELLA 20/20	Brown Queenie Yeh-Yeh	7"
ES7136	THE QUADRAJETS	My Car, My Spaceship	7"
ES7137	THE GIMMICKS	Dirty Inside!	7" EP
ES7138	THE SPITFIRES	Cut Me Some Slack	7"
ES7139	BROTHER BRICK	No Turning Back	7" EP
ES7140	FATAL FLYING GUILLOTEENS	Ask Marie Antoinette	7" EP
ES7141	THEE MICHELLE GUN ELEPHANT	West Cabaret Drive	7" EP

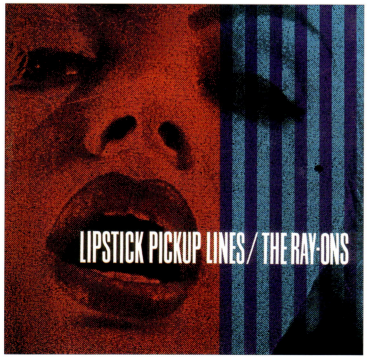

Design Art Chantry

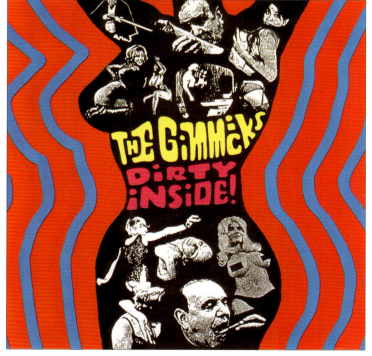

Design Art Chantry

CERTIFIED 100% APESHIT DISCOGRAPHY

Catalog No.	Artist	TITLE	FORMAT
ES7142	THE SOLEDAD BROTHERS	The Gospel According To John	7"
ES7143	THE NERVES	Midnight Sun	7"
ES7144	QUADRACOPTERS/HELLAJETS	Think it Over/I Wasn't Born in a Hallway	7"
ES7145	GASOLINE	Step On The Gas	7"
ES7146	THE BLOWTOPS	Menacing Sinstress	7" EP
ES7147	THE SWITCH TROUT	Under the Wire	7" EP
ES7148	THE SEWERGROOVES	7th Floor	7"
ES7149	THE MONKEYWRENCH	Sugar Man	7"
ES7150	THE GOLDEN GUINEAS	Shit or Bust!	7" EP
ES7151	THE VON ZIPPERS	Monkey on You	7"
ES7152	THE ROYAL FINGERS	Speed Crazy	7" EP
ES7153	TRICKY WOO	Trouble	7"
ES7154	BANTAM ROOSTER	I, Gemini	7"
ES7155	ZEN GUERRILLA	Dirty Mile	7"
ES7156	THE IMMORTAL LEE COUNTY KILLERS	Let's Get Killed	7"
ES7157	THE BLOW UP	Microscope	7"
ES7158	THE WEDNESDAYS	Spirit War	7"
ES7159	THE BASEBALL FURIES	I Hate Your Secret Club	7" EP
ES7160	THE MISTREATERS	Personal Space Invader	7" EP
ES7161	THE SWITCH TROUT	Sonic Masters	7"
ES7162	THE MOONEY SUZUKI	Hot/Shitter	7"
ES7163	THE INSOMNIACS	Maryanne Lightly	7"
ES7164	THE DIPLOMATS OF SOLID SOUND	Porkchop	7"
ES7165	THEE BUTCHER'S ORCHESTRA	In Glorious Rock and Roll	7" EP
ES7166	TOTAL SOUND GROUP DIRECT ACTION COMMITTEE	Total Sound Group Direct Action Committee	7"
ES7167	THE STAR SPANGLED BASTARDS	For a Ride	7"
ES7168	THE WEDNESDAYS	Mystery	7" EP
ES7170	THE KNOCKOUT PILLS	Parting Gift	7"

Estrus Promo Singles

MN71	THE MONO MEN	Here's How	7"
ES94017	THE MUMMIES	High Heel Sneakers	7"
ESP4	THE PHANTOM SURFERS	Play Bass with the Phantom Surfers	7"
ESP5	GRAVEL	Not Alive	7"
ESP6	SUPERCHARGER	Don't Mess Me Up	7"

Design Art Chantry

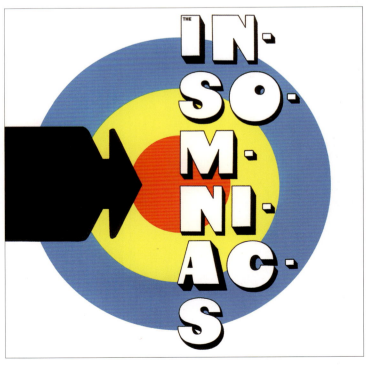

Design Art Chantry

CERTIFIED 100% APESHIT DISCOGRAPHY

Catalog No.	Artist	TITLE	FORMAT
ESP7	MAN OR ASTRO-MAN?	Amazing Thrills! In 3-Dimension	7" EP
ESP8	THE MAKERS	I Just Might Crack	7"
ESP9	THE TRASHWOMEN	Three Birds	7" EP
ESP10	THE MAKERS	Vegas	7"
ESP11	THE VON ZIPPERS	Not Worth Payin' For	7" EP
ESP3233	V/A	Sensational Sounds Of The 1995 Estrus Invitationals	7" EP

Reissued Singles

ES71R	THE MONO MEN	Burning Bush	7"
ES73R	GAME FOR VULTURES	Goin' My Way	7" EP
ES713R	THE PHANTOM SURFERS	Orbitron	7" EP
ES737R	JACKIE & THE CEDRICS	Thunder Struck!	7" EP
ES94017R	THE MUMMIES	Get Late!	7"
ES45001	THE MUMMIES	That Girl	7" EP
ES45002	THE MUMMIES	Food, Sickles, And Girls	7"

10" Releases

ES101	THE MONO MEN	Shut the Fuck Up!	10"
ES102	JACK O'FIRE	Six Super Shock Soul Songs	10"
ES103	THE INSOMNIACS	The Insomniacs	10"
ES104	THE MAKERS	The Devil's Nine Questions	10"
ES105	THE GALAXY TRIO	Saucers Over Vegas	10"
ES106	IMPALA	Kings of the Strip	10"
ES107	THE GALAXY TRIO	In the Harem	10"
ES108	THE MONO MEN	Live at Tom's Strip-N-Bowl	10"
ES109	THE STATICS	Pinball Junkies	10"
ES110	THE DRAGS	Dragsploitation…Now!	10"
ES111	THE CYBERMEN	The Cybermen	10"
ES112	THE NOMADS	Raw & Rare	10"
ES113	LORD HIGH FIXERS	Once Upon A Time Called…Right Now!	10"
ES114	MAD 3	Napalm in the Morning	10"
ES115	MADAME X	Madame X	10"
ES116	THE 1-4-5S	Rock n' Roll Spook Party	10"
ES117	THE SPLASH FOUR	Filth City	10"

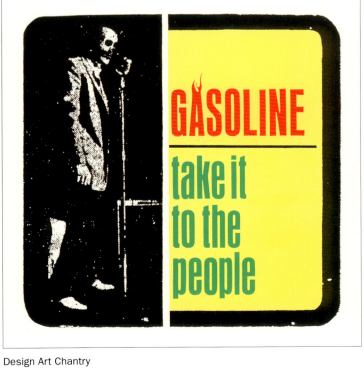

Design Art Chantry

Design Art Chantry

CERTIFIED 100% APESHIT DISCOGRAPHY

Catalog No.	Artist	TITLE	FORMAT
ES118	THE GIMMICKS	High Heels	10"
ES119	THE SEWERGROOVES	Three Time Losers	10"
ES1020	ESTRELLA 20/20	Afro Mexicana	10"
ES1021	GASOLINE	Take It To The People	10"

Full-Length Releases

Catalog No.	Artist	TITLE	FORMAT
PLES0024	V/A	Here Ain't the Sonics	LP
ES121/ESCD1	THE MONO MEN	Stop Draggin' Me Down	LP/CS/CD
ESCD2	MARBLE ORCHARD	Savage Sleep	-
ES007	THE BROOD	Vendetta!	LP
ES123	THE MONO MEN	Wrecker!	LP
ES124	THE MORTALS	Ritual Dimension of Sound	LP
ES125	THE PHANTOM SURFERS	Play the Music From the Big-Screen Spectaculars!	LP
ES126	GRAVEL	Break-A-Bone	LP
ES127	SUPERCHARGER	Goes Way Out!	LP
ES128	THE FALL-OUTS	Here I Come and Other Hits	LP
ES129	MAN OR ASTRO-MAN?	Is It…Man or Astro-Man?	LP
ES1210	THE WOGGLES	Teendanceparty!	LP
ES1211	GRAVEL	No Stone Unturned	LP
ES1212	THE MAKERS	Howl	LP
ES1213	JACK O'FIRE	The Destruction of Squaresville	-
ES1214	THE TRASHWOMEN	Spent the Night With…	LP
ES1215	MAN OR ASTRO-MAN?	Destroy All Astro-Men!	LP
ES1216	THE MORTALS	Bulletproof	LP
ES1217	THE WOGGLES	The Zontar Sessions	LP
ES1218	THE MONO MEN	Sin & Tonic	LP
ES1219	THE INSOMNIACS	Wake Up!	-
ES1220	THE MAKERS	All-Night Riot!	LP
ES1221	MAN OR ASTRO-MAN?	Project Infinity	LP
ES1222	TEENGENERATE	Smash Hits!	LP
ES1223	THE UNTAMED YOUTH	At the Fabulous El Morocco Lounge	LP
ES1224	IMPALA	Square Jungle	LP
ES1225	THE INHALANTS	The Inhalants	LP
ES1226	SATAN'S PILGRIMS	Soul Pilgrim	LP
ES1227	THE MAKERS	The Makers	LP

Design Art Chantry

Design Art Chantry

CERTIFIED 100% APESHIT DISCOGRAPHY

Catalog No.	Artist	TITLE	FORMAT
ES1228	THE MORTALS	Last Time Around	LP
ES1229	THE 1-4-5S	Rock Invasion	LP
ES1230	THE VOLCANOS	Surf Quake!	LP
ES1231	THE UNTAMED YOUTH	Planet Mace	LP
ES1232	THE MAKERS	Hunger	LP
ES1233	THE INSOMNIACS	Out of It	LP
ES1234	THE MONO MEN	Have a Nice Day, Motherfucker	LP
ES1235	THE SPLASH FOUR	Kicks in Style	LP
ES1236	THE CROWN ROYALS	All Night Burner	LP
ES1237	THE FELLS	The Fells	LP
ES1238	SUGAR SHACK	Five Weeks Ahead of My Time	LP
ES1239	THE DRAGS	Stop Rock and Roll	LP
ES1240	SUPERCHARGER	Supercharger	LP
ES1241	BLACK JACK	Black Jack	LP
ES1242	THE QUADRAJETS	Pay the Deuce	LP
ES1243	GASOLINE	Gasoline	LP
ES1244	SATAN'S PILGRIMS	Creature Feature	LP
ES1245	IMPALA	Play R&B Favorites	LP
ES1247	THE VON ZIPPERS	Bad Generation	LP
ES1248	THE MAKERS	Psychopathia Sexualis	LP
ES1249	THUNDERCRACK	Own Shit Home	LP
ES1250	THE SWITCH TROUT	Psycho Action!	-
ES1251	ELECTRIC FRANKENSTEIN	I Was A Teenage Shutdown	LP
ES1252	THE NOMADS	Big Sound 2000	LP
ES1253	T.V. KILLERS	Have A Blitz On You	LP
ES1254	THE VOLCANOS	Finish Line Fever	LP
ES1255	CROWN ROYALS	Funky-Do!	-
ES1256	COYOTE MEN, The	The Coyote Men VS El Mundo	-
ES1257	COYOTE MEN, The	Two Sides Of The Coyote Men	LP
ES1258	WATTS	Watts	LP
ES1259	THE NO-TALENTS	…Want Some More!	LP
ES1260	LORD HIGH FIXERS	Is Your Club A Secret Weapon?	LP w/gatefold
ES1261	FAMOUS MONSTERS	Around The World In 80 Bikinis!	-
ES1262	THE QUADRAJETS	When The World's On Fire	LP
ES1263	THE DRAGS	Set Right Fit to Blow Clean Up	LP
ES1264	THE SEWERGROOVES	Songs From The Sewer	LP

Design Art Chantry; illustration Jim Johannes

Design/illustration Frank Kozik

CERTIFIED 100% APESHIT DISCOGRAPHY

Catalog No.	Artist	TITLE	FORMAT
ES1265	FIREBALLS OF FREEDOM	Total Fucking Blowout	LP
ES1266	THE BOBBYTEENS	Fast Livin' & Rock N Roll	-
ES1267	SUGAR SHACK	Get Out of My World	LP
ES1268	THE GIMMICKS	Honeymoon's Over	LP
ES1269	THE MONKEYWRENCH	Electric Children	LP
ES1270	THE VON ZIPPERS	Blitzhacker	-
ES1271	THE SOLEDAD BROTHERS	Soledad Brothers	LP
ES1272	THE INSOMNIACS	Get Something Going!	LP
ES1273	THE MOONEY SUZUKI	People Get Ready	LP
ES1274	THE BOBBYTEENS	Not So Sweet	-
ES1275D	V/A	The Estrus Apeshit Rock Sampler (Vol. 2)	-
ES1276	THE FATAL FLYING GUILLOTEENS	The Now Hustle For New Diaboliks	LP
ES1277	THE IMMORTAL LEE COUNTY KILLERS	The Essential Fucked Up Blues	LP
ES1278D	MAN OR ASTRO-MAN?	Beyond the Black Hole	-
ES1279	FIREBALLS OF FREEDOM	Welcome To The Octagon	LP
ES1280	THE CHERRY VALENCE	The Cherry Valence	LP
ES1281	GASOLINE	Fake to Fame	LP
ES1282	FEDERATION X	American Folk Horror	LP
ES1283	TOTAL SOUND GROUP DIRECT ACTION COMMITTEE	Party Platform…Our Schedule Is Change	LP
ES1285	THE IMMORTAL LEE COUNTY KILLERS II	Love is a Charm of Powerful Trouble	LP
ES1286	THE CHERRY VALENCE	Riffin'	LP
ES1287	GAS HUFFER	The Rest Of Us	LP
ES1288	V/A	The Estrus Double Dynomite Sampler Vol.3	-
ES1289	THE SOLEDAD BROTHERS	Steal Your Soul and Dare Your Spirit to Move	LP
ES1290	SUGAR SHACK	Spinning Wheels	-
ES1291	THE VON ZIPPERS	The Crime is Now	-
ES1292	THUNDERCRACK	The Crack	-
ES1294	THE INSOMNIACS	Switched On!	LP
ES1295	THE FATAL FLYING GUILLOTEENS	Get Knifed	-
ES1296	THE MISTREATERS	Playa Hated to the Fullest	LP
ES1297	FEDERATION X	X Patriot	LP
ES1298	THE MIDNIGHT EVILS	Straight 'Til Morning	-
ES1299	THE BOBBYTEENS	Cruisin' For A Bruisin	-
ES2100	THE MUMMIES	Death By Unga Bunga!!	-
ES2101	THE DIPLOMATS OF SOLID SOUND	Let's Cool One!	-
ES2102	THE Dt's	Hard Fixed	-

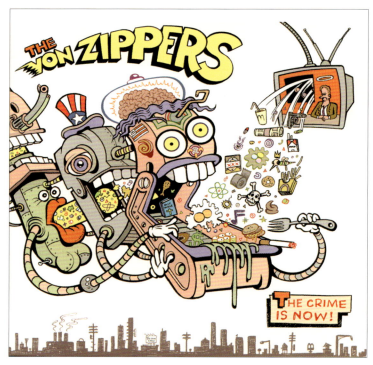

Design/illustration Pat Moriarity

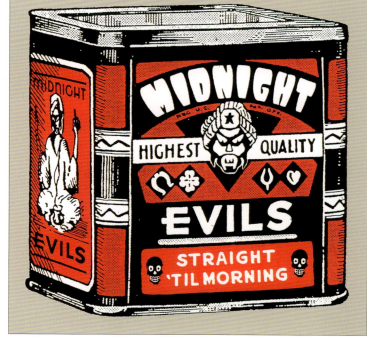

Design Art Chantry

CERTIFIED 100% APESHIT DISCOGRAPHY

Catalog No.	Artist	TITLE	FORMAT
ES2103	THE DEXATEENS	The Dexateens	-
ES2104	THE FALL-OUTS	Summertime	LP
ES2106	THE KNOCKOUT PILLS	1+1=Ate!	LP
ES2107	THE DEXATEENS	Red Dust Rising	-
ES2108	THE MIDNIGHT EVILS	Breakin' It Down	-
ES2109	DMBQ	The Essential Sounds From The Far East	LP
ES2110	THE DIPLOMATS OF SOLID SOUND	Destination…Get Down!	-
ES2111	GAS HUFFER	Lemonade for Vampires	-
ES2113	FEDERATION X	Rally Day	-
ES2115	V/A	The Estrus Kamikaze Ass Chomp n' Stomp CD Sampler Vol. 4	-
ES94015	THE MUMMIES	Play Their Own Records	LP
ES94016	THE MUMMIES	Runnin' On Empty Vol. 1	LP
ES94017	THE MUMMIES	Intro To The Mummies	7"
ES94018	THE MUMMIES	Runnin' On Empty Vol. 2	LP
FSCD1	FIRE SURVIVOR CDS		
	The Makers, The Mono Men, Man or Astro-Man?		

Box Sets/CDs/2x7"

ESDX5	V/A	The Estrus Cocktail Companion	CD Box
ESPD1	V/A	The Estrus Sampler: 26 Spicey Sizzlers	CD-only
ESBX1	V/A	The Estrus Lunch Bucket	3x7" Box set
ESBX2	V/A	The Estrus Combo Box	5x7" Box set
ESBX3	V/A	The Estrus Half Rack	3x7" Box set
ESBX4	V/A	The Estrus Gearbox	3x7" Box set
ESBX5	V/A	The Cocktail Companion	3x7" Box set
ESDX3	V/A	The Estrus Half Rack	CD box
ESDX4	V/A	Estrus Gearbox	CD box
ESX2	THE MUMMIES	Double Dumb Ass… In The Face	2x7"
ESX3	THE GALAXY TRIO	Cowboys and Cocktails	2x7"

Design/illustration Ed Fotheringham

Design Art Chantry

TAKIN' OUT THE TRASH BAGS By Chris Alpert Coyle

For what seemed like every other week for a year or so, I was unofficially Dave Crider's buyer for items being sold on Craigslist in the greater Seattle area. The process always began with a text message from Dave at five in the morning asking if a certain neighborhood in Seattle was "near" me. If the neighborhood was close, the next message would be about coordinating a pickup for an item he'd bought (or was planning to buy).

It wasn't always musical equipment being purchased. A bean bag chair in Normandy Park and an Apple TV in Belltown were just a couple of the non-rock items I snagged.

I was used to requests for furniture or electronics, so I couldn't help but think it was a typo or some sort of joke when I read a message asking if I could go pick up some "trash bags" from a guy living on Beacon Hill. If I chose to accept the assignment, I was to pick up 50 specialized trash bags made for a specific trash receptor in the Crider home. Though weird, custom trash bags for a particular receptacle made a little more sense. We can just assume that Dave accidentally stumbled on the ad while searching for Fender Groove Tubes or a wireless mouse.

For this pickup, acquiring the bags was a ludicrous adventure in itself; although not having the correct amount of cash and the wrong address was on me. Nevertheless, after acquiring the bags I gave Dave a rough estimate of the next time I'd be up in Bellingham to make the delivery. My timeline couldn't have been more than two or three weeks ahead; however, instead of waiting those days, Crider came up with an idea: Deliver the bags to Tom Price (legendary Seattle guitarist of the U-Men, Gas Huffer, and The Monkeywrench) because Tom's band (The Tom Price Desert Classic) was slated to play in Bellingham the following Friday. The absurdity of this favor was too good for me to pass up. Plus, I regarded (and still do) Tom as one of my favorite guitar players.

Dave coordinated everything. While I assumed that all I had to do was hand over the box of plastic bags to the TP/DC van en route to "the 'Ham"

for the gig, scheduling conflicts made it so that the only way the exchange would happen was if I were to deliver the bags personally to Tom's house on the day before the show.

The bag delivery favor quickly turned into an unexpected undertaking when my wife nabbed our car in the morning, leaving me with no way of getting to Tom's house other than to walk. Though a map would show the journey was just a hair under two miles, the quest was anything but a summertime stroll. For those who haven't been to West Seattle, there are some parts where one neighborhood block is at sea level and the next one over is 1,400 feet above. Tom lived in that part of West Seattle.

And it was August. And I was carrying an oddly shaped 12-pound box of boutique trash bags.

Sure enough, I show up at the home of one of my favorite guitar players drenched in sweat, winded, holding a box of 50 designer plastic trash bags for some robot trash can that probably tells you the weather too.

Anyway, the historic drop-off was made without too much awkwardness on my part, and the important bit is that I'm now part of grunge history. I did it, Mom. I delivered trash bags recently purchased by Estrus Records' head honcho and Mono Men captain Dave Crider to Seattle punk icon and legendary guitarist Tom Price.

This book wouldn't have been possible for me to write without the companionship and support of my ex-wife Bobbi Jo and my dog Casbah (RIP). It's dedicated to Tim Coyle (RIP), the bravest person I'll ever know.

A special thanks to Yak and Art for allowing me to write these nuggets of rock'n'roll adventure alongside Scott's wizardry. And, of course, I'm forever grateful to call Dave and Bekki Crider my dear friends.

HOW DID THIS HAPPEN? By Scott Sugiuchi

In 2015 I went to a book signing by Art Chantry at Seattle's Fantagraphics store. Art and I knew each other from the distant past via graphic design circles. Or was it music? I chatted him up, dropped off a couple of issues of my zine, "7x7 is," and left with a signed book. In the meantime, I released a single by Dave Crider's rockin' combo the Dt's on my own label, Hidden Volume. Sometime after that, I received an email from Art asking if I'd design a book about Estrus Records—and he said that both he and Crider would be involved. After picking up my eyeballs, I began a very long journey that would culminate in this book. I won't bore you with the exhaustive details of the process — I can only thank the people who helped along the way: Todd Carlis, Stuart Ellis, Bob Wojciechowski, Ken Chiodini, Trent Ruane, Bob Deck, Deke Dickerson, Rick Miller, Dave O'Halloran (What Wave Archive), John Gunsaulis, Darren Merinuk, Keith Marlowe, Tim Kerr, Pudd Sharp, Chet Weise; everyone who sent me pictures, images, and stories; All-world Estrus Museum Purveyor and tireless collector Hugo Moutinho, for the lists and infinite resources; the ridiculously talented and generous Alex Wald; and my lovely wife, Diana "is that book fucking done yet" Sugiuchi. Of course, the biggest love goes out to the following: Our publisher Yak El-Droubie of Korero Press for his Zen master-level patience (or is that English reserve?) and keen design guidance; partner-in-crime Chris Alpert "Sir Coyler" Coyle, the literal writing ENGINE behind this tome. It's almost unimaginable how Shovelin' could have happened without his research, words, and wit. Then there's Art Chantry and Dave Crider. Art, for his inspiration, encouragement, and for trusting me (me!) with designing everything; and Dave for his magnificent vision and ability to navigate any challenge (I learned that "fuck it" is the universal salve.) They say never meet your heroes because you'll always be disappointed. Not the case here. I can't overstate their wisdom, guidance, and sheer COOLNESS on this entire project. Thank you.

ESTRUS: SHOVELIN' THE SHIT SINCE '87   255

Dedicated to John "Mort" Mortensen

Korero Press Limited.
www.koreropress.com

This edition published in 2024
ISBN-13: 978-1-912740-36-9

Limited edition hardback published 2023
ISBN-13: 978-1-912740-24-6

A CIP catalogue record for this book is available from the British Library
© All rights reserved. No part of this book may be reproduced in any form without written permission from the publisher.

The best possible version of this spiffy son of a bitch couldn't have been done without the generosity of the following stooges:
Alan "Alwills" Williams, Alex Campos, Anthony Navarro, Ben Goetting, Brian Colantuno, Brodie, Carl Bedard, Carleton Mellot, Cash & Dennie Carter, Chris Cypert, Chris Fuller, Chris Harlow, Chris Shaughnessy, Christian Müller, Clif Morlan, Dan Spagnolo, Daryle Maciocha, Dr. Leopard Stolen from Reverb Brasil, Elmar Gimpl / Bachelor Records, Eric Action, Hardy G!!!!, Iain Burke, Isaac "Ike" Becker, J Castaldi, Jared, Jay Haskins, Jeffrey Everett, John Bohls, JSGrites, Ken Holewczynski, Kyle Christians, Les Scurry, Lil Tuffy, Mark Gwisdalla, Marty Halter, Mat Patalano, aka Summer Man, Michael "Murderhouse" Tkach, Michael Buchmiller, Michael Jalboot, Mike Tomei, Mike Winske, Mitch Laue, Nate Rhodes, Nils Erik Rye, Oliver Groth, Pat Sullivan, Rob Farrell, Rob Fletcher, Ryan Roullard, Sam Cowan, Scott Walcott, "Spiggot" Richardson, Sean Berry (Double Crown Records / The Continental Magazine), Steve Messerer, Steven B. Haslam, Tim Horner, Tom Chapman, Tomas Lindberg, Trad'r Don V of Our Big Luauski, Proprietor.

CREDITS

The authors would like to thank everyone who contributed photos, set lists, posters, and ephemera for *Shovelin' The Shit*. They've made every effort to identify and credit these sources; however, if they've missed you out, they apologize—and please know that you have their undying gratitude for your help in the production of this book.

PHOTOS
A. Patrick Adams, Alain Dauchy, Alex Wald, Andy Duvall, Andy Nelson, Anne Tangeman, Arthur S. Aubry, Beau Boyd, Beth Kerr, Bret Lunsford, Brian Teasley. Bryce Dunn, C. Zerling, Cam Garrett, Charles Peterson, Chelsea Mosher, Chris Fuller, Chris Hedlund, Dan Ball, Daniel Coston, Dave Ewing, Deke Dickerson, Dirty Harry Välimäki, Doug Rubenack, Eri Sekiguchi, Francisco Santelices, Hiro Estrella 20/20, Hugo Moutinho, Jack Pabis, Jacob Covey, Jason Stang, Jay Burnside, Jeanette Huddleston, Jeff Glave, Jenny Ankeny, Jessica Arp, Jilayne Jordan, Jim Blanchard, John Gunsaulis, John Mortensen, Johnny Bartlett, Keith Marlowe, Laurent Bigot, Ledge Morrisette, Leningradskoje Optiko Mechanitscheskoje Objedinenie, Louie The Letch. Mark Majors, Martin Vantomme, Marty Perez, Masao Nakagami, Megan Dooley, Michael Galinsky, Michael Palmer, Mike Grimm, Neil Chowdery, Nina Carter, Photobooth, Pudd Sharp, Rob Yazzie, Russell Quan, Sallie Mowles, Scott Lingren, Scott Pellet, Susan McKeever, Terry Allen, Tina Luchessi, Travis Haight, Trent Ruane, Vic Mostly, What Wave Archives, William Grapes, Ya Mummy

SET LISTS, POSTERS, TRASH
Alex Wald, Art Chantry, Blair Buscareno, Bob Wojciechowski, Buffi Aguero, Chet Weise, Chris "COOP" Cooper, Darren Merinuk, Dave Crider, David Wojciechowski, Devlin Thompson, Hugo Moutinho, Jeff Glave, Joe Belock, Jr., Ken Chiodini, Kyle Christians, Lance Lindell, Mari Tamura, Matt Becher, Mel Bergman, Ryan Roullard, Sam Leyja, Sammy James, Sean Berry, Stuart Ellis, Ted Miller, Tim Steele, Todd Caris, William Grapes, Zack Static